BILLY PHELAN'S GREATEST GAME

Also by William Kennedy

THE INK TRUCK
LEGS

BILLY PHELAN'S GREATEST GAME

WILLIAM KENNEDY

THE VIKING PRESS   New York

First published in 1978 by The Viking Press
625 Madison Avenue, New York, N.Y. 10022
Published simultaneously in Canada by
Penguin Books Canada Limited

LIBRARY OF CONGRESS CATALOGING IN PUBLICATION DATA
Kennedy, William, 1928–
    Billy Phelan's greatest game.
    I. Title.
PZ4.K3615Bi   [PS3561.E428]   813'.5'4   77-28374
ISBN 0-670-16667-7

Printed in the United States of America
Set in Linotype Electra

For Brendan Christopher Kennedy, a nifty kid

The great archetypal activities of human society are all permeated with play from the start.

—JOHAN HUIZINGA

The "eternal child" in man is an indescribable experience, an incongruity, a disadvantage, and a divine prerogative; an imponderable that determines the ultimate worth or worthlessness of a personality.

—CARL JUNG

Because the city of Albany exists in the real world, readers may be led to believe that the characters who populate the Albany in this book are therefore real people. But there are no authentically real people in these pages. Some local and national celebrities are so indelibly connected to the era of the story that it would have been silly not to present them under their real names. But wherever a character has a role of even minor significance in this story, both name and actions are fictional. Any reality attaching to any character is the result of the author's creation, or of his own interpretation of history. This applies not only to Martin Daugherty and Billy Phelan, to Albany politicians, newsmen, and gamblers, but also to Franklin D. Roosevelt, Thomas E. Dewey, Henry James, Damon Runyon, William Randolph Hearst, and any number of other creatures of the American imagination.

WILLIAM KENNEDY

BILLY
PHELAN'S
GREATEST
GAME

1

Martin Daugherty, age fifty and now the scorekeeper, observed it all as Billy Phelan, working on a perfect game, walked with the arrogance of a young, untried eagle toward the ball return, scooped up his black, two-finger ball, tossed it like a juggler from right to left hand, then held it in his left palm, weightlessly. Billy rubbed his right palm and fingers on the hollow cone of chalk in the brass dish atop the ball rack, wiped off the excess with a pull-stroke of the towel. He faced the pins, eyed his spot down where the wood of the alley changed color, at a point seven boards in from the right edge. And then, looking to Martin like pure energy in shoes, he shuffled: left foot, right foot, left-right-left and slide, right hand pushing out, then back, like a pendulum, as he moved, wrist turning slightly at the back of the arc. His arm, pure control in shirtsleeves to Martin, swung forward, and the ball glided almost silently down the polished alley, rolled through the seventh board's darkness, curving minimally as it moved, curving more sharply as it neared the pins, and struck solidly between the headpin and the three pin, scattering all in a jamboree of spins and jigs.

"Attaway, Billy," said his backer, Morrie Berman, clapping twice. "Lotta mix, lotta mix."

1

"Ball is working all right," Billy said.

Billy stood long-legged and thin, waiting for Bugs, the cross-eyed pinboy, to send back the ball. When it snapped up from underneath the curved wooden ball return, Billy lifted it off, faced the fresh setup on alley nine, shuffled, thrust, and threw yet another strike: eight in a row now.

Martin Daugherty noted the strike on the scoresheet, which showed no numbers, only the eight strike marks: bad luck to fill in the score while a man is still striking. Martin was already thinking of writing his next column about this game, provided Billy carried it off. He would point out how some men moved through the daily sludge of their lives and then, with a stroke, cut away the sludge and transformed themselves. Yet what they became was not the result of a sudden act, but the culmination of all they had ever done: a triumph for self-development, the end of something general, the beginning of something specific.

To Martin, Billy Phelan, on an early Thursday morning in late October, 1938, already seemed more specific than most men. Billy seemed fully defined at thirty-one (the age when Martin had been advised by his father that he was a failure).

Billy was not a half-bad bowler: 185 average in the K. of C. league, where Martin bowled with him Thursday nights. But he was not a serious match for Scotty Streck, who led the City League, the fastest league in town, with a 206 average. Scotty lived with his bowling ball as if it were a third testicle, and when he found Billy and Martin playing eight ball at a pool table in the Downtown Health and Amusement Club, the city's only twenty-four-hour gamester's palace, no women, no mixed leagues, please, beer on tap till 4:00 A.M., maybe 5:00, but no whiskey on premises, why then Scotty's question was: Wanna bowl some jackpots, Billy? Sure, with a twenty-pin spot, Billy said. Give you fifty-five for three games, offered the Scotcheroo. Not enough, but all right, said Billy, five bucks? Five bucks fine, said Scotty.

And so it was on, with the loser to pay for the bowling, twenty cents a game. Scotty's first game was 212. Billy turned in a sad 143, with five splits, too heavy on the headpin, putting him sixty-nine pins down, his spot eliminated.

Billy found the pocket in the second game and rolled 226. But Scotty had also discovered where the pocket lurked, and threw 236 to increase his lead to seventy-nine pins. Now in the eighth frame of the final game, the match was evening out, Scotty steady with spares and doubles, but his lead fading fast in front of Billy's homestretch run toward perfection.

Word of a possible 300 game with a bet on it drew the bar stragglers, the fag-end bowlers, the night manager, the all-night pinboys, even the sweeper, to alleys nine and ten in the cavernous old room, spectators at the wonder. No one spoke to Billy about the unbroken string of strikes, also bad luck. But it was legitimate to talk of the bet: two hundred dollars, between Morrie Berman and Charlie Boy McCall, the significance being in the sanctified presence of Charlie Boy, a soft, likeable kid gone to early bloat, but nevertheless the most powerful young man in town, son of the man who controlled all the gambling, all of it, in the city of Albany, and nephew of the two politicians who ran the city itself, all of it, and Albany County, all of that too: Irish-American potentates of the night and the day.

Martin knew all the McCall brothers, had gone to school with them, saw them grow up in the world and take power over it. They all, including young Charlie Boy, the only heir, still lived on Colonie Street in Arbor Hill, where Martin and his father used to live, where Billy Phelan used to live. There was nothing that Charlie Boy could not get, any time, any place in this town; and when he came into the old Downtown alleys with Scotty, and when Scotty quickly found Billy to play with, Charlie just as quickly found Morrie Berman, a swarthy ex-pimp and gambler who would bet on the behavior of bumblebees. A week ago Martin had seen Morrie open a welsher's forehead with a shotglass at Brockley's bar on Broadway over a three-hundred-dollar dart game: heavy bettor, Morrie, but he paid when he lost and he demanded the same from others. Martin knew Morrie's reputation better than he knew the man: a fellow who used to drink around town with Legs Diamond and had hoodlums for pals. But Morrie wasn't quite a hoodlum himself, as far as Martin could tell. He was the son of a politically radical Jew, grandson of a superb old Sheridan Avenue tailor. In Morrie the worthy Berman family strain had gone slightly askew.

The bet between Charlie Boy and Morrie had begun at one hundred dollars and stayed there for two games, with Martin holding the money. But when Morrie saw that Billy had unquestionably found the pocket at the windup of the second game, he offered to raise the ante another hundred; folly, perhaps, for his boy Billy was seventy-nine pins down. Well yes, but that was really only twenty-four down with the fifty-five-pin spot, and you go with the hot instrument. Charlie Boy quickly agreed to the raise, what's another hundred, and Billy then stood up and rolled his eight strikes, striking somberness into Charlie Boy's mood, and vengeance into Scotty's educated right hand.

Martin knew Scotty Streck and admired his talent without liking him. Scotty worked in the West Albany railroad shops, a short, muscular, brush-cut, bandy-legged native of the West End German neighborhood of Cabbagetown. He was twenty-six and had been bowling since he was old enough to lift a duckpin ball. At age sixteen he was a precociously unreal star with a 195 average. He bowled now almost every night of his life, bowled in matches all over the country and clearly coveted a national reputation. But to Martin he lacked champion style: a hothead, generous neither with himself nor with others. He'd been nicknamed Scotty for his closeness with money, never known to bet more than five dollars on himself. Yet he thrived on competition and traveled with a backer, who, as often as not, was his childhood pal, Charlie McCall. No matter what he did or didn't do, Scotty was still the best bowler in town, and bowling freaks, who abounded in Albany, gathered round to watch when he came out to play.

The freaks now sat on folding chairs and benches behind the only game in process in the old alleys, alleys which had been housed in two other buildings and moved twice before being installed here on State Street, just up from Broadway in an old dancing academy. They were venerable, quirky boards, whose history now spoke to Martin. He looked the crowd over: men sitting among unswept papers, dust, and cigar butts, bathing in the raw incandescence of naked bulbs, surrounded by spittoons; a nocturnal bunch in shirtsleeves and baggy clothes, their hands full of meaningful drink, fixated on an ancient game with origins in Christian ritual, a game brought to this city centuries ago by nameless old Dutchmen and now a captive of the indoor sports of the city. The game abided in such windowless, smoky lofts as this one, which smelled of beer, cigar smoke and alley wax, an unhealthy ambience which nevertheless nourished exquisite nighttime skills.

These men, part of Broadway's action-easy, gravy-vested sporting mob, carefully studied such artists of the game as Scotty, with his high-level consistency, and Billy, who might achieve perfection tonight through a burst of accuracy, and converted them into objects of community affection. The mob would make these artists sports-page heroes, enter them into the hall of small fame that existed only in the mob mind, which venerated all winners.

After Billy rolled his eighth strike, Scotty stood, danced his bob and weave toward the foul line, and threw the ball with a corkscrewed arm, sent it spinning and hooking toward the one-three pocket. It was a perfect hit, but a dead one somehow, and he left the eight and ten pins perversely standing: the strike split, all but impossible to make.

"Dirty son of a biiiiiitch!" Scotty screamed at the pair of uncooperative pins, silencing all hubbub behind him, sending waves of uh-oh through the spectators, who knew very well how it went when a man began to fall apart at the elbow.

"You think maybe I'm getting to him?" Billy whispered to Martin.

"He can't even stand to lose a fiver, can he?"

Scotty tried for the split, ticking the eight, leaving the ten.

"Let's get it now, Scotty," Charlie Boy McCall said. "In there, buddy."

Scotty nodded at Charlie Boy, retrieved his ball and faced the new setup, bobbed, weaved, corkscrewed, and crossed over to the one-two pocket, Jersey hit, leaving the five pin. He made the spare easily, but sparing is not how you pick up pinnage against the hottest of the hot.

Billy might have been hot every night if he'd been as single-minded as Scotty about the game. But Martin knew Billy to be a generalist, a man in need of the sweetness of miscellany. Billy's best game was pool, but he'd never be anything like a national champion at that either, didn't think that way, didn't have the need that comes with obsessive specialization. Billy roamed through the grandness of all games, yeoman here, journeyman there, low-level maestro unlikely to transcend, either as gambler, card dealer, dice or pool shooter. He'd been a decent shortstop in the city-wide Twilight League as a young man. He was a champion drinker who could go for three days on the sauce and not yield to sleep, a double-twenty specialist at the dart board, a chancy, small-time bookie, and so on and so on and so on, and why, Martin Daugherty, are you so obsessed with Billy Phelan? Why make a heroic *picaro* out of a simple chump?

Well, says Martin, haven't I known him since he was a sausage? Haven't I seen him grow stridently into young manhood while I slip and slide softly into moribund middle age? Why, I knew him when he had a father, knew his father too, knew him when that father abdicated, and I ached for the boy then and have ever since, for I know how it is to live in the inescapable presence of the absence of the father.

Martin had watched Billy move into street-corner life after his father left, saw him hanging around Ronan's clubroom, saw him organize the Sunday morning crap game in Bohen's barn after nine o'clock mass, saw him become a pinboy at the K. of C. to earn some change. That was where the boy learned how to bowl, sneaking free games after Duffy, the custodian, went off to the movies.

Martin was there the afternoon the pinboys went wild and rolled balls up and down the middle of the alleys at one another, reveling in a boyish exuberance that went bad when Billy tried to scoop up one of those missiles like a hot grounder and smashed his third finger between that onrushing ball and another one lying loose on the runway. Smash and blood, and Martin moved in and took him (he was fourteen, the same age as Martin's own son is this early morning) over to the Homeopathic Hospital on North Pearl Street and saw to it that the intern called a surgeon, who came and sewed up the smash, but never splinted it, just wrapped it with its stitches and taped it to Billy's pinky and said: That's the best anybody can do with this mess; nothing left there to splint. And Billy healed, crediting it to the influence of the healthy pinky. The nail and some bone grew back crookedly, and Martin can now see the twist and puff of Billy's memorable deformity. But what does a sassy fellow like Billy need with a perfectly formed third finger? The twist lends character to the hand that holds the deck, that palms the two-finger ball, that holds the stick at the crap table, that builds the cockeyed bridge for the educated cue.

If Martin had his way, he would infuse a little of Billy's scarred sassiness into his own son's manner, a boy too tame, too subservient to the priests. Martin might even profit by injecting some sass into his own acquiescent life.

Consider that: a sassy Martin Daugherty.

Well, that may not be all that likely, really. Difficult to acquire such things.

Billy's native arrogance might well have been a gift of miffed genes, then come to splendid definition through the tests to which a street like Broadway puts a young man on the make: tests designed to refine a breed, enforce a code, exclude all simps and gumps, and deliver into the city's life a man worthy of functioning in this age of nocturnal supremacy. Men like Billy Phelan, forged in the brass of Broadway, send, in the time of their splendor, telegraphic statements of mission: I, you bums, am a winner. And that message, however devoid of Christ-like other-cheekery, dooms the faint-hearted Scottys of the night, who must sludge along, never knowing how it feels to spill over with the small change of sassiness, how it feels to leave the spillover there on the floor, more where that came from, pal. Leave it for the sweeper.

Billy went for his ball, kissed it once, massaged it, chalked and toweled his right hand, spat in the spittoon to lighten his burden, bent slightly at the waist, shuffled and slid, and bazoo-bazoo, boys, threw another strike: not *just* another strike, but a titanic blast this time which sent all pins flying pitward, the cleanest of clean hits, perfection unto tidiness, bespeaking power battening on power, control escalating.

Billy looked at no one.

Nine in a row, but still nobody said anything except hey, and yeah-yeah, with a bit more applause offered up. Billy waited for the ball to come back, rubbing his feet on the floor dirt just beyond the runway, dusting his soles with slide insurance, then picked up the ball and sidled back to the runway of alley nine for his last frame. And then he rolled it, folks, and boom-boom went the pins, zot-zot, you sons of bitches, ten in a row now, and a cheer went up, but still no comment, ten straight and his score (even though Martin hadn't filled in any numbers yet) is 280, with two more balls yet to come, twenty more pins to go. Is Billy Phelan ready for perfection? Can you handle it, kid? What will you do with it if you get it?

Billy had already won the match; no way for Scotty to catch him, given that spot. But now it looked as if Billy would beat Scotty without the spot, and, tied to a perfect game, the win would surely make the sports pages later in the week.

Scotty stood up and walked to the end of the ball return to wait. He chalked his hands, rubbed them together, played with the towel, as Billy bent over to pick up his ball.

"You ever throw three hundred anyplace before?" Scotty asked.

"I ain't thrown it here yet," Billy said.

So he did it, Martin thought. Scotty's chin trembled as he watched Billy. Scotty, the nervous sportsman. Did saying what he had just said mean that the man lacked all character? Did only relentless winning define his being? Was the fear of losing sufficient cause for him to try to foul another man's luck? Why of course it was, Martin. Of course it was.

Billy threw, but it was a Jersey hit, his first crossover in the game. The ball's mixing power overcame imprecision, however, and the pins spun and rolled, toppling the stubborn ten pin, and giving Billy his eleventh strike. Scotty pulled at the towel and sat down.

"You prick," Morrie Berman said to him. "What'd you say that to him for?"

"Say what?"

"No class," said Morrie. "Class'll tell in the shit house, and you got no class."

Billy picked up his ball and faced the pins for the last act. He called out to Bugs, the pinboy: "Four pin is off the spot," and he pointed to it. Martin saw he was right, and Bugs moved the pin back into proper position. Billy kissed the ball, shuffled and threw, and the ball went elegantly forward, perfect line, perfect break, perfect one-three pocket hit. Nine pins flew away. The four pin never moved.

"Two-ninety-nine," Martin said out loud, and the mob gave its full yell and applause and then stood up to rubberneck at the scoresheet, which Martin was filling in at last, thirty pins a frame, twenty-nine in the last one. He put down the crayon to shake hands with Billy, who stood over the table, ogling his own nifty numbers.

"Some performance, Billy," said Charlie Boy McCall, standing to stretch his babyfat. "I should learn not to bet against you. You remember the last time?"

"Pool match at the K. of C."

"I bet twenty bucks on some other guy."

"Live and learn, Charlie, live and learn."

"You were always good at everything," Charlie said. "How do you explain that?"

"I say my prayers and vote the right ticket."

"That ain't enough in this town," Charlie said.

"I come from Colonie Street."

"That says it," said Charlie, who still lived on Colonie Street.

"Scotty still has to finish two frames," Martin announced to all; for Scotty was already at alley ten, facing down the burden of second best. The crowd politely sat and watched him throw a strike. He moved to alley nine and with a Jersey hit left the baby split. He cursed inaudibly, then made the

10

split. With his one remaining ball he threw a perfect strike for a game of 219, a total of 667. Billy's total was 668.

"Billy Phelan wins the match by one pin, without using any of the spot," Martin was delighted to announce, and he read aloud the game scores and totals of both men. Then he handed the bet money to Morrie Berman.

"I don't even feel bad," Charlie Boy said. "That was a hell of a thing to watch. When you got to lose, it's nice to lose to somebody who knows what he's doing."

"Yeah, you were hot all right," Scotty said, handing Billy a five-dollar bill. "Really hot."

"Hot, my ass," Morrie Berman said to Scotty. "You hexed him, you bastard. He might've gone all the way if you didn't say anything, but you hexed him, talking about it."

The crowd was already moving away, back to the bar, the sweeper confronting those cigar butts at last. New people were arriving, waiters and bartenders who would roll in the Nighthawk League, which started at 3:00 A.M. It was now two-thirty in the morning.

"Listen, you mocky bastard," Scotty said, "I don't have to take any noise from you." Scotty's fists were doubled, his face flushed, his chin in vigorous tremolo. Martin's later vision of Scotty's coloration and form at this moment was that of a large, crimson firecracker.

"Hold on here, hold on," Charlie McCall said. "Cool down, Scotty. No damage done. Cool down, no trouble now." Charlie was about eight feet away from the two men when he spoke, too far to do anything when Morrie started his lunge. But Martin saw it coming and jumped between the two, throwing his full weight into Morrie, his junior by thirty pounds, and knocking him backward into a folding chair, on which he sat without deliberation. Others sealed off Scotty from further attack and Billy held Morrie fast in the chair with two hands.

"Easy does it, man," Billy said, "I don't give a damn what he did."

"The cheap fink," Morrie said. "He wouldn't give a sick whore a hairpin."

Martin laughed at the line. Others laughed. Morrie smiled. Here was a line for the Broadway annals. Epitaph for the Scotcheroo: It was reliably reported during his lifetime that he would not give a sick whore a hairpin. Perhaps this enhanced ignominy was also entering Scotty's head after the laughter, or perhaps it was the result of *his* genetic gift, or simply the losing, and the unbearable self-laceration that went with it. Whatever it was, Scotty doubled up, gasping, burping. He threw his arms around his own chest, wobbled, took a short step, and fell forward, gashing his left cheek on a spittoon. He rolled onto his side, arms still aclutch, eyes squeezing out the agony in his chest.

The mob gawked and Morrie stood up to look. Martin bent over the fallen man, then lifted him up from the floor and stretched him out on the bench from which he had risen to hex Billy. Martin blotted the gash with Scotty's own shirttail, and then opened his left eyelid. Martin looked up at the awestruck mob and asked: "Anybody here a doctor?" And he answered himself: "No, of course not," and looked then at the night manager and said, "Call an ambulance, Al," even though he knew Scotty was already beyond help. Scotty: Game over.

How odd to Martin, seeing a champion die in the embrace of shame, egotism, and fear of failure. Martin trembled at a potential vision of himself also prostrate before such forces, done in by a shame too great to endure, and so now is the time to double up and die. Martin saw his own father curdled by shame, his mother crippled by it twice: her own and her husband's. And Martin himself had been bewildered and thrust into silence and timidity by it (but was that the true

12

cause?). Jesus, man, pay attention here. Somebody lies dead in front of you and you're busy exploring the origins of your own timidity. Martin, as was said of your famous father, your sense of priority is bowlegged.

Martin straightened Scotty's arm along his side, stared at the closed right eye, the half-open left eye, and sat down in the scorekeeper's chair to search pointlessly for vital signs in this dead hero of very recent yore. Finally, he closed the left eye with his thumb.

"He's really gone," he told everybody, and they all seemed to wheeze inwardly. Then they really did disperse until only Charlie Boy McCall, face gone white, sat down at Scotty's feet and stared fully at the end of something. And he said, in his native way, "Holy Mother of God, that was a quick decision."

"Somebody we should call, Charlie?" Martin asked the shocked young man.

"His wife," said Charlie. "He's got two kids."

"Very tough. Very. Anybody else? What about his father?"

"Dead," said Charlie. "His mother's in Florida. His wife's the one."

"I'll be glad to call her," Martin said. "But then again maybe you ought to do that, Charlie. You're so much closer."

"I'll take care of it, Martin."

And Martin nodded and moved away from dead Scotty, who was true to the end to the insulting intent of his public name: tightwad of heart, parsimonious dwarf of soul.

"I never bowled a guy to death before," Billy said.

"No jokes now," Martin said.

"I told you he was a busher," Billy said.

"All right but not now."

"Screw the son of a bitch," Morrie said to them both, said it softly, and then went over to Charlie and said, "I know he was your friend, Charlie, and I'm sorry. But I haven't liked him for years. We never got along."

13

"Please don't say any more," Charlie said with bowed head.

"I just want you personally to know I'm sorry. Because I know how close you two guys were. I'da liked him if I could, but Jesus Christ, I don't want you sore at me, Charlie. You get what I mean?"

"I get it. I'm not sore at you."

"I'm glad you say that because sometimes when you fight a guy his friends turn into your enemies, even though they got nothin' against you themselves. You see what I mean?"

"I see, and I've got nothing against you, Morris. You're just a punk, you've always been a punk, and the fact is I never liked you and like you a hell of a lot less than that right now. Good night, Morris."

And Charlie Boy turned away from Morrie Berman to study the corpse of his friend.

Martin Daugherty, infused with new wisdom by the entire set of events, communicated across the miles of the city to his senile father in the nursing home bed. You see, Papa, Martin said into the microphone of the filial network, it's very clear to me now. The secret of Scotty's death lies in the simple truth uncovered by Morrie Berman: that Scotty would not give a sick whore a hairpin. And Papa, I tell you that we must all give hairpins to sick whores. It is essential. Do you hear me? Can you understand? We must give hairpins to sick whores whenever they require them. What better thing can a man do?

2

Martin Daugherty, wearing bathrobe and slippers, sat at his kitchen table, bleeding from sardonic wounds. In the name of the Father, in the name of the Son, who will savor the Father when the Son is gone? He salted his oatmeal and spiced it with raisins, those wrinkled and puny symbols of his own dark and shriveling years. He chewed a single raisin, thinking of Scotty dead, his own son gone to the seminary. But the boy was alive and free to change his mind in time, and the bitter-sweetness of this thought flowed on his tongue: treasure lurking among the wrinkles.

"You're mad entirely," Mary Daugherty said when she saw him smiling and chewing, grim and crazy. She broke into laughter, the lilt of Connacht, a callous response to madness in her morning kitchen.

"You can bet your sweet Irish ass I'm mad," Martin said. "I dreamed of Peter, carried through the streets by pederast priests."

That stopped her laughter, all right.

"You're at the priests again, are you? Why don't you let it alone? He may not even take to it."

"They'll see he does. Fill him full of that windy God shit, called to the front, cherub off Main Street. Give the helping hand to others, learn to talk to the birds and make a bridge to

15

the next world. Why did God make you if it wasn't to save all those wretched bastards who aren't airy and elite enough to be penniless saviors?"

"You're worried he'll be penniless, is that it?"

"I'm worried he'll be saved entirely by priests."

The boy, Peter, had been sitting in a web of ropes, suspended beyond the edge of the flat roof of home. Billy Phelan, in another suspended web, sat beside Peter, both of them looking at Martin as they lounged in the ropes, which were all that lay between them and the earth. Martin marveled at the construction of the webs, which defied gravity. And then Peter leaped off the web, face forward, and plummeted two stories. His body hit, then his head, two separate impacts, and he lay still. Two priests in sackcloth scooped him into a wheelbarrow with their shovels and one of them pushed him off into the crowded street. Billy Phelan never moved from his web. Martin, suddenly on the street, followed the wheelbarrow through the rubble but lost it. In a vacant lot he confronted a band of children Peter's age. They jogged in an ominous circle which Martin could not escape. A small girl threw a stone which struck Martin on the head. A small boy loped toward Martin with an upraised knife, and the circle closed in. Martin rushed to meet the knife-wielding attacker and flew at the boy's chest with both feet.

He awoke and squinted toward the foot of the bed, where the figure of an adolescent, wearing a sweater of elaborate patterns, leaned back in a chair, feet propped on the bedcovers. But the figure was perhaps beyond adolescence. Its head was an animal's, with pointed snout. A fox? A fawn? A lamb? Martin sat up, resting on his elbow for a closer look. The figure remained in focus, but the head was still blurred. Martin rubbed his eyes. The figure leaned back on the legs of the chair, feet crossed at the ankles, leisurely observing Martin.

And then it vanished, not as a dream fading into wakefulness, but with a filmmaker's magic: suddenly, wholly gone.

Martin, half-erect, leaning on his elbow, heard Mary say the oatmeal was on the table. He thought of the illustrated Bible he had leafed through when he'd come home after Scotty's death, compulsively searching through the Old Testament for an equivalent of the man's sudden departure. He had found nothing that satisfied him, but he'd put out the light thinking of the engraving of Abraham and the bound Isaac, with the ram breaking through the bushes, and he had equated Isaac with his son, Peter, sacrificed to someone else's faith: first communion, confirmation, thrust into the hands of nuns and priests, then smothered by the fears of a mother who still believed making love standing up damned you forever.

Had Martin's fuzzy, half-animal bedside visitor been the ram that saved Isaac from the knife? In a ski sweater? What did it have to do with Peter? Martin opened the Bible to the engraving. The sweatered animal at bedside bore no resemblance to the ram of salvation. Martin re-read what he had written years ago above the engraving after his first reading of the Abraham story: We are all in conspiracy against the next man. He could not now explain what precisely he had meant by that phrase.

It had been years since the inexplicable touched Martin's life. Now, eating his oatmeal, he examined this new vision, trying to connect it to the dream of Peter falling out of the web, to Peter's face as he left home two days before, a fourteen-year-old boy about to become a high school sophomore, seduced by God's holy messengers to enter a twig-bending pre-seminary school. Peter: the centerpiece of his life, the only child he would have. He raged silently at the priests who had stolen him away, priests who would teach the boy to pile up a fortune from the coal collection, to scold the poor for their

17

indolence. The assistant pastor of Sacred Heart Church had only recently sermonized on the folly of striving for golden brown toast and the fatuity of the lyrics of "Tea for Two." There was a suburban priest who kept a pet duck on a leash. One in Troy chased a nubile child around the parish house. Priests in their cups. Priests in their beggars' robes. Priests in their eunuch suits. There were saints among them, men of pure love, and one such had inspired Peter, given him the life of Saint Francis to read, encouraging selflessness, fanaticism, poverty, bird calls.

Months ago, when he was shaping his decision, the boy sat at this same kitchen table poking at his own raisins, extolling the goodness of priests. Do you know any good men who aren't priests? Martin asked him.

You, said the boy.

How did I make it without the priesthood?

I don't know, but maybe sometimes you aren't good. Are you always good?

By no means.

Then did you ever know any men good enough to talk to the birds?

Plenty. Neil O'Connor talked to his ducks all day long. After four pints Marty Sheehan'd have long talks with Lackey Quinlan's goose.

But did the birds talk back?

You couldn't shut them up once they got going, said Martin.

Balance: that was what he wanted to induce in Peter. Be reverent also in the presence of the absence of God.

"I just don't want them to drown him in their holy water," Martin said to Mary Daugherty. "And I don't want him to be afraid to tell them to shove their incense up their chalices if he feels like coming home. There'll be none of that failed priest business in this house the way it was with Chickie

Phelan." (And Martin then sensed, unreasonably, that Chick would call him on the telephone, soon; perhaps this morning.) "His mother and sisters wanted Chick to bring a little bit of heaven into the back parlor, and when he couldn't do it, they never forgave him. And another thing. I always wanted Peter to grow up here, grow up and beget. I don't want to see the end of the Daughertys after the trouble of centuries took us this far."

"You want another Daugherty? Another son? Is that what you're saying to me?"

"It's that I hate to see the end of a line. Any line. Think of all the Daughertys back beyond Patrick. Pirates stole *him* you know, made him a slave. That's how *he* got into the saint business."

"Ah," said Mary, "you're a talky man."

"I am."

"Are you through now?"

"I am."

"Why don't you be talky like that with the boy?"

"I was."

"You told him all that?"

"I did."

"Well, then?" said the wife and mother of the family. "Well?"

"Just about right," said Martin.

The talk had calmed him, and real and present things took his attention: his wife and her behind, jiggling while she stirred the eggs. Those splendid puffs of Irish history, those sweet curves of the Western world, sloping imagistically toward him: roundaceous beneath the black and yellow kimono he'd given her for the New York vacation. The memory of coupling in their stateroom on the night boat, the memory of their most recent coupling—was it three, four days ago?—suggested to

Martin that screwing your wife is like striking out the pitcher. Martin's attitude, however, was that there was little point in screwing anyone else. Was this a moralistic judgment because of his trauma with Melissa Spencer, or merely an apology for apathetic constancy? Melissa in his mind again. She would be in town now with the pseudoscandalous show. She would not call him. He would not call her. Yet he felt they would very probably meet.

The phone rang and Miss Irish Ass of 1919 callipygiated across the room and answered it. "Oh yes, yes, Chick, he's here, yes. Imagine that, and he was just talking about you."

"Well, Chickie," said Martin, "are you ready for the big move today? Is your pencil sharpened?"

"Something big, Martin, really big."

"Big enough," said Martin; for Chick had been the first to reveal to him the plan concocted by Patsy McCall, leader of the Albany Democratic Party, to take control of the American Labor Party's local wing on this, the final day of voter registration. Loyal Democrats, of which Chick was one, would register A.L.P., infiltrate the ranks, and push out the vile Bolsheviks and godless socialists who stank up the city with their radical ways. Patsy McCall and his Democrats would save the city from the red stink.

"No, Martin, it's not that," Chick said. "It's Charlie Boy. The police are next door, and Maloney too. Him and half the damn McCall family's been coming and going over here all night long. He's gone, Martin. Charlie's gone. I think they grabbed him."

"Grabbed him?"

"Kidnapped. They've been using the phone here since four-thirty this morning. A regular parade. They'll be back, I know it, but you're the one should know about this. I owe you that."

"Are you sure of this, Chickie?"

"They're on the way back now. I see Maloney coming down

their stoop. Martin, they took Charlie out of his car about four o'clock this morning. His mother got up in the night and saw the car door wide open and nobody inside. A bunch of cigarettes on the running board. And he's gone. I heard them say that. Now, you don't know nothing from here, don't you know, and say a prayer for the boy, Martin, say a prayer. Oh Jesus, the things that go on."

And Chick hung up.

Martin looked at the kitchen wall, dirty tan, needing paint. Shabby wall. Shabby story. Charlie Boy taken. The loss, the theft of children. Charlie was hardly a child, yet his father, Bindy McCall, would still think of him as one.

"What was that?" Mary asked.

"Just some talk about a story."

"Who or what was grabbed? I heard you say grabbed."

"You're fond of that word, are you?"

"It's got a bit of a ring to it."

"You don't have to wait for a ring to get grabbed."

"I knew that good and early, thanks be to God."

And then, Martin grabbed the queenly rump he had lived with for sixteen years, massaged it through the kimono, and walked quickly out of the kitchen to his study. He sat in the reading rocker alongside a stack of Albany newspapers taller than a small boy, and reached for the phone. Already he could see the front pages, the splash, boom, bang, the sad, sad whoopee of the headlines. The extras. The photos. These are the McCall brothers. Here a recap of their extraordinary control of Albany for seventeen years. Here their simple homes. And now this. Here Charlie Boy's car. Here the spot where. Here the running board where the cigarettes fell. Here some famous kidnappings. Wheeeeee.

Martin dialed.

"Yeah," said Patsy McCall's unmistakable sandpaper voice box after the phone rang once.

"Martin Daugherty, Patsy."

"Yeah."

"I hear there's been some trouble."

Silence.

"Is that right or wrong?"

"No trouble here."

"I hear there's a lot of activity over at your place and that maybe something bad happened."

Silence.

"Is that right or wrong, Patsy?"

"No trouble here."

"Are you going to be there a while? All right if I come down?"

"Come down if you like, Martin. Bulldogs wouldn't keep the likes of you off the stoop."

"That's right, Patsy. I'll be there in fifteen minutes. Ten."

"There's nothing going on here."

"Right, Patsy, see you in a little while."

"Don't bring nobody."

In his bedroom, moving at full speed, Martin took off his blue flannel bathrobe, spotted with egg drippings and coffee dribbles, pulled on his pants over the underwear he'd slept in and decided not to tell his wife the news. She was a remote cousin to Charlie's mother and would want to lend whatever strength she had to the troubled family, a surge of good will that would now be intrusive.

The McCalls' loss intensified Martin's own. But where his was merely doleful, theirs was potentially tragic. Trouble. People he knew, sometimes his kin, deeply in trouble, was what had often generated his inexplicable visions. Ten years without this kind of divination, now suddenly back: the certainty Chick would call; the bizarre bedside visitor heralding the unknown; the death of Scotty followed by the kidnapping of Charlie. Coincidental trouble.

The inexplicable had first appeared a quarter century ago in late October, 1913, when, fresh from a six-month journalistic foray in England and Ireland, Martin found himself in Albany, walking purposefully but against logic north on North Pearl Street, when he should have been walking west on State Street toward the Capitol, where he had an appointment to interview the new governor, a namesake, Martin H. Glynn, an Albany editor, politician, and orator interested in Ireland's troubles. But a counterimpulse was on him and he continued on Pearl Street to the Pruyn Library, where he saw his cousin, a fireman with steamer eight, sitting on the family wagon, the reins of the old horse sitting loosely on his knees. He was wearing his knitted blue watch cap, a familiar garment to Martin. As their eyes met, the cousin smiled, lifted a pistol from his lap, pointed it at the horse, then turned it to his right temple and pulled the trigger. He died without further ado, leaving the family no explanation for his act, and was smiling still when Martin caught the reins of the startled horse and reached his cousin's side.

Nothing like that happened to Martin again until 1925, the year he published his collection of short stories. But he recognized the same irrational impulse when he was drawn, without reason, to visit the lawyer handling his father's libel suit against an Albany newspaper, which had resurrected the old man's scandal with Melissa. Martin found the lawyer at home, in robust health, and they talked of Martin's father, who at that point was living in New York City. Two hours after their talk the lawyer died of a heart attack walking up Maiden Lane, and the task of finding a new lawyer for his father fell to Martin.

That same year Martin tuned in the radio at mid-morning,

an uncharacteristic move, and heard of the sinking of the excursion steamer *Sweethearts* in the Hudson River below Kingston. He later learned that a girl he once loved had gone down with the boat. He began after this to perceive also things not related to trouble. He foresaw by a week that a *Times-Union* photographer would win six thousand dollars in the Albany baseball pool. He was off by only one day in his prediction of when his father would win the libel suit. He knew a love affair would develop between his wife's niece from Galway and an Albany bartender, two months before the niece arrived in Albany. He predicted that on the day of that love's first bloom it would be raining, a thunderstorm, and so it was.

Martin's insights took the shape of crude imagery, like photographs intuited from the radio. He came to consider himself a mystical naturalist, insisting to himself and to others that he did not seriously believe in ghosts, miracles, resurrection, heaven, or hell. He seasoned any account of his beliefs and his bizarre intuition with a remark he credited to his mother: There's no Santa Claus and there's no devil. Your father's both. He dwelled on his visions and found them comforting, even when they were false and led him nowhere and revealed nothing. He felt they put him in touch with life in a way he had never experienced it before, possessor of a power which not even his famous and notorious father, in whose humiliating shadow he had lived all his years, understood. His father was possessed rather by concrete visions of the Irish in the New World, struggling to throw off the filth of poverty, oppression, and degradation, and rising to a higher plane of life, where they would be the equals of all those arrived Americans who manipulated the nation's power, wealth, and culture. Martin was bored with the yearnings of the immigrant hordes and sought something more abstract: to love oneself and one's opposite. He preferred personal insight to social justice, though he wrote of both frequently in his column, which was a confusion of radicalism, spiritual exploration, and foolery. He was a comedian who sympathized with Heywood Broun, Tom Mooney, and all Wobblies, who drank champagne with John McCormack, beer with Mencken, went to the track with Damon Runyon, wrote public love letters to Marlene Dietrich whenever her films played Albany, and who viewed America's detachment from the Spanish Civil War as an exercise in evil by omission.

He also wrote endlessly on a novel, a work he hoped would convey his version of the meaning of his father's scandalous life. He had written twelve hundred pages, aspiring to perhaps two hundred or less, and could not finish it. At age fifty he viewed himself, after publication of two books of non-fiction, one on the war, the other a personal account of the Irish troubles, plus the short story collection and innumerable articles for national magazines, as a conundrum, a man unable to define his commitment or understand the secret of his own navel, a literary gnome. He seriously valued almost nothing he wrote, except for the unfinished novel.

He was viewed by the readers of the *Times-Union*, which carried his column five days a week, as a mundane poet, a penny-whistle philosopher, a provocative half-radical man nobody had to take seriously, for he wasn't quite serious about himself. He championed dowsing and ouija boards and sought to rehabilitate Henry James, Sr., the noted Albanian and Swedenborgian. He claimed that men of truest vision were, like James, always considered freaks, and he formed the International Brotherhood of Crackpots by way of giving them a bargaining agent, and attracted two thousand members.

His column was frequently reprinted nationally, but he chose not to syndicate it, fearing he would lose his strength, which was his Albany constituency, if his subject matter went national. He never wrote of his own gift of foresight.

The true scope of that gift was known to no one, and only his family and a few friends knew it existed at all. The source of it was wondered at suspiciously by his Irish-born wife, who had been taught in the rocky wastes of Connemara that druids roamed the land, even to this day.

The gift left Martin in 1928 after his fortieth birthday debauch with Melissa, the actress, his father's erstwhile mistress, the woman who was the cause of the paternal scandal. Martin returned home from the debauch, stinking of simony, and severely ill with what the family doctor simplistically diagnosed as alcoholic soak. Within a week Martin accurately sensed that his mystical talent was gone. He recuperated from the ensuing depression after a week, but rid himself of the simoniacal stink only when he acceded to his wife's suggestion, and, after a decade of considering himself not only not a Catholic but not even a Christian, he sought out the priest in the Lithuanian church who spoke and understood English only primitively, uttered a confession of absurd sins (I burned my wife's toenail parings three times) and then made his Easter Duty at Sacred Heart Church, driving out the odor of simony with ritual sacrilege.

He shoved his arms into the fresh shirt Mary Daugherty had ironed. A fresh shirt every day, Mary insisted, or you'll blow us all out the window with the B.O. Martin pushed into his black shoes, gone gray with months of scuffs and the denial of polish, threw a tie once around his neck in a loose knot, and thrust himself into his much abused suit coat. A sughan, Mary said. You've made a sughan of it. Ah well, all things come alike to all, the clean and the unclean, the pressed and the unimpressed.

In the bathroom he brushed away the taste of oatmeal, splashed his face with cold water, flattened his cowlick with the hairbrush, and then salt-stepped down the stairs, saying as he sped through the kitchen: "I've got a hell of a story, I think, Mary. I'll call you."

"What about your coffee? What about your eggs?"

But he was already gone, this aging firefly who never seemed to his wife to have grown up quite like other men, gone on another story.

Martin Daugherty had once lived in Arbor Hill, where the McCalls and the Phelans lived, but fire destroyed the house of his childhood and adolescence, and the smoke poisoned Katrina Daugherty, his mother, who escaped the flames only to die on the sidewalk of Colonie Street in her husband's arms, quoting Verlaine to him: "... you loved me so!" "Quite likely—I forget."

The fire began in the Christian Brothers School next door, old Brother William turned to a kneeling cinder by the hellish flames. The fire leaped across the alley and consumed the Daugherty house, claiming not only its second victim in Martin's mother, but also his father's accumulation of a lifetime of books, papers, and clippings that attested to his fame and infamy, and two unfinished plays. Edward Daugherty left Arbor Hill forever after the fire and moved into the North End of the city, politely evicting the tenants in his own father's former home on Main Street.

This was the house Edward Daugherty's parents had built on the edge of the Erie Canal the year before Martin was born, and had lived in until they died. After Edward's first stroke, Martin moved into the house also, with his wife and son, to nurse his father back to independence. But the man was never to be well again, and Martin remained in the house even until now, curator of what he had come to call the Daugherty Museum.

Martin parked his car on Colonie Street in front of the

vacant lot where his former home had stood before it burned. He stepped out onto the sidewalk where he'd once pitched pennies and election cards, and the charred roots of his early life moved beneath his feet. Chick Phelan peered out of the upstairs bay window of the house next to the empty lot. Martin did not wave. He looked fleetingly at the outline of the foundation of the old place, slowly being buried by the sod of time.

Patsy McCall's house was kitty-corner to the empty lot and Martin crossed the street and climbed the stoop. He, the Phelans, the McCalls (Bindy lived two doors above Patsy), and all the other youths of the street had spent uncountable nights on this stoop, talking, it now seemed, of three subjects: baseball, the inaccessibility of the myriad burgeoning breasts that were poking themselves into the eyeballs and fluid dreams of every boy on the street, and politics: Would you work for Billy Barnes? Never. Packy McCabe? Sure. Who's the man this election? Did you hear how the Wally-Os stole a ballot box in the Fifth Ward and Corky Ronan chased 'em and got it back and bit off one of their ears?

Martin looked at his watch: eight thirty-five. He rang the doorbell and Dick Maloney, district attorney of Albany County, a short, squat man with an argumentative mouth, answered.

"You're up early, Dick, me boy."

"Am I?"

"Are you in possession of any news?"

"There's no news I know of."

And Maloney pointed toward the dining room, where Martin found Patsy and Matt McCall, the political leaders of the city and county for seventeen years. Cronies of both brothers sat with them at the huge round table, its white tablecloth soiled with coffee stains and littered with cups, ashes, and butts. On the wall the painted fruit was ripening in the bowl and the folks were still up at Golgotha. Alongside hung framed, autographed photos of Jim Jeffries, Charlie Murphy of Tammany, Al Smith as presidential candidate, and James Oliver Plunkett, who had inscribed the photo with one of his more memorable lines: "Government of the people, by the people who were elected to govern them."

"Morning, gentlemen," Martin said with somber restraint.

"We're not offering coffee," said Patsy, looking his usual, overstuffed self. With his tight haircut, rounded jowls, and steel-rimmed specs, this Irish-American chieftain looked very like a Prussian puffball out of uniform.

"Then thanks for nothing," said Martin.

The cronies, Poop Powell, an ex-hurley player and ex-cop who drove for the McCalls, and Freddie Gallagher, a childhood pal of Matt's who found that this friendship alone was the secret of survival in the world, rose from the table and went into the parlor without a word or a nod. Martin sat in a vacated chair and said to Patsy, "There's something tough going on, I understand."

"No, nothing," said Patsy.

The McCalls' faces were abulge with uncompromising gravity. For all their power they seemed suddenly powerless confronting personal loss. But many men had passed into oblivion for misjudging the McCalls' way with power. Patsy demonstrated it first in 1919 when he campaigned in his sailor suit for the post of city assessor and won, oh wondrous victory. It was the wedge which broke the hold the dirty black Republican sons of bitches had had on the city since '99. Into the chink Patsy made in the old machine, the Democrats, two years later, drove a new machine, the Nonesuch, with the McCalls at the wheel: Patsy, the savior, the *sine qua non*, becoming the party leader and patron; Matt, the lawyer, be-

29

coming the political strategist and spokesman; and Benjamin, called Bindy, the sport, taking over as Mayor of Nighttime City.

The three brothers, in an alliance with a handful of Protestant Yankee aristocrats who ran the formal business of the city, developed a stupendous omnipotence over both county and city, which vibrated power strings even to the White House. Democratic aspirants made indispensable quadrennial pilgrimages to genuflect in the McCall cathedral and plead for support. The machine brushed the lives of every Albany citizen from diapers to dotage. George Quinn often talked of the day he leaped off the train at Van Woert Street, coming back in uniform from France, and was asked for five dollars by John Kelleher on behalf of Patsy's campaign for the assessorship. George gave not five but fifteen and had that to brag about for the rest of his life.

"I have to say it," Martin said, looking at Patsy, his closest friend among the brothers. "There's a rumor around that Charlie was kidnapped last night."

The gravity of the faces did not change, nor did the noncommittal expressions.

"Nothing to that," said Matt, a tall, solid man, still looking like the fullback he once was, never a puffball; handsome and with a movie actor's crop of black hair. When he gained power, Matt put his college football coach on the Supreme Court bench.

"Is Charlie here?" Martin asked him.

"He went to New York," Matt said.

"When was that?"

"None of your goddamn business," said Patsy.

"Patsy, listen. I'm telling you the rumor is out. If it's fake and you don't squelch it, you'll have reporters crawling in the windows."

"Not these windows I won't. And why should I deny something that hasn't happened? What the hell do you think I am, a goddamn fool?"

The rising anger. Familiar. The man was a paragon of wrath when cornered. Unreason itself. He put Jigger Begley in tears for coming drunk to a rally, and a week later Jigger, Patsy's lifelong friend, quit his job in the soap factory, moved to Cleveland, and for all anybody knew was there yet. Power in the voice.

Martin's personal view was this: that I do not fear the McCalls; that this is my town as much as theirs and I won't leave it for any of them. Martin had committed himself to Albany in part because of the McCalls, because of the promise of a city run by his childhood friends. But he'd also come back to his native city in 1921, after two years with the A.E.F. and a year and a half in Ireland and England after that, because he sensed he would be nothing without his roots, and when, in 1922, he was certain of this truth he went back to Ireland and brought Maire Kiley out of her Gaelic wilderness in Carraroe, married her in Galway, and came to Albany forever, or at least sixteen years now seemed like forever. So to hell with Patsy and his mouth and the whole bunch of them and their power. Martin Daugherty's complacency is superior to whatever abstract whip they hold over him. But then again, old fellow, there's no need to make enemies needlessly, or to let the tone of a man's voice turn your head.

"One question then," Martin said with his mildest voice, "and then I'm done with questions."

The brothers waited solemnly.

"Is Bindy in town?"

"He's in Baltimore," said Matt. "At the races with his wife."

Martin nodded, waited, then said, "Patsy, Matt. You say there's nothing going on and I have to accept that, even though Maloney looks like he's about to have twins on the stair carpet. But very obviously something *is* happening, and you don't want it out. All right, so be it. I give you my word, and I pledge Em Jones's word, that the *Times-Union* will not print a line about this thing, whatever it is. Not the rumor, not the denial of the rumor, not any speculation. We will not mention Charlie, or Bindy, or either of you in any context other than conventional history, until you give the go-ahead. I don't break confidences without good reason and you both know that about me all my life. And I'll tell you one more thing. Emory will do anything in his power to put the newspaper behind you in any situation such as the hypothetical one we've not been discussing here. I repeat. Not discussing. Under no circumstances have we been discussing anything here this morning. But if the paper can do anything at all, then it will. I pledge that as true as I stand here talking about nothing whatsoever."

The faces remained grave. Then Patsy's mouth wrinkled sideways into the makings of a small grin.

"You're all right, Martin," he said. "For a North Ender."

Martin stood and shook Matt's hand, then Patsy's.

"If anything should come up we'll let you know," Matt said. "And thanks."

"It's what's right," Martin said, standing up, thinking: I've still got the gift of tongues. For it was as true as love that by talking a bit of gibberish he had verified, beyond doubt, that Charlie Boy McCall had, indeed, been grabbed.

"You know I saw Charlie last night down at the Downtown alleys. We were there when Scotty Streck dropped dead. I suppose you know about that one."

"We knew he was there," Patsy said. "We didn't know who else."

"We're working on that," Matt said.

"I can tell you who was there to the man," Martin said, and he ticked off names of all present except the sweeper and one bar customer, whom he identified by looks. Matt made notes on it all.

"What was Berman doing there?" Patsy asked.

"I don't know. He just turned up at the bar."

"Was he there before Charlie got there?"

"I can't be sure of that."

"Do you think he knew Charlie would be at the alleys?"

"I couldn't say."

"Do you know Berman?"

"I've been in his company, but we're not close."

"Who is close to him?"

Martin shook his head, thinking of faces but connecting no one intimately to the man. Then he said, "Billy Phelan seems to know him. Berman backed him in last night's match and did the same once before, when Billy played pool. He seems to like Billy."

"Do you trust Phelan?" Matt asked.

"No man in his right mind would trust him with his woman, but otherwise he's as good as gold, solid as they come."

"We want to keep tabs on that Berman fellow," Patsy said.

"You think he's connected to this situation?" and both Patsy and Matt shrugged without incriminating Berman, but clearly admitting there certainly was a situation.

"We're keeping tabs on a lot of people," Patsy said. "Can you ask young Phelan to hang around a while with Berman, the next few days, say, and let us know where he goes and what he says?"

"Ahhhhh," said Martin, "that's tricky but I guess I can ask."

"Don't you think he'll do it?"

"I wouldn't know, but it is touchy. Being an informer's not Billy's style."

"Informer?" said Patsy, bristling.

"It's how he might look at it."

"That's not how I look at it."

"I'll ask him," Martin said. "I can certainly ask him."

"We'll take good care of him if he helps us," Matt said. "He can count on that."

"I don't think he's after that either."

"Everybody's after that," Patsy said.

"Billy's headstrong," Martin said, standing up.

"So am I," said Patsy. "Keep in touch."

"Bulldogs," said Martin.

3

Martin drove downtown and parked on Broadway near the Plaza, as usual, and headed, he thought, for the *Times-Union*. But instead of turning up Beaver Street, he walked south on Broadway, all the way to Madison Avenue. He turned up Madison, realizing then that he was bound for Spanish George's bar. He had no urge to drink and certainly no reason to confront either George or any of his customers, especially at this hour. George, notorious in the city's South End, ran a bar and flophouse in Shanks's old three-story livery stable. He had come to America from Spain to build the Barge Canal and stayed on to establish an empire in the dregs, where winos paid to collapse on his cots after they had all but croaked on his wine.

The sour air assaulted Martin as he stepped inside the bar, but he understood the impulse that was on him and did not retreat. His will seemed unfettered, yet somehow suspended. He knew he was obeying something other than will and that it might, or might not, reveal its purpose. In the years when this came as a regular impulse, he often found himself sitting in churches, standing in front of grocery stores, or riding trolleys, waiting for revelation. But the trolley often reached the end of the line and took him back to his starting point without producing an encounter, and he would resume the previous path of his day, feeling duped by useless caprice. Yet the encounters which did prove meaningful, or even prophetic of disaster or good fortune, were of such weight that he could not help but follow the impulse once he recognized it for what it was. He came to believe that the useless journeys did not arise from the same source as those with genuine meaning, but were rather his misreadings of his own mood, his own imagination, a duping of self with counterfeit expectations. Five such fruitless trips in four days after his debauch made him aware his gift had fled. Now, as he gagged on the wine-pukish rancidity of George's, on the dead-rat stink and the vile-body decay that entered your system with every breath, he was certain that the impulse was the same as it had always been, whether true or false; and what he was doing was giving his mystical renewal a chance to prove itself. He ordered a bottle of beer and when George was looking elsewhere he wiped its neck clean with his handkerchief and drank from the bottle.

"I don't see you too much," George said to him.

George was, as usual, wearing his filthy sombrero and his six-gun in the embroidered leather holster, and looked very like a Mexican *bandido*. The gun, presumably, was not loaded, or so the police had ordered. But any wino aggressive on muscatel could not be so sure of that, and so George, by force of costume alone, maintained order on his premises.

"That's true, George," Martin said. "I keep pretty busy uptown. Not much on this edge of things lately."

"I see you writing in the paper."

"Still at it. Right you are."

"You never write me a story any more."

"I've done you, George, again and again. You've ceased to be newsy. If you decide to renovate the premises and put in a bridal suite, then maybe I'll work up a story."

"No money in that stuff."

"You're probably right. Honeymooners are bum spenders. But business is good, I suppose?"

"Always lousy. You like a sandwich? Fry an egg for you?"

"I just had breakfast, thanks. The beer is fine."

"Okay," George said, and he pushed Martin's dollar back to him.

Martin sensed a presence then and looked toward the door to see a tall, shambling man in a suit coat of brown twill, collar up, lighting a cigarette as he moved toward the bar. Despite what the years had done to the man, Martin instantly recognized Francis Phelan, Billy's father, and he knew his own presence here had a purpose. Forced confluence of Martin and the Phelans: Billy and Chick, now Francis, and yet more than that. The McCalls were part of it. And Martin's father, too, in his bed of senility; and Melissa, in town in the old man's play. A labyrinth.

"Francis," said Martin, and Francis turned and squinted through half-waking eyes, pitiable visage. Martin vividly remembered the original: Franny Phelan: Albany's best-known ballplayer in his time. And he remembered too the dreadful day in 1901 when the scabs and the militia were trying to drive a single trolley through a mob on Broadway in front of Union Station, and Franny, in front of the Railroad YMCA, hurling a smooth round stone like a fast ball, and laying open the skull of the scab conductor. The militia fired wildly into the crowd as other stones flew, and in retaliation for the dead scab, two men who had nothing to do with the violence, a businessman and a shopper, were shot dead. And Franny became a fugitive, his exile proving to be the compost for his talent. He fled west, using an alias, and got a job in Dayton playing pro ball. When he came home again to live, he returned to life on the road every summer for years, the last three as a big leaguer with Washington. Franny Phelan, a razzmatazz third baseman, maestro of the hidden ball trick.

Such a long time ago. And now Franny is back, the bloom of drink in every pore, the flesh ready to bleed through the sheerest of skin. He puffed his cigarette, dropped the lit match to the floor, inhaled, and then looked searchingly at Martin, who followed the progress of the match, watched its flame slowly burn out on the grease of George's floor.

"Ah, how are you Martin?" Francis said.

"I'm well enough, Fran, and how are you keeping yourself?"

"Keeping?" He smiled. "Orange soda, with ice," he told George.

"What color orange has your money got?" George said.

"Take it here," said Martin, pushing the dollar back to George. And George then poured Francis a glass of soda over ice, a jelly glass with a ridged rim.

"It's been years," Martin said. "Years and years."

"I guess so," said Francis. He sipped the soda, once, twice. "Goddamn throat's burning up." He raised the glass. "Cheers."

"To you," Martin said, raising the bottle, "back in Albany."

"I only came to vote," said Francis, smiling.

"To vote?"

"To register. They still pay for that here, don't they?"

"Ah, yes, of course. I understand. Yes, I believe they do."

"I did it before. Registered fourteen times one year. Twenty-eight bucks."

"The price is up to five now. It must've been a long while ago you did that."

"I don't remember. I don't remember much of anything any more."

"How long has it been? Twenty years, it must be."

"Twenty-two. I do remember that. Nineteen-sixteen."

"Twenty-two years. You see the family?"

"No, I don't go through that business."

"I talked to Chick this morning."

"Fuck him."

"Well, I always get along pretty well with him. And he always thought well of you."

"Fuck 'em all."

"You don't see your kids either?"

"No, I don't see nobody." He sipped the soda. "You see the boy?"

"Quite often. He's a first-rate citizen, and good looking, with some of your features. I was with him last night. He bowled two-ninety-nine in a match game."

"Yeah."

"You want to see him? I could set that up."

"No, hell no. None of that old shit. That's old shit. I'm out of it, Martin. Don't do nothin' like that to me."

"If you say so."

"Yeah, I do. No percentage in that."

"You here for a while?"

"No, passing through, that's all. Get the money and get gone."

"Very strange development, running into you here. Anything I can do for you, Franny?" Franny, the public name. What a hell of a ball player, gone to hell.

"I could use a pack of smokes."

"What's your brand?"

Francis snorted. "Old Golds. Why not?"

Martin pushed a quarter at George and George fished for the cigarettes and bounced them on the bar in front of Francis.

"That's two I owe you, Martin. What're you doin' for yourself?"

"I write for the morning paper, a daily column."

"A writer like your father."

"No, not like that. Not anything like that. Just a column."

"You were always a smart kid. You always wrote something. Your father still alive?"

"Oh yes," and ancient times rolled back, the years before and after the turn of the century when the Phelans and Daughertys were next-door neighbors and Martin's mother was alive in her eccentric isolation. Francis was the handyman who fixed whatever went wrong in the Daugherty home, Edward Daugherty cosmically beyond manual labor, Martin a boyish student of Francis's carpentry skills as he put on the new roof or enlarged the barn to house two carriages instead of one. He was installing a new railing on the back stoop the summer morning Martin's mother came down that same stoop naked, bound for the carriage barn with her shopping bag. Francis wrapped her in a piece of awning and walked her back into the house, the first indication to anyone except Edward Daugherty that something was distracting her.

Edward Daugherty used Francis as the prototype for the fugitive hero in his play about the trolley strike, *The Car Barns*, in which heroic Francis, the scab-killer, was immortalized. Legends and destinies worked out over the back fence. Or over a beer and an orange soda.

"He's in a nursing home now," Martin said of his father. "Pretty senile, but he has his moments when a good deal of it comes back. Those are the worst times."

"That's how it goes," Francis said.

"For some people."

"Yeah. Some don't get that far."

"I have the feeling I ought to do something for you, Fran," Martin said. "Something besides a pack of cigarettes and a glass of soda. Why do I feel that?"

"Damned if I know, Martin. Nothing I want out of you."

"Well, I'm around. I'm in the book, up on Main Street in the North End now. And you can always leave a message at the *Times-Union*."

"Okay, Martin, and thanks for that," and Francis extended his right hand, which was missing two joints on the index

40

finger. He will throw no more baseballs. Martin shook the hand and its stumpy digit.

"Don't blow any whistles on me, Martin. I don't need that kind of scene."

"It's your life," Martin said, but even as he said it he was adding silently: but not entirely yours. Life hardly goes by ones.

Martin bought an *Armstrong* at Jerry's newsroom, just up from the paper, and then an egg sandwich and coffee to go at Farrell's lunchroom, three doors down, and with breakfast and horses in hand he crossed Beaver Street, climbed the paintless, gray, footworn, and crooked staircase to the *Times-Union* city room, and settled in at his desk, a bruised oak antique at which the Albany contemporaries of Mark Twain might have worked. Across the room Joe Leahy, the only other citizen on duty and a squeaker of a kid, was opening mail at the city desk and tending the early phone. The only other life sign was the clacking of the Associated Press and International News Service teletypes, plus the Hearst wire, which carried the words of The Chief: editorials, advisories, exclusive stories on Marion Davies.

Martin never looked at the machine without remembering the night Willie Powers, the night slot man, went to lunch and came back pickled, then failed to notice an advisory that The Chief was changing his front-page editorial on Roosevelt, changing it drastically from soft- to hard-line antipathy, for the following day. Willie failed to notice not only the advisory but also the editorial which followed it, and so the *Times-Union* the next morning carried The Chief's qualified praise of F.D.R., while the rest of the Hearst press across the nation carried The Chief's virulent attack on the president, his ancestors, his wife, his children, his dog.

There is no record of Hearst's ever having visited the *Times-*

41

Union city room, but a week later, during a stopover at the Albany station on the Twentieth Century, The Chief received Emory Jones, who presented him with the day's final edition, an especially handsome, newsy product by local standards. The Chief looked at the paper, then without a word let it fall to the floor of his private compartment, and jumped up and down on it with both feet until Emory fled in terror.

Martin fished up salt, pepper, saccharin, and spoon to garnish his sandwich and coffee and, as he ate, studied the entries in the *Armstrong*. There in the third at Laurel loomed a hunch, if ever a hunch there was: Charley Horse, seven-to-one on the morning line. He circled it, uncradled the phone receiver and dialed the operator: Madge, lively crone.

"Any messages for me, kiddo?"

"Who'd call you, you old bastard? Wait while I look. Yes, Chick Phelan called. Not that long ago. He didn't leave a number."

"You heard from Emory? He coming in?"

"Not a word from him."

"Then give me a line."

Martin dialed home and told Mary the news and swore her to secrecy. Then he called Chick's home. The phone rang but nobody answered. He dialed the home of Emory Jones, the Welsh rarebit, the boss of bosses, editor of editors, a heroic Hearstian for almost as many years as Hearst had owned newspapers, a man who lived and died for the big story, who coveted the Pulitzer Prize he would never win and hooted the bootlickers and eggsuckers who waltzed off with it year after year. Martin would now bring him the word on the Charlie Boy story, fracture his morning serenity.

Martin remembered the last big Albany story, the night word arrived that a local man wanted for a triple murder in Canada would probably try to return to the U.S. Which border crossing he had in mind was uncertain, so Em Jones studied the map and decided the fellow would cross at Montreal. But on the off chance he would go elsewhere Emory also alerted border police at Niagara Falls, Baudette, Minnesota, and Blaine, Washington, to our man perhaps en route. When the four calls were made Emory sat down at the city desk, lit up a stogie, and propped up his feet to wait for the capture. We got him surrounded, he said.

"Em, that you?"

"Ynnnnnh."

"I've got a bit of news."

"Ynnnh."

"Charlie McCall was kidnapped during the night."

Emory yawned. "You drunken son of a bitch."

"I'm not drunk, nor have I been, nor will I be."

"Then you mean it? You mean it?" Emory stood up. Even through the telephone, Martin observed that.

"I just left Patsy and Matt, and Maloney too, all at Patsy's house, and I pledged in your name we wouldn't run a story on it."

"Now I know you're lying." Emory sat down.

"Emory, you better get down here. This town is getting ready to turn itself inside out."

The editor of editors fell silent.

"You really do mean it?"

"Whoever grabbed Charlie meant it, too."

"But you didn't tell Patsy that about no story. You wouldn't say that."

"I did."

"You needle-brained meathead. What in the sweet Christ's name possessed you?"

"My Celtic wisdom."

"Your Celtic ass is right between your eyes, that's your

wisdom. I'm coming down. And you better figure a way to undo that pledge, for your own sake. And this better be real. Is it real?"

"Em, are your teeth real?"

"Half and half."

"Then Em, this story is even more real than your teeth."

Martin found two more Chuck and Charlie horses in the *Armstrong*, checked his wallet, and lumped all but his last ten on the bunch, across the board, plus a parlay. Never a hunch like this one. He called the bets in to Billy Phelan, the opening move in his effort to bring Billy into the McCall camp, not that Billy would require much persuasion. Billy was a Colonie Streeter, was he not? Grew up three doors up from Patsy and next door to Bindy, knew Charlie Boy all his life. But Billy was an odd duck, a loner, you bet, erratic in a way Martin was not. Billy was self-possessed, even as a boy, but then again he had to be, did he not? Fatherless from age nine, when Francis Phelan left home, left wife, son, and daughter forever, or at least until this morning.

Martin's problem was similar, but turned inside out: too much father, too much influence, too much fame, too much scandal, but also too much absence as the great man pursued his greatness. And these, my friends, are forces that deprived a young man of self-possession and defined his life as a question mark, unlike Billy Phelan's forces, which defined *his* life as an exclamation point.

When his bets were made Martin swallowed the last of his coffee and went to the morgue and pulled all files on the McCalls. They should have had a file cabinet to themselves, given the coverage of their lives through the years, but thieves walked abroad. No clips remained of Patsy's victory in 1919, or even of the Democratic sweep of the city in 1921. Stories on the 1931 legislative probe into the city's assessment racket were gone. So were all reports on Patsy's doing six months for contempt in the baseball-pool scandal.

This was historical revisionism through burglary. Had free-lancers looking for yet another magazine piece on the notorious McCalls done the filching? Or was it McCall loyalist reporters, who doubled on the city payroll as sidewalk inspectors? The lightfingering effectively kept past history out of the ready reach of reform-minded newsmen, or others snooping on behalf of uplift: Tom Dewey, the redoubtable D.A., for instance, who was making noises like a governor: Elect me, folks, and I'll send the McCall bunch swirling down the sinkhole of their own oily unguents.

Joe Leahy saw Martin shuffling through the McCall files and wondered aloud, "What's up with them?"

"Ahh," said Martin with theatrical weariness, "a backgrounder on them and the A.L.P. Big power move that comes to a head tonight when the enrollment figures come in."

"The McCalls taking on the reds? Can they really do it?"

"The power of prayer is with them. The bishop's behind Patsy all the way."

"You writing something for the first edition?"

"Nothing for the first. When it happens, it happens."

Martin turned back to the folders and Leahy walked off, a good Catholic boy who loved Franco and hated the reds. Untrustworthy with anything meaningful. Martin leafed through the Charlie Boy file, all innocuous stuff. Promoted to major in the National Guard. Engaged to sweet-faced Patricia Brennan. Initiated into the B.P.O.E. lodge number forty-nine. Named vice-president of the family brewery. Shown visiting Jimmy Braddock in his dressing room in Chicago before the fight with Joe Louis. Shown with his favorite riding horse, a thoroughbred named Macushla, birthday gift from Uncle Patsy of political fame, who keeps horses on a small Virginia farm.

45

Charlie was pudgy, the face of a smiling marshmallow on the torso of a left tackle. There he stood in his major's suit, all Sam Browne and no wrinkles. Where are you this minute, Charlie Boy? Tied to a bed? Gun at your brain? How much do they say your life is worth? Have they already killed you?

Martin remembered Charlie's confirmation, the boy kissing the bishop's ring; then at the party Bindy gave afterward at the Hampton Hotel, the bishop kissing Bindy's foot. That was the year the McCalls all but donated the old city almshouse to the Catholic diocese as a site for the new Christian Brothers Academy, the military high school where Charlie would become a cadet captain. Martin's wife, Maire, now called Mary, a third or maybe fourth cousin to Bindy's wife, sang "Come Back to Erin" at the confirmation party, accompanied on the piano by Mrs. Dillon, the organist at St. Joseph's Church, whose son was simple-minded. And Mary, when the bishop congratulated her on her voice and patted her on the hand, felt fully at home in America for the first time since Martin had snatched her away from Ireland.

Martin's recollection of Charlie Boy on that afternoon was obscured by memories of Bindy and Patsy and Matt, whom he saw yet at a table in a far corner, objects of veneration, Albany's own Trinity.

The perils of being born, like himself, to a man of such fame and notoriety sent Martin into commiseration with Charlie. Bindy was an eminence, the power on the street. "Celebrated sporting figure" and "a member of the downtown fraternity" was as far as the papers ever went by way of identifying him. Cautious journalism. No one mentioned his direct power over the city's illegal gambling. No editor would let a writer write it. It was the received wisdom that no one minds the elephant in the parlor if nobody mentions it's there. Martin's own decision to tell Patsy there would be no story on the kidnapping: Was that conspiratorial genuflection? No end to the veneration of power, for the news is out: The McCalls hurl thunderbolts when affronted.

The memory of their confrontation with *The Albany Sentinel* was still fresh. *The Sentinel* had prospered as an opposition voice to the McCalls in the early days of the machine, but its success was due less to its political point of view than to the gossip it carried. In 1925 the paper dredged up "The Love Nest Tragedy of 1908" involving Edward Daugherty and Melissa Spencer, purporting to have discovered two dozen torchy love letters from the famous playwright to the now beloved star of the silent screen. The letters were crude forgeries and Melissa ignored them. But Edward Daugherty halted their publication with an injunction and a libel suit. Patsy McCall saw to it that the judge in the case was attuned to the local realities, saw to it also that a hand-picked jury gave proper consideration to Patsy's former Colonie Street neighbor. *The Sentinel* publicly admitted the forgery and paid nominal libel damages. But it then found its advertisers withdrawing *en masse* and its tax assessment quintupled. Within a month the ragbag sons of bitches closed up shop and left town, and moral serenity returned to Albany as McCall Democracy won the day.

"Aren't you a little early this morning?"

Marlene Whiteson, a reporter whose stories were so sugary that you risked diabetic coma if you read them regularly, stood in front of Martin's desk, inside her unnecessary girdle, oozing even at this hour the desire but not quite the will, never quite the will, to shed those restrictive stays, leap onto the desk, and do a goat dance with him, or with anyone. But Marlene was an illusionist, her sexuality the disappearing rabbit: Now you see it, now you don't. Reach out to touch and find it gone, back inside her hat. The city room was full of hopefuls, ready to do Marlene, but as far as Martin knew, he himself came closest to trapping the rabbit on a night six years past when both of them worked late and he drove her home, circuitously. Need one explain why he stopped the car, stroked her cheek? She volunteered a small gift of smooch and said into his ear, Oh, Martin, you're the man I'd like to go to Pago Pago with. Whereupon he reached for her portions, only to be pushed away, while she continued nevertheless with bottomless smooch. Twist my tongue but stroke me never. Oh the anomaly. Coquettes of the world, disband; you have nothing to gain but saliva.

"What goodies do you have for us today?" Martin asked her.

"I have a message for you, as a matter of fact. Did you see this morning's paper?"

"I was just about to crack it."

"I have a story in about Melissa Spencer. She sends you greetings and hopes she gets a chance to see you. She also asked about your father."

"Ah. And is she well?"

"She looks absolutely gorgeous. For forty-nine. She is some sexy dame."

"How long will she be here?"

"Just a week."

Martin knew that. He had known for weeks she was starring in the touring production of his father's great work, *The Flaming Corsage*, the play Edward Daugherty had written in order to transform his melodramatic scandal with Melissa and her jealous lesbian lover, and the consequent destruction of his career and his wife, into anguished theatrical harmony. He used both Martin's mother, Katrina, and the young Melissa as models for the two principal women in the play, and, not unnaturally, Melissa, as a young actress, yearned to incarnate the role she had inspired in life.

Now, at forty-nine, no longer disguisable as the pristine Melissa of 1908, she was appearing in the play for the first time, but as the hero's reclusive, middle-aged wife. The casting, the result of assiduous pursuit of the part by Melissa herself, had the quality of aged perfume about it: yesterday's scarlet tragedy revived for an audience which no longer remembered this flaming, bygone sin, but for whom the reversal of roles by the famed Melissa was still quaintly scandalous. Melissa had acted in the play for six months on Broadway before taking it on the road, her comeback after a decade of invisiblity: one of the most animatedly lovely stars of the silent screen back once more in the American embrace, this time visible, all but palpable, in the flesh.

"She really is interested in seeing you," Marlene said, opening the morning paper to her interview with Melissa and spreading it on Martin's desk. "She's keeping a ticket in your name at the box office, and she wants you to go backstage after the curtain." Marlene smiled and raised her sexual eyebrow. "You devil," she said, moving away from Martin's desk.

Martin barely managed a smile for the world champion of sexual fatuity. How surprised she would be at what Melissa could do with the same anatomical gifts as her own. He looked at Melissa's photo in the paper and saw Marlene was right. Melissa was still beautiful. When time descends, the ego forfends. But Martin could not read her story now. Too distracted to resurrect old shame, old pleasure. But Martin, you will go backstage one night this week, will you not? He conjured the vision of the naked, spread-eagled Melissa and his phone rang. Chick Phelan on the line.

"I saw you go in across the street, Martin. What'd they say?"

"Not much except to confirm what you said."

"Now they've cut off all the phones on the block. I'm in Tony Looby's store down on Pearl Street."

Chick, the snoop, grateful to Martin for introducing him to Evelyn Hurley, the love of his life, whom he is incapable of marrying. Chick will reciprocate the favor as long as love lasts.

"They probably don't want any busybodies monitoring their moves and spreading the word all over town. Anything else going on?"

"People coming in here know something's up but they don't know what."

"Just keep what you know under your hat, Chickie, for Charlie's sake as well as your own. My guess is they're afraid for his life. And keep me posted."

Martin called Walter Bradley, the Albany police chief.

"Walter, I hear the phones are out on Colonie Street."

"What's that to me? Call the phone company."

"We've been told, Walter, that something happened to Charlie McCall. I figured you'd know about it."

"Charlie? I don't know anything about that at all. I'm sure Patsy'd tell me if something was going on. I talk to Patsy every morning."

"I talked to him myself just a while ago, Walter. And you say there's nothing new? No kidnapping for instance?"

"No, no, no, no kidnapping, for chrissake, Martin. No kidnapping, nothing. Nothing at all. Everything's quiet and let's keep it that way."

"You get any other calls about Charlie?"

"No, goddamn it, no. I said nothing's going on and that's all there is to it. Now I'm busy, Martin."

"I'll talk to you later, Walter."

In minutes Martin's phone rang again, Freddie Dunsbach of the United Press.

"Martin, we've had a tip Patsy McCall's nephew was kidnapped."

"Is that so?"

"It's so and you know it."

"Who said I know it?"

"I called Patsy. He denied it and then said to call you."

50

"Me? Why me?"

"I thought you could tell me that. Right now we've got an eight-hour jump on you, Martin, or are you putting out an extra? You can't keep a story like this all to yourself."

"There's no story, Freddie."

"You really haven't heard about it?"

"I've heard a wild rumor, but we don't print rumors."

"Since when?"

"Blow it out your ass, Fred." And Martin hung up. The phone rang right back.

"Martin, I'm sorry. That was a joke."

"I accept your groveling apology. What do you want?"

"Why did Patsy tell me to call you?"

"Damned if I know. Maybe to get rid of you."

"I think we're going with the rumor, as an editor's advisory. Our source is a good one."

"That's a bad idea."

"We can't sit on it."

"You can if it means Charlie's life."

"This is too big. Hell, this is national."

Martin snorted. Freddie Dunsbach, boy bureau chief. Arrogant yokel.

"It's all of that. But let me ask you. How long've you been in this town?"

"Almost a year."

"Then you ought to know that if the McCalls are quiet on this thing, and the police are quiet, there's one hell of a reason. Patsy must've sent you to me because I told him I wouldn't print any rumors. I see the significance escapes you, but Patsy's concern is obviously for the safety of Charlie, if Charlie has in fact been kidnapped, which is really not provable if nobody admits it."

"Does he expect us to bury our heads and ignore the story?"

"What Patsy expects is known only to the deity, but I

51

know what I'd expect if I broke this story and Charlie was murdered because of it. Would you know what to expect in a case like that?"

Freddie was silent.

"Freddie, would you?"

"You're talking about reprisals for reporting the news."

"You ever hear about the time Bindy McCall beat a man half to death for insulting his wife? What do you suppose he'd do to somebody who caused the death of his only son? The only child in the whole McCall family."

"You can't run a news organization on that basis."

"Maybe you can't. Maybe a five-minute beat—which is about all you'd get since we'd put it on the I.N.S. wire as soon as the word was out—is worth Charlie's life. Kidnappers are nasty bastards. You know what happened to Lindbergh's kid, don't you? And he was just a baby who couldn't recognize anybody."

"Yeah, there's something in that."

"There's more than you think. We could've had an extra out an hour ago with the rumor. But who the hell wins that kind of game?"

"I see, but—"

"Listen, Fred, I don't run the show here. You talk to Emory when he comes in. He'll be calling the shots for us and I think I know what he's going to do, which is nothing at all until there's a mighty good reason to print something."

"It's going to be all over the world in a couple of hours."

"Not unless you send it."

"I'll talk to Emory."

"You do that."

Martin dialed Patsy, and the great gravelbox answered, again on the first ring.

"Are you sending people to me for a reason, Patsy?"

"You'll keep 'em quiet."

"Hey, this thing is already spreading all over town. Some of these birds don't give a damn about anything but news. They'll blow it wide open unless they're convinced there's a hell of a good reason not to."

Silence.

"Call Max at the office in five minutes."

In five minutes precisely Martin called Max Rosen, law partner to Matt McCall.

"The story is this, Martin," Max said. "I answered a call here forty-five minutes ago. A man's voice told me to tell Patsy and Matt they'd picked up their nephew and wanted a quarter of a million ransom, a ridiculous figure. Half an hour ago we had a letter from them, with Charlie's signature, saying the same thing. They said if we told the police or put out any publicity that they'd kill Charlie. Patsy wants you to inform the rest of the press about this. He won't talk to anyone but you, and neither will I, nor anyone else in the family. We're not telling Chief Bradley much of anything, so don't bother him any more. I don't need to tell you what this means, do I, Martin, this confidence in you?"

"No need."

"When there's something to be said it will be said to you, provided you can convince the rest of the press to preserve silence."

"I'll do what I can, Max. But it's quite a big world out here. Full of nosy, irresponsible newspapermen."

"The family knows that."

"Do they also know I don't work miracles for a living?"

"I think they presume you do now."

Emory Jones's hair was white, with vague, yellowish implications that he might once have been the fair-haired boy of somebody, a mother perhaps, somewhere. He said, whenever the whiteness of his hair arose for discussion, that pea-

53

brained reporters who didn't know the doughnut from the hole had given it to him prematurely. For years he had put up with them, he argued, because he had a basically sacrificial nature. He outlasted almost all of them, he argued further, because he had the forbearance of Jesus Christ in the face of the drooling, foaming, dementia praecox activity that passed for reporting on his one and only newspaper. The noted cry: "That son of a bitch doesn't know the goddamn dough-nut from the goddamn hole!" emanating from editor Jones's cubicle, meant a short professional life for somebody.

Martin Daugherty placed Emory in this context as he spotted the white hair, saw Emory rumbling across the crooked, paintless, freshly swept wooden floor of the city room. Here he came: pear-shaped, bottom-heavy, sits too much, unhealthy fear of exercise in the man, choler rising, executorially preempted by Martin's pledge, unspeakably happy at the unfortunate turn of events that had already boiled his creative fluids, which fluids, Martin could see, were percolating irrationally in his eyeballs.

Martin remembered a comparable frenzy in Emory's past: the period when Legs Diamond had been an Albany celebrity; the most outlandishly sensational running news event in the modern history of Albany. Emory, who whipped his slaves like a galleymaster to ferret out every inch of copy the story could bear, finally triumphed prophetically the night Diamond was acquitted of a kidnapping charge. He oversaw personally the hand-setting of the great fist-sized wooden type he saved for major natural catastrophes, armistices, and The Chief's sneezes: DIAMOND SLAIN BY ENEMIES; for the rumor had been abroad in Albany for twelve hours, and was indeed current the length of the Eastern seaboard and as far west as Chicago, that Diamond was, on that particular night, truly a terminal target. Emory had the headline made up a full six hours before Diamond was actually shot dead in his bed on

Dove Street by a pair of gunmen. It was then used on the extra that sold twenty thousand copies.

Martin had already calculated that the extra that never was on Charlie Boy would have sold even more. When the news on Charlie did break, the coverage would dwarf the Diamond story. There had never been anything like this in Albany's modern history, and Martin knew Emory Jones also knew this, knew it deeply, far down into the viscous, ink-stinking marrow of his editorial bones.

"Did you undo that goddamn pledge?" were Emory's first words.

"No."

"Then get at it."

"It's not possible, Emory."

Emory moved his cigar in and out of his mouth, an unnerved thumbsucker. He sat down in the wobbly chair alongside Martin's decrepit desk, blew smoke at Martin, and inquired: "Why in the sacred name of Jesus is it not possible?"

"Because I don't think you're interested in being the editor who put the bullet in Charlie McCall's brain. Or are you?"

Martin's explanation of the sequence of events forced Emory to recapitulate the future as he had known it all morning. Martin let him stew and then told him: "Emory, you're the man in charge of this silence, whether you like it or not. You're the man with the reputation, the journalistic clout. You're the only one in town who can convince the wire services and whoever's left among the boys up in the Capitol press room to keep their wires closed on this one for a little while. They'll do it if you set the ground rules, make yourself chairman of the big secret. Maybe set a time limit. Two days? Four? A week?"

"A week? Are you serious?"

"All right, two days. They'll do it as a gentleman's agreement if you explain the dread behind it. You'll be a genuine hero to the McCalls if you do, and that's worth money to this newspaper, if I'm not mistaken."

"Keep your venal sarcasm under your dirty vest."

"It's not sarcasm. It's cynical humanism."

"Well, hell, I don't want to murder anybody. At least not Charlie."

"I knew you'd get the picture."

"But what will I tell them?"

"Emory, I have faith that you'll think of something. We both know you've got more bullshit than the cattle states."

"Maybe Dunsbach's already put it out."

"Maybe. Then your problem is solved, even if his isn't. But I doubt it. I was persuasive."

"Then you do it."

"I can't do it, Emory. I'm just a piss-ant columnist, not an omnipotent editor."

"Willard Maney will go along. He's an Albanian."

"And a McCall fancier."

"And Foley at the News."

"Another kinsman."

"But those bastards up at the Capitol. I don't know them. You know them. You play cards with them when you're supposed to be out getting under the news."

"Use my name up there if you like."

"The wire services can pass the word up there."

"Exactly. And the boys will very likely follow suit. Despite what you think, they're a decent bunch. And Emory, it's really not your responsibility anyway what out-of-town writers do. Then it's on them, and on their children. And what the hell, even an editor's advisory like Dunsbach's talking about wouldn't be all that bad if they made it clear to their clients that Charlie's life was at stake. Which is now a rotten fact."

"That poor bastard. What he must be going through."

"He may already be gone."

Martin looked at the clippings on his desk, Charlie's face staring up from one as he attends a Knights of Columbus party. On almost any given evening when Charlie walked into the K. of C., somebody would make a fool of himself over this gentle young man who might carry a word of good will back to his father and uncles. Life preservation. Money in the bank for those who make their allegiance known. Shake the hand of the boy who shakes the hand of the men who shake the tree from which falls the fruit of our days. Poor sucker, tied to a bed someplace. Will I live through the night? Will they shoot me in the morning? Where is my powerful father? Where are my powerful uncles? Who will save the son when the father is gone? Pray to Jesus, but where is Jesus? Jesus, Charlie, sits at my desk in the person of an equivocating Welsh rarebit who doesn't understand sons because he never had any. But he understands money and news and power and decency and perhaps such things as these will help save the boy we remember. We are now scheming in our own way, Charlie, to keep you in our life.

"I was putting together a backgrounder on Charlie," Martin said, breaking the silence. "Is there anything else you want me to do? There's also that A.L.P. business today."

"The hell with that stuff now."

"It's pretty big, you know. Quite a show of power."

"They're a handful of reds, that's all."

"They're not reds, Emory. Don't you fall for that malarkey. Probably only two or three are really Communists."

"They're pinks, then. What's the difference?"

"We can discuss this fine point of color another time, but it's definitely worth a story, and good play, no matter what else happens along with it."

"Whatever happens I don't want you on it. You stay on Charlie."

"Doing what?"

"Find the kidnappers, what the hell else?"

"Find the kidnappers."

"Check around Broadway. That's where they hang out."

"Check around Broadway."

"And don't get lost. Call me every hour. Every half-hour."

"Every half-hour."

And then Emory Jones, sucking on his stogie, rumbled off and slammed the door of his cubicle, then sat at his desk and picked up the phone to begin spreading the blanket of silence over a story whose magnitude punified even his own recurring glory dreams of news at its colossally tragic best.

4

"P lease don't talk about me when I'm gone," Mildred
Bailey was singing over WHN, with the Paul Whiteman band behind her. And Billy Phelan, writing horses
in his, or, more precisely, his sister's and brother-in-law's living
room, wearing pants, socks, and undershirt, no shoes or belt,
remembered the time she came to town with Whiteman.
Played the Palace. She always sang like a bird to Billy's ear, a
hell of a voice. Hell of a voice. Sounded gorgeous. And then
she showed up fat. Dumpy tub of lard. Whiteman too, the
tub. Billy remembered the night he played games with Whiteman at the crap table in Saratoga. He was dealing at Riley's
Lake House, youngest dealer in town that season, 1931, and
of course, of course he knew who Whiteman was when the
big boy rolled the dice and lost the last of his wad.

"Let's have five hundred in chips, sonny, and an I.O.U,"
Whiteman said.

"Who the hell are you? I don't know you," Billy said.
Sonny me, you son of a bitch. Hubie Maloy, the crazy, was at
the table that night. From Albany. Always carried a gun. But
Billy liked him. Hubie smiled when Whiteman called Billy
sonny. Big-timer, throwing his weight around, that big gut,
and figures everybody on earth knows his mustache.

"I'm Paul Whiteman."

"Wyman?"

"Whiteman. Whiteman."

"Ohhhhh yeah, Whiteman. You're the guy's got that hill-billy band playing over at Piping Rock. You don't mean nothing to me, bud. Go see the manager if you want chips."

They fired Billy twenty minutes later. Orders from above. From those who didn't want to make enemies of Paul the Man. Lemon Lewis came over to the table and said, "I hate to do it, Billy, but we gotta can you. I'll call over to Newman's and the Chicago Club, see what they got going."

And two hours after that Billy was back to work, with cards this time, sleek and sharp, full of unpredictable combinations. Billy, maybe the best dealer around, pound for pound, you name the game, such a snappy kid, Billy.

He was in Saratoga that year because one night a month earlier he was hanging around Broadway in Albany when Bindy McCall came by, Bindy, in the tan fedora with the flowerpot crown, had connections and investments in Saratoga gambling, a natural by-product of his control of all the action in Albany, all of it: gambling houses, horse rooms, policy, clearing house, card games, one-armed bandits, punch boards. Playing games in Albany meant you first got the okay from Bindy or one of his lieutenants, then delivered your dues, which Bindy counted nightly in his office on Lodge Street. The tribute wasn't Bindy's alone. It sweetened the kitty for the whole McCall machine.

Billy touched Bindy's elbow that night.

"Hey, Billy."

"Got a second, Bin? I need some work. Can you fix me up for Saratoga next month?"

"What can you do?"

"Anything."

"Anything at all?"

"Craps, poker, blackjack, roulette. I can deal, handle the stick."

"How good are you?"

"Haven't you heard?"

Bindy chuckled.

"I'll ask around someone who has. See Lemon Lewis."

"All right, Bindy, fine. Obliged. Can I touch you for fifty?"

Bindy chuckled again. Billy's got brass. Bindy reached for the roll and plucked a fifty out of the middle.

"Use it in good health."

"Never felt better," said Billy. "I pay my debts."

"I know you do. I know that about you. Your father paid his debts, too. We played ball together when we were kids. He was one hell of a player. You ever hear from him?"

"We don't hear."

"Yeah. That's an odd one. See Lewis. He'll fill you in."

"Right, Bin."

Billy saw Lewis an hour later at the bar in Becker's and got the word: You deal at Riley's.

"What about transportation?" Billy asked. "How the hell do I get from Albany to Saratoga every night?"

"Jesus, ain't you got a car?"

"Car? I never even had roller skates."

"All right. You know Sid Finkel?"

Billy knew Sid, a pimp and a booster and a pretty fair stickman. Put his kid through dentists' school with that combination.

"Look him up. I'll tell him to give you a lift."

"I'll half the gas with him," Billy said.

"That's you and him. And don't forget your source," and Lemon hit himself on the chest with his thumb.

"Who the hell could forget you, Lemon?" Billy said.

It went fine for Billy for two weeks and then came the Whiteman scene and Billy went from Riley's to the Chicago

Club, on earlier hours. The Club got a big play in the afternoon, even though the horses were running at the track. So Billy had to find new transportation because Sid Finkel stayed on nights. Was Billy lucky? He certainly was. Angie Velez saw him dealing at the Chicago Club and when he took a break, she asked him for a light.

"You weren't out of work long," she said.

"Who told you I was out of work?"

"I was there when you gave it to Whiteman. Funniest damn thing I've heard in years. Imagine anybody saying that to Paul Whiteman. You're the one with the hillbilly band. I laughed right out loud. He gave me an awfully dirty look."

Billy smiled at this new dish. Then he asked her name and bought her a drink and found she was married but only dabbled in that. Hubby was a gambler, too. Brought her to Saratoga for a week, then left her there to play while he went home to run his chunk of Rochester, what a town. No town like Albany. Rochester is where you might go on the bum, only might, if they kicked you out of Albany. Billy couldn't imagine life outside Albany. He loved the town. And half-loved you too, Angie, now that you're here. "Are you a spic?"

"I'm Irish, baby. Just like you. One of the Gagen girls. My old man's a Cuban."

She was playing kneesies with him by then.

"You keep that up, you're liable to get raped."

"Room two-forty-six in the Grand Union." And she proved it with the key. That was the beginning of Billy's private taxi service between Albany and Saratoga for the rest of the month. Other things began that season in Saratoga: Billy's reputation as the youngest of the hot numbers at any table, never mind the game. Big winner. I could always get a buck, Billy said. What the hell, I know cards and dice.

Of course, at the end of the season Billy was broke. Playing both sides of the table.

Now Mildred Bailey was all through and Clem McCarthy was barking in with the race results on WHN, and can you believe what is happening to Billy? Friar Charles wins, the son of a bitch, five-to-two, the son of a bitch, *the son of a bitch!* Martin Daugherty, what in Christ's name are you doing to Billy Phelan?

Here's how it looked to this point: Martin bet ten across the board on Charley Horse, who wins it, four-to-one; puts a tenner across also on Friar Charles and now wins that one, too; and has a third tenner going across on Hello Chuckie in the sixth at Pimlico, and Hello Chuckie is two-to-one on the morning line. There is more. Martin also *parlayed* the three horses for yet another ten.

Now, Billy knows that Martin is a hell of a sport, always pays, and loses more than he wins, which has always been pleasant for Billy, who takes a good bit of his play. But my Jesus Christ almighty, if he wins the third, plus the three-horse parlay, Billy is in trouble. Billy doesn't hold every bet he takes. You hold some, lay off some. You hold what you think you can cover, maybe a little more, if you're brassy like Billy. Billy lays some off with his pal Frankie Buchanan, who has the big book in Albany. But mother pin a rose on Billy. For bravery. For Billy is holding *all* of Martin's play. Didn't lay off a dime. Why? Because suckers and losers bet three-horse parlays. I'll hold them all day long, was Billy's philosophy until a few minutes ago when Clem McCarthy came on with the Friar Charles news. And now Billy is sitting at his card table in the front room. (Billy came here to Thanksgiving dinner six years ago and never went back downtown to his furnished room.) His money sits on the floor, next to his bridge chair, in a Dyke cigar box, Dykes being the cigar the McCall machine pushed in all the grocery and candy stores in town.

Billy himself sits under the big, shitty print of Mo the Kid in the gold frame. Billy's fingers are working with his number two Mongol pencil on the long yellow pad, and his eyes keep peeking out through the curtains on the front windows in case state cops step on his stoop, in which case Billy would be into the toilet p.g.d.q., those horse bets would be on their way down the city conduits toward the river, and even the most enterprising raider could not then bring them back and pin them on Billy's chest.

Stan whatsisname, the WHN disk jockey, was talking about Bob Crosby and Billy felt good hearing that because he knew Crosby, had heard him in Saratoga, danced to his music with Angie, talked music with him when he played The Edgewood over in Rensselaer. "Between the Devil and the Deep Blue Sea" Crosby was playing now. The phone rang and Billy turned Crosby down. Frankie Buchanan with the results of the fifth at Arlington Park, Friar Charles official now. Billy then told Frankie about Martin Daugherty's very weird parlay.

"You're the weird one," said Frankie, who was as weird as they come. One of the best-liked guys in Albany, Frankie, and yet he couldn't take the public. He'd come out at night for ham and eggs, and you'd have to sit with him in his car behind the Morris diner while he ate off a paper plate. Crazy bastards in this world.

"You want to give me the third horse or part of that parlay?"

"No," said Billy, "I can't believe the son of a bitch can pick three in a row, and parlay them, too. I never seen it done. I believe in luck but not miracles."

"Okay, pal," said Frankie, "it's all yours." And he left Billy wondering if he was really crazy. Billy could cut the mustard if the third horse ran out of the money, because the day's play was good. But if Martin Daugherty wins the parlay, Billy, it's up in the seven, eight hundreds, even if nobody else wins a nickel. And Billy Boy, you don't have that kind of cash. So why, oh why, is darlin' Billy doing it? Well, it's a gamble, after all. And Billy is certainly a gambler. Nobody will argue that. And Billy is already feeling the pressure rise in his throat, his gut, under his armpits, under his teeth and behind his jockey shorts. Christ, it tickles me somewhere, Billy thinks, and the money doesn't matter. Pressure. Sweet pressure. Here we go again, folks.

Crosby was just winding up "Deep Blue Sea." Billy remembered listening to it with Angie, saw her face. And then it was Morey Amsterdam on the radio. Popped into the studio as usual to ad lib with Stan. I gotta go up to the sixth floor, Amsterdam was saying. They're gonna lay a rug up there and I wanna see how they do it.

Telephone. Martin Daugherty.

"Yeah, Friar Charles wins it, Martin, so you got something good going. Shows seven dollars, four dollars, and three-forty. Tote it up, Martin, you're the money machine today."

Stan was telling a caller, if you don't like my show, you crumb, don't listen, but if you want to make more of it than that I'll meet you at five o'clock out in the alley behind the studio and knock your brains out. And he gave the address. Wireheaded bastard, that Stan. Billy liked his style.

Then it was quiet with no phones and only Earl (Fatha) Hines—a kid, really, so why do they call him Fatha?—playing something wild, and somebody in the chorus, when he started to move it, really move it, yelling out, "Play it Fatha . . . play it till nineteen ninety-nine." And Billy smiles, taps his foot, feels the jazz, feels, too, that good old, good old pressure beginning to cut a pulpy wedge out of his fat-assed day.

Simpson, that bum, rang Billy's bell, looking for his sawbuck. Billy saw him coming up the walk, fished a tenner out of the cigar box, folded it once and put it in his right hip pocket.

Ten down the sewer. But Billy had to pay. Tribute to Pop O'Rourke, Democratic leader of the Ninth Ward, who, six months ago, when Billy announced plans to write horses, approved the venture during Billy's formal call. The payoff? Give ten a week to Simpson, Pop said. He's down on his luck. He'll come by every week for it. Fair enough, Billy said. What else could he say? And he was still paying out the tenner.

"Hello, Bill, how you doin'?" Simpson said when Billy opened the door just enough to make it clear that it was not a welcoming gesture. The Simp's sport shirt was at least four days soiled and he needed a shave. Holes in the elbows of his sweater, boozer's look and the breath'd knock over two mules.

"Life's still tough," Billy said to him.

"I thought maybe I'd come in and sit a while," Simpson said as Billy was reaching for the ten in his pocket. And that line stopped Billy's hand.

"What?"

"Keep you company a while. I ain't doin' nothin', just hangin' around Brady's. Might as well chew the fat. You know."

"No, I don't know nothing like that," Billy said. "You ain't coming in now or ever." He opened the door all the way, stepped out, grabbed Simpson's dirty shirt, and lifted him backward down the stairs. "Now get off this stoop and stay off. Next time you put a foot on it I'll knock your ass the other side of Pearl Street."

"Don't get hot, Bill. I just wanna come in and talk."

"I don't let bums in my home. Who the hell do you think you're conning? From now on I don't even want to see you on this side of the street."

"Where's my ten?"

"You blew it, bum."

And Billy slammed the door and called Pop O'Rourke.

"And he says he wants to keep me company for the day,

chew the fat. Listen, Pop, I respect you, but that bum is looking to see my action. I have a good half hour, he'll want twenty instead of ten. Don't send him back, Pop, and I mean that. I don't like his slimy looks and I never did. I hit him once, I'll knock him off the stoop altogether. There's five steps and he'd clear the whole five if I hit him. I'll break both his arms, Pop. I don't want the bum ringing my bell."

"Take it easy, Billy. He won't be back. He did wrong. He's a greedy person. I'll tell him."

"Fine, Pop. Do you want me to send you the tenner?"

"No, not at the moment. I'll let you know if there's any other needy case around."

"I'm a needy case, Pop."

"But there are rules, Billy."

"I play by them."

"That's the good boy. Just don't get excited. I underwent a heart attack that way, and I can tell you that getting excited is one of the worst, one of the very worst things a man can do to himself. It takes you over when you don't expect it. Very sudden and we don't anticipate a thing. It's a terrible thing to do to yourself, getting too overly worked up, Billy. I wouldn't do it again for any man."

"I'll catch you later, Pop. Thanks."

"Billy, I'm very glad you called me."

Billy hung up and scraped the horseshit out of his ear.

The first of Billy's family came home at three-forty. Daniel Quinn, age ten, resident little kid returning from fourth grade at Public School Twenty across the street, found his uncle on the couch with *True Detective* open on his chest, the lights out, shades drawn more than usual, the *Telegraph*, the *Armstrong*, the New York *News* and *Daily Mirror* on the floor beside the card table.

"That you, kid?"

"It's me, Unk. Aren't you working?"

"Get lost. I'm half asleep. Catch you later."

And the boy went upstairs. But Billy's eyes were open again, his gaze again on the shitty print of Mo the Kid, more properly titled "The Young Mozart," hanging in an enormous gold frame above the couch. There sat the precocious composer, exceptionally upright, playing, no doubt, a tune of his own making, on a spinet in a drawing room baroquely furnished with gilded mirrors, heavy drapes, fringed oriental rug. The room was busy with footstools, ornamental screens, and music sheets strewn across the floor. The ladies in long, flowered gowns and chokers, clutching single sheets of music, and an older gentleman in a wig, breeches, and buckled shoes like the composer, all sat listening as the young Mo sent out his life-giving music. The three gave off non-human smiles, looking glazed and droopy, as if they'd all been at the laudanum.

The print would not have been on the wall, or in the house, if Billy had had his way. It was a gift to his sister, Peg, from their Aunt Mary, a reclusive old dame who lived in the old family home on Colonie Street, raised canaries, and had a secret hoard of twenty-dollar gold pieces she parceled out on birthdays. The picture always reminded Billy of his ill treatment by the people in that house after his father ran away and left him and his sister and their mother; ran away and stayed away eighteen years, and neither Billy, Peg, nor their mother ever heard from him again. In 1934 he came back, not to his own home but to that goddamn house of his sisters and brothers, his visit culminating in inadequately explained rejection and flight, and further silence. And so Billy hated the house for that reason, and also for the uncountable other reasons he had accumulated during his years as a never-quite-welcome nephew (nasty son of nasty Francis). The house was as worthless as the stupid picture in which Kid Mo offered up his stupid, invisible music to a roomful of dope fiends.

The picture would not leave his mind, even after he'd closed his eyes, and so Billy picked up the magazine and looked again at the about-to-be-raped model, fake-raped, with slip on the rise revealing thigh, garter, seamed stockings. In high heels, with her rouged lips, artful hair, artificial fear on her face, she cowered on the bed away from the hovering shadow of the artificial rapist. The change of vision from Mo to rape worked, and Billy slept the fearful sleep of an anxious loser.

Peg's keys, clinking at the keyhole, woke him.

Plump but fetching, graying but evergreen, Margaret Elizabeth Quinn was returning from her desk in the North End Tool Company, where she was private secretary to the owner.

"It's dark in here," she said. "What happened to the lights?"

"Nothing," Billy said as she switched on the bridge lamp.

"Is Danny home?"

"Upstairs."

"What's new? You have a decent day?"

"Great day."

"That's nice."

"No it's not."

"Did Mama call?"

"No."

"The receiver's off the hook."

"I know it."

"How could she call if the receiver's off the hook."

"She couldn't."

Peg cradled the receiver and took off her black-and-white checked shorty coat and black pillbox hat.

"You want pork chops?" she asked.

"No."

"Liver? That's the choice."

"Nothing, no."

"You're not eating?"

"No, the hell with it."

"Oh, that's a beautiful mood."

"I'm beautiful out of business is what I am."

Peg sat on the edge of the rocker, formidable lady in her yellow, flowered print, full knees up, glasses on, lipstick fresh, fingernails long and crimson, solitaire from husband George small but respectably gleaming under the bridge light, hair marcelled in soft finger wave. Billy's beautiful sister.

"What's this you're saying?"

And he told her the Martin story: that, believe it or not, his three horses all came home. Some joke, eh kid? Sextuple your money, folks. Place your bets with Brazen Billy Boy, who lives the way we all love to live—way, way, way up there beyond our means.

Peg stood up, saying nothing. She pushed open the swinging door to be greeted by a near-frenzied collie, all but perishing from his inability to disgorge affection. From the refrigerator she took out the pork chops and put them into two large frying pans over a low flame on the gas stove. Then she went back to Billy, who was pouring a shot of Wilson's into a soiled coffee cup with a dry, brown ring at the bottom. The phone rang and Peg answered, then handed the instrument to Billy, who closed his eyes to drive out all phone calls.

"Yeah," he said into the mouthpiece. And then, "No, I'm closed down. No. NO, GODDAMN IT, NO! I mean I'm CLOSED. Out of business and you owe me fifty-four bucks and I need it tonight so goddamn get it up. I'll be down." And he slammed the receiver onto the hook.

"Wasn't that Tod?"

"Yeah."

"You don't have to eat *his* head off because you lost some money."

"Lost some money? I'm dumped, broke. I can't work. Do you get that picture?"

"You've been broke before? You're broke most of the time."

"Ah, shut up, this is bad news."

"What possessed you to hold a three-horse parlay? I wouldn't even make that mistake."

"I make a lot of mistakes you wouldn't make."

"It doesn't make sense, with your bankroll."

"I can't explain it."

Billy gulped the Wilson's and the phone rang. Martin Daugherty. Peg handed him the phone.

"Yes, Martin, you're a lucky son of a bitch. Nobody in their right mind bets three-horse parlays. I know it, Martin. Yeah, sure I'll be downtown tonight. I'll have some of it for you. No, I haven't got it right this minute. Collections are slow, nobody paying this month. But you'll get paid, Martin. Billy Phelan pays his debts. Yeah, Martin, I held it all myself. Thanks, I'm glad you feel bad. I wish I could get mad at you, you son of a bitch. Knock your teeth out and make you spend your winnings on the dentist. What do I make it? What do you make it? Right. That's exactly right, Martin—seven eighty-eight eighty-five. Yeah, yeah. Yeah. See you tonight around Becker's, or maybe the poker game in Nick's cellar. Yeah, you son of a bitch, you sleep with the angels. What hotel they staying at?"

The kitchen gave off the rich odor of seared pork. Peg came out of it in her apron, carrying a long fork. At the foot of the stairs she called, "Danny," and from a far height in the attic came a "Yeah?" and then she said "Supper," and the door slammed and the steps of Daniel Quinn could be heard, descending from his aerie.

"How much cash do you actually have?" Peg asked.

"About a hundred and seventy," Billy said. "Can you spare anything?"

Peg almost smiled. She sniffed and shook her head. "I'll see."

"George is doing all right, isn't he?" George wrote numbers.

"He's doing swell. He lost three dollars yesterday on the day."

"Yeah. We all got a problem."

"All of us," Peg said. "George wants to talk to you about a new book. Somebody named Muller."

"I'm here if he wants me."

"What about this money you owe? How will you raise it?"

"I can always raise a buck."

"Can you raise six hundred?"

"What does *that* mean, can I? I've got to. What do you do when you lose? You pay."

"The Spider never loses," Danny Quinn said as he hit the last step down.

Billy drew the bath water, hot as he could stand for his hemorrhoid, back again. Got to get some exercise, Billy. Three baths a day in the hottest, the doc said, the sweat already forming on Billy's face, as he drew the hottest of hot baths. Has that guy Billy got any money? Has he! He's got piles! And he's in hot water, too, I'll say. Might be all washed up. He really took a bath, all right. But you never can tell about a fellow like Billy, because he runs hot and cold.

Billy eased into the water and spread his cheeks so the heat would rise up the back alley and draw some bloody attention to that oversized worm of a vein which was sticking its nose out, itching the goddamn ass off Billy. Are itchy assholes hereditary? But itchy no more right now. Now soothed. Now hot stuff. Now easy livin'. And Billy settles back against the tub and forgets about his asshole and its internal stresses and considers the evening ahead of him.

He will wear his navy blue gabardine and the new silk shirt he got at Steefel's through Harvey Hess. A fast half-dozen shirts for Billy and six, too, for Harv, who glommed them, wrapped them, and put them down as paid for in Billy's name, and all Billy had to do was go in and pick up his order. How sweet. Billy gave Harvey all his legitimate clothing action, or as much as Steefel's could handle, and why not? For wasn't Harvey Billy's grandest fish?

Harvey.

Why hadn't Billy thought of him before this? Harvey was of the opinion he could actually beat Billy at pool. Even after maybe two hundred games and yet to win even one. Still, Harv could say, I'll beat you yet, Billy, I'm learning and you got to admit that. Billy would admit anything to Harvey as long as he kept coughing up fivers and tenners. Such a mark. Billy remembered the night he and Tod had heavy dates with showgirls from the Kenmore and then Tod says, Billy, we can't keep those dates tonight. Why not? says Billy. Because, says Tod, it's payday at Steefel's.

Billy put Harvey on his list of problem solvers. He already had $170. He would get $54 from Tod. Peg would be good for maybe $10, maybe only $5 if it was as tough with George as she said it was. And it had to be because Peg was no bull-shitter. So the arithmetic comes to maybe $234. And if Billy nailed Harvey for, let's be conservative, $25, that's $259, say $260 round figures; which means Billy still has to come up with say $530 round figures to pay off Martin. Quite a challenge, Billy, $530, and the first time in your life you ever went out at night and absolutely had to come up with five big ones. Always a first for everything. But Billy can raise a buck, right, Billy?

Billy saw the top half of his torso in the bathroom cabinet mirror. The vision always reduced him to a corpse, being washed and powdered in an undertaker's basement, like Johnny Conroy. He always turned the image quickly back to life, pulling chest hair to feel pain, pressing a finger against shoulder flesh to see it whiten, then return to rich redness, moving his mouth, showing his teeth, being alive in a way he wasn't sure his father still was. Is death hereditary?

Johnny Conroy: the corpse in Cronin's funeral parlor, 1932, raised with Billy on Colonie Street, wild kid. Used to run with Billy after the action, any action, run to the cliff at the tail end of Ten Broeck Street and leap, leap, faaaaaaaaalllll, and lose the pursuit, faaaaaaaaalllll into the great sandpile in Hogan's brickyard, scramble off, free.

Johnny Conroy, free to die in the gutter over stolen booze, and they waked him at Cronin's.

Billy and Tod were taking Hubie Maloy home that night from Becker's, crazy Hubie who said, Let's stop and see Johnny, my old pal. But they're closed now, it's two in the morning, said Billy. I wanna go in, said Hubert, the wild filbert. And so Tod stopped the car and Hubert got out and went around the back of Cronin's and crawled in a window and in a few minutes had opened the side door for Tod and Billy, and in they went, half drunk or Billy wouldn't have done it. A burglary rap for sure. And there was Johnny in the open coffin with one basket of flowers, only one, ready for planting in the ay-em.

He don't look so bad, Tod said.

He don't look so bad for a corpse, Billy said.

And that's when Hubert undid Johnny's tie. And Billy watched it happen because he didn't understand Hubert's plan. Then Hubert pulled Johnny up from the casket and for the first time Billy really understood the word "stiff." Hubert took off Johnny's coat and shirt, and by then Billy and Tod were out the door and back in Toddy's car, parked safely up the street.

Hubert's nuts, said Tod.

Playful, Billy said and couldn't even now say why that word occurred to him. Maybe because he still, even now, liked Hubert, liked crazies.

Well, I don't play with him no more, said Toddy. He's got no respect.

And Billy said, You could say that. Because he had to admit it was true. Five minutes go by and Hubert puts out the light in Cronin's and comes out with all Johnny's burial clothes under his arm, suit, tie, even the shoes. He owed me, the bastard, Hubert says, and if I waited any longer I'd never even collect this much. And Hubert kept the shirt and tie for his own and sold the suit and shoes for twenty bucks the next afternoon at The Parody Club, to a grifter passing through with a carny. On Broadway they laughed for weeks over poor Johnny and, worse, poor old Cronin, who had an attack and damn near died when he walked in and saw the naked corpse, standing with his back against the coffin, all his bullet holes showing. For Hubert didn't tell folks he also took Johnny's underwear. Always said he wasn't wearing any.

Billy shaved and wet his straight black hair, brushed it back with the little part at the left, and was padding barefoot toward his bedroom, wrapped in a towel, when the phone rang. He waited and listened while Peg got it again. Ma. Billy stayed at the top of the stairs.

"We're fine, Mama, and how are things there? Good. Yes, everything is all right. Billy is getting dressed to go out, and George won't be home for an hour. The office is quite busy, yes, which is a nice change. You what, made an apple pie? Oh, I wish I had some. But it burned? Oh that's too bad. But it tastes good anyway. And now Minnie and Josie want to bake pies, too. Well, I hope I get a piece of somebody's pie. I bet yours'll be the best. Yes, Mama, Billy's working. He's going out tonight and pick up some money. Yes, it is nice . . ."

In his room Billy took out the navy blue gabardine and the silk shirt and the newest blue bow tie with the white polka dots. He fished in the drawer for the pair of solid blue socks with the three blue dots on the sides and took his black shoes with the pointed toes out of the closet. Billy never went out without being really dressed. But really. George was the same, and Peg and Ma, too. But George was too flashy. Dress conservative and you'll always be well dressed. George always imitated Jimmy Walker, ever since he worked for him up at the Capitol. He'd see Walker's picture in the paper in a sport coat with patch pockets and he'd be downtown buying one the next day. I never imitated anybody, was Billy's thought. I never even imitated my father. They couldn't even tell me how he looked dressed up, except what Ma said, he was so handsome. George is all right. George is a father. A good one. Billy hoped George would get the new book from Muller, but he didn't know who the hell Muller was.

Billy took his trig gray fedora out of the hatbox and thought: pies. And pictured Pete the Tramp stealing two steaming pies off a kitchen windowsill, then running off and eating them behind a fence.

Billy looked at himself in the full-length mirror on the back of the closet door. He looked good. Maybe handsome to some. Not like a man who owed seven eighty-eight to anybody. Whataya think, because Billy owes a few bucks he can't look good?

"Aren't you eating *anything?*" Peg said when he went downstairs.

"I'll grab something downtown."

She didn't make him ask. She fished in the apron pocket

and handed him the bill, folded in a square. A twenty. He kissed her quick and patted her corset.

"That's all I can give you," she said.

"I didn't expect so much. You're a classy dame."

"Class runs in this family," she said.

5

Billy got off the Albany-Troy bus at Broadway and Clinton Avenue and walked up Clinton, past Nick Levine's haberdashery, where the card game would be. He walked toward the theaters, three of them on Clinton Square, and stopped at The Grand. Laughton in his greatest role. As Ginger Ted. Ragged son of trouble. A human derelict on the ebb tide of South Sea life. Surpassing such portrayals as Captain Bligh, Henry VIII, Ruggles of Red Gap. An experience definitely not to be missed. *The Beachcomber*. Billy made a note to avoid this shit. Fats Laughton in a straw hat on the beach. He walked around the box office to check the coming attractions in the foyer. A Warner Baxter thing. Costume job with that lacy-pants kid, Freddie Bartholomew. Billy had already avoided that one at the Palace, coming back for a second run now. The Grand, then, a wipeout for two weeks. Billy headed for the restaurant.

There were four restaurants within a block of each other on Clinton Square but Billy, as always, went to the Grand Lunch next door to The Grand, for it had the loyalty of the nighttime crowd, Billy's crowd. Dan Shugrue, well liked, ran it, and Toddy Dunn worked the counter starting at six, an asset because he spoke the language of the crowd, which turned up even in daylight for the always-fresh coffee and the poppy-seed rolls, the joint's trademark, and because since Prohibition the place never closed and nobody had to remember its hours. Also there was Slopie Dodds, the one-legged Negro cook, when he worked, for he was not only a cook but a piano player who'd played for Bessie in her early years, and he did both jobs, whatever the market dictated. Nobody believed he'd played for Bessie until it came out in a magazine, but Billy believed it because you don't lie about that kind of thing unless you're a bum, and Slopie was a straight arrow, and a good cook.

The place was brightly lighted, globes washed as usual, when Billy walked in. Toddy, behind the counter, gave him half a grin, and Slopie gave him a smile through the kitchen door. Billy didn't expect the grin from Tod. Billy also saw his Uncle Chick sitting alone at one of the marble-topped booth tables, having coffee and doughnuts before going to work at the *Times-Union* composing room. It was the first time Billy had seen Chick in months, six, eight months, and even that was too soon.

"Hello, Chick," he said, said it aloofly from the side of his mouth, that little hello that hits and runs.

"Howsa boy, Billy, howsa boy? Long time no see."

"All right, Chick."

Billy would have kept walking, but his uncle's gaze stayed on him, looking at those clothes, so spiffy, so foreign because of that; and so Billy spoke compulsively. "How you been?" A man's got to be civil.

"Fine and dandy. Sit down."

"I got some business here a minute," and Billy's hand said, I'll be back, maybe. He walked to the counter, where Tod was already drawing a coffee, dark. Tod also shoved a spoon and an envelope at him.

"Forty there," Tod said, jaunty in his counterman's white military cap of gauze and cardboard. "All I can come up with."

Billy didn't touch the envelope.

"That phone call," Billy said.

"Forget it. Peg called me."

"She tell you what happened?"

"All but the numbers."

"Seven eighty-eight eighty-five. How do you like that, doctor?"

"You got a reason to be edgy."

"I'm through till I pay it off and get another bankroll."

"You got no reserve at all?"

"A wipeout."

"Then what's next?"

"I thought I'd look up Harvey. You want to make the call?"

"For when?"

"When, hell. Now. I'm there if he wants me."

Tod looked at his watch. "Five to six. He's home by now. Shit. I got to work. I'll miss it."

"I'll tell you about it. But I wanna make the game at Nick's."

"How you gonna play with no money?"

"I got almost two bills."

"And you got this forty," and Tod shoved the envelope closer.

"Two-thirty then. I play with half that. I can't afford to lose more than that. I got to save something for Martin, unless I can swing him."

"I'll call Harvey, good old Harv."

"Hey, you hear I rolled two-ninety-nine last night? I beat Scotty Streck and the son of a bitch dropped dead from shock."

"I saw the obituary in the afternoon paper. It didn't mention you. Two-ninety-nine? What stood up?"

"The four pin. Gimme a western." Billy pocketed the envelope and carried the coffee to Chick's table, thinking: I could grunt and Toddy'd get the message. Talk to Chick all week and he'll ask you is this Thursday. Chick wasn't dumb, he was ignorant. Anybody'd be ignorant living in that goddamn house. Like living in a ditch with a herd of goats. Years back, Chick got baseball passes regular from Jack Daley, the *Times-Union's* sports editor. The Albany Senators were fighting Newark for first place and Red Rolfe was with Newark, and George McQuinn and others who later went up with the Yankees. Chick gave the passes for the whole Newark series to young Mahan, a tub-o'guts kid whose mother was a widow. Billy always figured Chick was after her ass. Chick gave Billy a pass two weeks later to see Albany play the cellar club. Who gave a damn about the cellar club? Billy can't even remember now which club it was. Shove your pass, Nasty Billy told his uncle.

"You're all dressed up," Chick said, chuckling. "Are you going to work?"

"Not to give you a short answer to a snotty question, but what the hell is it to you? What am I supposed to do, dress like a bum? Look like you?"

"All right, Billy, I was only kidding."

"The hell you were."

"Dress any way you want. Who cares?"

"I do what I want, all right."

"Calm down, Billy, and answer me a question. You seen Charlie McCall lately?"

"I saw him last night. He bet against me in a bowling match."

"You hear anything about him?"

"Since last night? Like how he slept?"

"No, no."

"What the hell you asking then?"

"Can you keep a secret?"

"I'd be dead if I couldn't."

"I hear Charlie's in bad trouble. I hear maybe he was kidnapped last night."

Billy stared Chick down, not speaking, not moving except to follow Chick's eyes when they moved. Chick blinked. *Kidnapped.* With Warner Baxter.

"You heard what I said?"

"I heard."

"Don't that mean anything to you?"

"Yeah, it means something. It means I don't know what the hell it means. You got this straight or you making it up?"

"I'm telling you, it's a secret. I shouldn't have said anything, but I know you know Charlie and thought maybe you heard something."

"Like who kidnapped him?"

"Hey, come on, Billy. Not so loud. Listen, forget it, forget I said anything." Chick bit his doughnut. "You heard any news about your father?"

"Wait a minute. Why is it a secret about Charlie?"

"It's just not out yet."

"Then how come you know?"

"That's a secret, too. Now forget it. What about your father?"

"Nothing. You know any secrets about him?"

"No, no secrets. Nothing since he came to see us."

"And you kicked him out."

"No, Billy, we wanted him, I wanted him to stay. Your Uncle Peter and I went all over town looking for him. You know it was your Aunt Sate had the fight with him. They always fought, even as kids. He was gone before we even knew he was out of the house."

"Bullshit, Chick."

"Nobody can talk to you, Billy. Nobody ever could."

"Not about him they can't."

"There's a lot you don't know."

"I know how he was treated, and how I was treated because of him."

"You don't know the half of it."

Somebody said, "Haw! My mother just hit the numbers!" And Billy turned to see a boy with a broken front tooth, about fifteen, brush cut, sockless, in torn sneakers, beltless pants, and a ragged cardigan over a tank-top undershirt with a hole in the front. His jackknife, large blade open, danced in his hand, two tables away.

"Saunders kid," Chick said softly.

"Who?"

Chick whispered. "Eddie Saunders. Lives up on Pearl Street near us. He's crazy. Whole family's crazy. His father's in the nut house at Poughkeepsie."

"She had a dollar on it," Eddie Saunders said. "Four forty-seven. Gonna get five hundred bucks. Haw!" With his left foot he nudged a chair away from a nearby table, then slashed its leatherette seat twice in parallel cuts.

"Gonna get me some shoes," he said. "Gonna go to the pitchers."

A lone woman in a corner made little ooohing sounds, involuntary wheezes, as she watched the boy. Billy thought the woman looked a little like Peg.

"Who'd she play the numbers with, Eddie?" Billy asked the kid.

The boy turned and studied Billy. Billy stood up. The boy watched him closely as he moved toward the counter and said to Tod, "Where's my western? And gimme a coffee." And then he turned to the kid.

"I asked who she played the numbers with, Eddie."

"The grocery."

"That's big news. Bet your mother feels good."

"She does. She's gonna buy a dress."

Eddie tapped the knife blade on the marble table top and let it bounce like a drum stick. Billy took the ironstone mug of coffee and the western off the glass counter and moved toward the boy. When he was alongside he said, "You oughta close that knife."

"Nah."

"Yeah, you should."

"You won't make me." And Eddie made little jabs at the air about two feet to the right of Billy's stomach.

"If you don't close it," Billy said, "I'll throw this hot coffee in your eyes. You ever have boiling hot coffee hit you in the eyes? You can't see nothing after that."

Eddie looked up at Billy, then at the mug of steaming coffee in his right hand, inches from his face. He looked down at his knife. He studied it. He studied it some more. Then he closed the blade. Billy set his western on the table and reached out his left hand.

"Now give me the knife."

"It's mine."

"You can have it later."

"No."

"You rather have coffee in the face and then I beat the shit out of you and get the knife anyway?"

Eddie handed the knife to Billy, who pocketed it and put the coffee on the table in front of Eddie. He put the western in front of him. "Have a sandwich," Billy said. He pushed the sugar bowl toward the kid and gave him a spoon a customer had left at the next table.

"Now behave yourself," Billy said, and he went back to his table. "Will you for chrissake gimme a western?" he said to Tod.

The dishwasher came in the front door with the Clinton Square beat cop, Joe Riley. Riley had his hand on his pistol.

People were leaving quickly. Tod came around the counter and explained the situation to Riley, who took Eddie's knife from Billy and then took Eddie away.

"That was clever, what you did," Chick said.

"Toddy taught me that one. I seen him use it on nasty drunks two or three times."

"All the same it was clever, and dangerous, with that knife and all. You never know what crazy people will do. It was clever."

"I'm a clever son of a bitch," Billy said, and he reached for Chick's check and pocketed it. One up on you, Chick, you sarcastic prick. "Doughnuts are on me, Chick."

"Why thanks, Billy, thanks. Take care of yourself."

Tod came around the counter with two coffees in one mitt and Billy's western in the other. He sat down.

"You play a nice game of coffee."

"I had a good teacher. You call Harvey?"

"Yeah. He'll be down at Louie's." Tod looked at his watch. "Fifteen minutes from now. Damn, I wish I didn't have to work. I love to see old Harvey in action. He makes me feel smart."

"Listen, you know what I heard? Charlie McCall was snatched."

"No. No shit?"

"And I just saw him last night. He backed Scotty against me in this match."

"That'll teach him."

"They must've grabbed him after he left the alleys."

"Wow, that's a ballbuster. Broadway'll be hot tonight."

"Too bad I gotta play cards. Be fun just floatin' tonight." Billy finished his coffee and then gave both his own and Chick's food checks to Tod, who knew how to make them disappear. "Now I gotta go get fresh money."

When Billy walked into Louie's pool room on Broadway across from Union Station, Daddy Big, wearing his change apron and eyeshade, was leaning on a cue watching Doc Fay, the band leader, run a rack. Tomorrow night, Billy would likely face the Doc here in the finals of a six-week-old round robin. There were four players left and Billy and the Doc could beat the other two left-handed. But Billy and the Doc were also near equals in skill. They beat each other as often as they were beaten: Doc, a flashy shooter; Billy, great control through position and safe shots. Doc, as usual, was playing in his vest. Billy watched him mount the table with one leg, flatten out, stretch his left arm as far as it would take him, with the intention of dropping the fourteen ball into the far corner, a double combination shot he'd never try in a match unless he was drunk, or grandstanding. Ridiculous shot, really, but zlonk! He sank it. Sassy shooter, the Doc, no pushover.

Only one of the other ten tables was busy, Harvey Hess at that one, revving up his sucker suction. Billy could feel it pulling him, but he resisted, walked over to Daddy Big, whose straight name was Louis Dugan, known from his early hustling days because of his willingness to overextend the risk factor in any given hustle—once spotting a mark eighty-four points in a game of one hundred—as Daddy Big Ones, which time shortened to Daddy Big. He'd grown old and wide, grown also a cataract on one eye that he wouldn't let anybody cut away. The eye was all but blind, and so focusing on the thin edge of a master shot was no longer possible for him, which meant that Daddy Big no longer hustled. Now he racked for other hustlers and their fish, for the would-bes, the semi-pros, the amateurs who passed through the magically dismal dust of Louie's parlor.

Daddy Big had run Louie's since the week he came out of Comstock after doing two for a post-office holdup flubbed by

Georgie Fox, a sad, syphilitic freak with mange on his soul. Because Fox had lifted Daddy Big's registered pistol to pull the job, then dropped it in a scuffle at the scene, Daddy ended up doing the two instead of Georgie, whom the police never connected to the job. But Bindy McCall, Daddy's cousin, made the connection, and sent out the word: Mark Fox lousy; which swiftly denied Georgie the Syph access to all the places the Broadway crowd patronized: the gin mills, the card games, the gambling joints, the pool rooms, the restaurants, the night clubs, even the two-bit whorehouses Georgie had never learned to live without. He lived two years like a mole, and then, the week before Daddy Big was due to return to Albany and perhaps find a way to extract some personal compensation for lost time from him, Georgie walked into Fobie McManus's grill on Sheridan Avenue, bought a double rye for himself and one for Eddie Bradt, the barman, and said to Eddie: "I'm all done now," and he then walked west to the Hawk Street viaduct, climbed its railing, and dropped seventy feet to the middle of the granite-block pavement below, there to be scraped up and away, out of the reach of Daddy Big forever. Bindy's reward to Daddy for time lost was the managership of this pool room, which Bindy had collected during Daddy's absence as payment on a gambling debt. And Daddy had a home ever after.

"Hey, Daddy," Billy said, "the Doc monopolizing the action?"

"He's got an idea he's Mosconi."

"He thinks he can spot Mosconi."

"I know some I can spot. And beat," the Doc said, smiling at Billy. Good guy, the Doc. The ladies love his curls.

"Tomorrow you get your chance," Billy said, "if you got the money to back up the mouth."

"I'll handle all you can put on the table. That's if you don't lose your first match."

"I lose that, I'll get a job," Billy said.

"You want a game here, Billy?" Daddy Big asked. "I'm just keeping a cue warm."

Daddy slurred when he spoke, half in the bag already. By midnight, he'd be knee-walking, with no reason to stay sober any more. Also, his teeth clicked when he talked, prison dentures. Sadistic bastards pulled all his teeth when they had him down. Yet he's still living, and Georgie Fox is gone. Georgie, turned into a cadaver in shoe leather, had hit Billy many a time for coffee money, and Billy'd peel off a deuce or a fin for the bum, even though he was a bum. Georgie was dead long before he hit the pavement, sucked dry by Bindy's order. Why didn't they just beat on him a little, Billy wondered. Lock him up or take away what he owned? But they took away the whole world he lived in. Billy always hated a freak, but he couldn't hate Georgie. I ain't et in two days, Billy. Billy can still remember that line. But Billy also says: You know what you do when you lose, don't you, Georgie? Do you hear me, freak? You pay.

"I already got a game," Billy told Daddy, nodding his head in Harvey's direction.

The Doc heard that and looked up from the cue ball. He glanced at Harv, then smiled at Billy. "So you do have dough, then," he said.

"A hungry chicken picks up a little stray corn once in a while. How much we on for tomorrow night?"

"Fifty all right? And fifty more if my backer shows up?"

"Fifty definite, fifty maybe. You got it."

Billy moved close to Daddy Big and spoke in a whisper. "I heard something maybe you know already. About Charlie McCall."

"Charlie?"

"That somebody put the snatch on him."

"What the hell you say?" said Daddy, near to full volume. "What, what?"

"It's what I hear, a rumor. More than that I don't know."

"Who told you?"

"What am I, a storyteller? I heard it."

"I didn't hear that. I know Bindy good as any man. You hear anything like that, Doc?"

The Doc gave a small shake of his head and listened.

"It's all I know," Billy said.

"I don't believe it. Sounds like goatshit," Daddy said. "If that happens, I'd know about it. I'll call Bindy."

"Let me know," Billy said.

"Hey, Billy," Harvey called across the empty table. "You gonna play pool or you gonna talk?"

Billy looked at the Doc and said under his breath: "Fish get hungry, too." He clapped the Doc on the shoulder and watched Daddy Big waddling toward the pay phone. Then he went over to Harvey's table to reel in the catch.

Harvey Hess, a dude who wore good suits but fucked them up with noisy neckties and loud socks, had bitten the hook one night eight, ten months back when he saw Billy playing in Louie's and asked for a game. Billy recognized him immediately as a sucker. Billy recognized suckers the way he recognized cats. Harvey almost won that first game. The games were for a deuce after the first free one, and on subsequent days went up to five. Hearing rumors of Billy's talent did not put Harvey off. He merely asked for a spot. Ten points, then fifteen, and lately twenty, which made Harvey almost win.

Billy watched Harvey show off for him, finishing off two balls, both easy pickin's. Then Daddy Big came over to rack the balls, mark down the time, and give Billy the word that Bindy's line was busy. Harvey spoke up: "Give me thirty-five points and I'll play you for twenty-five bucks."

"Who the hell you think I am?" Billy said. "You think I'm Daddy Big here, giving the game away?"

"Thirty-five," said hard-hearted Harvey.

"Thirty," Billy said. "I never spotted anybody thirty-five."

"Thirty-five."

"Thirty-two I give you, for thirty-two bucks, buck a point."

"You're on," said Harv, and Billy felt the sweet pressure on the way. Harvey almost won, but it was Billy, finally, one hundred to ninety-two, winging it with a run of thirty-two in mid-game to come from behind twenty points. Daddy Big came back and told Billy: "I knew that was goatshit about Charlie Boy. Bindy said he heard the rumor, too, and to kill it. He talked to Charlie in New York an hour ago."

"What's this about Charlie?" Harvey asked. "I sold him a gray sharkskin last week."

"It's nothin'," said Daddy. "Billy here's spreading the news he was kidnapped, but I just talked to Bindy and he says it's goatshit."

"I took the third degree at the K. of C. with him," Harvey said.

"I'll tell you why I bought it," Billy said, shrugging. "I heard a rumor last summer Bindy was going to be snatched, so the Charlie thing made sense to me."

"Who snatched? I never heard nothing like that," said Daddy.

"It was all over Broadway."

"So was I, but I never heard it."

"I heard it."

"I never heard it either," Harvey said.

"So you bums don't get around. What're we doing here, playing pool or strollin' down memory lane?"

"I'll play you one more, Billy, but I want forty points now.

You're hot tonight. I never saw anybody run thirty-two before. You ran my whole spot. That's hot in my book."

"I got to admit I'm feeling good," Billy said. "But if the spot goes to forty, so does the bet."

"Thirty-five," said Harv. "I'm getting low."

"All right," Billy said, and he broke with a deliberately bad safe shot, giving Harvey an opening target. Harv ran four and left an open table. Billy ran ten, re-racked, ran four more, and missed on purpose, fourteen to four, and said: "Harv, I'm on. What can I say? I'll even it up some and give you eight more points, forty-eight spot."

"You give me eight more?"

"For another eight bucks."

Harvey checked his roll, studied the table.

"No, no bet. I got a feelin' I ain't gonna lose this one, even though you got the lead, Billy. I'm feelin' good, too. I'm gettin' limber. Keep the bet where it is. You can't stay lucky forever."

Lucky. The line blew up in Billy's head. He wanted the rest of Harvey's roll, but time was running. Nick's card game at nine-thirty with big money possible, and Billy wanted a cold beer before that. Yet you can't call Billy lucky, just lucky, and get away with it. Billy's impulse was to throw the game, double the bet, clean out Harvey's wallet entirely, take away his savings account, his life insurance, his mortgage money, his piggy bank. But you don't give them that edge even once: I beat Billy Phelan last week. No edge for bums.

Harvey faced the table. The seven ball hung on the lip, but was cushioned, and the cue ball sat on the other side of the bunch, where Billy, you clever dog, left it. No shots, Harv, except safe. Sad about that seven ball, Harv. But wait. Is Harv lining up to break the bunch? Can it be? He'll smash it? Not possible.

"What're you doing?"

"Playing the seven."

Billy laughed. "Are you serious?"

"Depth bomb it. The four will kiss the seven and the bunch'll scatter."

"Harv, are you really calling that, the four to the seven?"

"I call the seven, that's enough."

"But you can't hit it." Billy laughed again. He looked again at the bunch, studying the angle the four would come off the end. No matter where you hit the bunch, the four would not kiss the seven the right way. Not possible. And Harvey hesitated.

"You don't want me to play this shot, do you, Billy? Because you see it's a sure thing and then I'll have the bunch broken, a table full of shots. That's right, isn't it?"

Billy closed his eyes and Harvey disappeared. Who could believe such bedbugs lived in a civilized town? Billy opened his eyes at the sound of Harvey breaking the bunch. The four kissed the seven, but kissed it head on. The seven did not go into the corner pocket. The rest scattered, leaving an abundant kindergarten challenge for Billy.

"You do nice work, Harv."

"It almost worked," said Harv, but the arrogance was draining from his face like a poached egg with a slow leak.

"Why didn't you play a safe shot?"

"When I've got a real shot?"

"A real shot? Willie Hoppe wouldn't try that one."

"I saw you break a bunch and kiss one in."

"You never saw me try a shot like that, Harv."

"If you can do it, I can do it too, sooner or later."

Billy felt it rising. The sucker. Lowlife of Billy's world. Never finish last, never be a sucker. Don't let them humiliate you. Chick's face grinned out of Harvey's skull. Going to work, Billy? Lowlife. Humiliate the bastard.

"Harv, you got to play safe even when you're ahead. Didn't you learn anything playing against me?"

"I learned plenty."

"You didn't learn enough."

And Billy leaned into the action and ran the table and broke a new rack and ran that and part of another. He missed a tough one and Harv sank eight and then Billy got at it and finished it off, a hundred to Harvey's twelve, which, with his forty-point spot was still only fifty-two. Billy put his cue in the rack, feeling he'd done his duty. Suckers demand humiliation and it is the duty of people like Billy to answer their demand. Suckers must be stomped for their love of ignorance, for expecting too much from life. Suckers do not realize that a man like Billy spent six hours a day at pool tables all over Albany for years learning how to shed his ignorance.

Doc Fay watched the finale, shaking his head at what he heard from Harvey's mouth. Harvey paid Billy the thirty-five dollars and put on his hat and suit coat. Billy actually felt something for Harvey then.

"You know, Harv," he said, putting his hand on the sucker's shoulder, "you'll never beat me."

"You're good, Billy. I see how you play safe till the bunch breaks and then you get a streak going. I see how you do it."

"Harv, if you play from now till you're ninety-nine (play it, Fatha), you still won't know how I do it."

"I'll get you, Billy," Harv said, backing toward the door. "One of these nights I'll get you." And then he was gone, only his monkey smirk still hanging there by the door above the image of his orange and purple tie. Doc Fay broke up with laughter.

"I thought for a minute there, Billy, you were wising up the sucker," the Doc said.

"You can't wise up a sucker," said Billy.

"Absolutely. It's what I said to myself when Harv says he

knows how you do it. I said, Doc, you know and *Billy* knows."

"What do we know?"

"That a sucker don't get even till he gets to heaven."

"Right," Billy said. "I learned that in church."

6

Red Tom Fitzsimmons, the four-to-two man at Becker's, a good fellow, stood behind his mustache and amidst his brawn in a fresh apron, arms folded, sleeves rolled, waiting for thirst to arise anew in his four customers. Martin Daugherty sat at the end of the bar underneath the frame of the first dollar Becker's ever made, and at the edge of the huge photo of Becker's thirtieth anniversary outing at Picard's Grove on a sunny day in August of 1932, which adorned the back bar. The photographer had captured two hundred and two men in varying degrees of sobriety, in shirtsleeves, sitting, kneeling, standing in a grassy field, clutching their beer, billowy clouds behind and above them. Emil Becker ordered a wall-sized blowup made from the negative and then spent weeks identifying all present by full name, and writing an index, which he framed and hung beside the blowup, which covered the wall like wallpaper.

Emil Becker died in 1936 and his son, Gus, put a check mark alongside his name, and a gold star on his chest in the photo. Customers then wanted the same done for other faithful departed, and so the stars went up, one by one. There were nineteen gone out of two hundred in six years. Martin Daugherty was in the photo. So was Red Tom. So was Billy Phelan, and Daddy Big, and Harvey Hess. So was Bindy

McCall and his son, Charlie. So was Scotty Streck. The star was already shining on Scotty's chest and the check mark alongside his name.

Martin looked at Red Tom, and at his mustache: in the photo and the real thing. It was a mustache of long standing, brooded over, stroked, waxed, combed, pampered.

"That mustache of yours, Fitzsimmons," said Martin, "is outlandish. Venturesome and ostentatious."

"Is that so?"

"Unusually vulgar. Splendid too, of course, and elegant in a sardonic Irish way. But it surely must be unspeakable with tomato juice."

"Give up and have a drink," Red Tom said, pouring a new bourbon for Martin.

"It's pontifical, it's arrogant. It obviously reflects an intemperate attitude toward humankind. I'd say it was even intimidating when found on a bartender, a mustache like that."

"Glad you like it."

"Who said I liked it? Listen," Martin said, now in complete possession of Red Tom's attention, "what do you hear about Charlie McCall?"

Red Tom eyed the other customers, moved in close. "The night squad was here asking your kind of question, Bo Linder and Jimmy Bergan."

"You tell them anything a fellow like myself should know?"

"Only that the word's out that he's gone."

"Gone how?"

"Disappeared, that's all."

"What about Jimmy Hennessey?"

"Hennessey? What's he got to do with it?"

"Maybe something."

"I haven't laid eyes on Hennessey in months."

"Is he all right?"

"Last I heard, he was drying out. Fell down the church steps and landed in front of Father O'Connor, who says to him, Hennessey, you should stop drinking. Hennessey reaches his hand up to the priest and says, I'm waiting for help from the Holy Ghost. He's in the neighborhood somewhere, says O'Connor. Ask him to pick you up. And he steps over Hennessey's chest."

"He must be dried out by now. The McCalls put his name on a go-between list."

"A go-between list?"

"It'll be in the morning paper. Our guess is they're trying to find an intermediary to talk with the kidnappers about the ransom."

Martin put the list on the bar and ran down the names: Joe Decker, a former soft-shoe artist who ran the Double Dot nightclub on Hudson Avenue; Andy Kilmartin, the Democratic leader of the Fifth Ward; Bill Shea, a Bindy McCall lieutenant who ran the Monte Carlo, the main gambling house in the city; Barney O'Hare, a champion bootlegger who served four terms as Patsy McCall's man in the State Assembly and no longer had need of work; Arnold Carroll, who ran the Blue Elephant saloon; Marcus Gorman, the town's best-known criminal lawyer, who defended Legs Diamond; Butch McHale, a retired welterweight and maybe the best fighter ever to come out of Albany, who ran the Satin Slipper, a speakeasy, after he quit the ring; Phil Lynch, who ran the candy store that was Bindy's headquarters for numbers collections and payoffs downtown; Honey Curry, a hoodlum from Sheridan Avenue, who did four years for a grocery store stickup; Hennessey, an ex-alderman who was one of Patsy's political bagmen until he developed the wet spot on his brain; Morrie Berman, the ex-pimp and gambler; and Billy Phelan.

"Kilmartin never comes in any more," Red Tom said. "O'Hare comes in for a nightcap after he gets laid. Gorman hasn't been in here since old man Becker told him and Legs Diamond he didn't want their business. Most of the others are in and out."

"Lately?"

"All but Curry. No show for a long while."

"Billy been in tonight yet?"

"He's about due."

"I know. I whipped him today with a parlay. I think I hurt him."

"He knows how to get well. You say this list is in the paper?"

Martin told him how the coded list arrived at the *Times-Union* as a classified ad and was spotted by a lady clerk as oddball enough to send up to Emory Jones for a funny feature story. The message was to CHISWICK, the names in scrambled numbers. Emory solved it instantly: A as 1, B as 2, the moron code. And when Martin next communicated, Emory had him check out everyone on the list. Max Rosen admitted the list was connected to the kidnapping but would say no more and didn't have to. Martin spent an hour in the phone booth discovering that none of those listed was available. Not home. In Miami. Away for the month. Except for Hennessey and Curry, whose phones didn't answer, and Billy and Morrie, whose recent movements Martin knew personally.

"Who's Curry hang around with these days?"

"He's cozy with Maloy, used to be. But he's always with a dame."

"And Maloy?"

"I heard he was hanging out with a bunch down in Jersey. Curry too."

Billy Phelan came in then. Martin saw him touch Red Tom for what looked like a twenty before he even looked the place over. Then he sat down beside Martin.

"Luckiest man in North America," Billy said.

"A connoisseur of horseflesh."

"With a horseshoe up your ass."

"Talent makes its own luck, Billy. Like somebody bowling two-ninety-nine."

"Yeah. I got a partial payment for you." Billy signaled Red Tom for a refill for Martin and a beer for himself, and put an envelope in front of Martin. He kept his hand on it.

"I need a bankroll for Nick's game tonight. If I hold on to this and I win I pay you off entirely."

"And if you lose, I lose this."

"You don't lose. Billy pays his debts."

"I mean this month."

"All right, Martin, you need the cash, take it. I'm not arguing. I just work a little longer."

"Keep the roll and maybe we'll both get our dues paid. But I have a question. What do you hear about Charlie McCall, apart from what we both know about last night?"

"Jesus, this is my big Charlie McCall day. Why the hell does everybody think I know what Charlie's up to?"

"Who's everybody?"

"Nobody."

"Some significant people in town obviously think you might be able to help find him, one way or another."

"Find him? He ain't lost."

"Haven't you heard?"

"I heard he got snatched, but I just found out upstairs that's not straight. Daddy Big got it right from Bindy. Charlie's in New York. All I heard was a rumor."

"Your rumor was right."

"They took him, then? That's it?"

"Correct."

"Daddy Big and his goatshit."

"What goatshit?"

"Just goatshit. What about significant people?"

"Your name's in the paper that comes out tonight, one of twelve names, all in a code in a classified ad, which is obviously a message to the kidnappers about go-betweens. Nobody said anything to you about this?"

"Nobody till now."

"You weren't on the original list. The ad came in about two this afternoon and I just found out your name was added about half an hour ago." Martin told the ad story again, and Billy knew all the names. He signaled for a beer.

"I got a message for you," Red Tom said when he brought Billy's beer. "Your friend Angie was in today. She's at the Kenmore."

"She say anything?"

"She said she needs her back scratched."

"That's not what she wants scratched."

"Well, you're the expert on that," said Red Tom, and he went down the bar.

Billy told Martin, "I don't belong on that list. That's either connected people or hoodlums. I pay off the ward leader, nickel and dime, and I vote the ticket, that's my connection. And I never handled a gun in my life."

"You classify Berman as a hoodlum?"

"Maybe not, but he sure ain't no altar boy."

"You know him pretty well?"

"Years, but we're not that close."

"You know everybody on Broadway and everybody knows you. Maybe that's why you're on the list."

"No, I figured it out. Daddy Big got me on it. If it come in half an hour ago, that's all it could be. Something I said about a plan to snatch Bindy last year. You know that rumor."

"No. What was it?"

"Fuck, a rumor. I'm the only one heard it? What is this? It was all over the goddamn street. Tom, you heard that rumor about Bindy last year?"

"What rumor?"

"Around August. Saratoga season. Somebody was gonna snatch him. You heard it."

"I never heard that. Who was gonna do it?"

"How the fuck do I know who was gonna do it?"

"It's your rumor."

"I heard a goddamn rumor, that's all. I paid no attention, nothing ever happened. Now, because I heard a rumor last August, I'm on the McCalls' shit list?"

"This is no shit list," Martin said.

When Red Tom went to serve another customer, Billy said, "They think I'm in on it."

"I don't think that's true," Martin said, "but it does make you a pretty famous fellow tonight in our little community. A pretty famous fellow."

"Know where I first heard about Charlie? From my Uncle Chick, who don't even know how to butter bread right. How the hell did he hear about it? He asks me what I know about Charlie and all I know is last night at the alleys and then you and all your Charlie horses. You knew it then, didn't you?"

"Maybe."

"Maybe, my fucking noodle."

"Maybe, your fucking noodle then."

"I'm standing with Charlie horses and you know the guy's glommed."

"And that explains why I won?"

"Sure it explains why you won, you prick."

"I didn't win anything yet," and Martin pushed the envelope toward Billy.

"Right. Poker time. Money first, Charlie later."

101

"Morrie Berman'll be in that game, right?"

"That's what he said last night."

"Look, pay attention to what he says. Anything. It's liable to be very important."

"What do you know that I don't?"

"That's an intriguing question we can take up some other time, but now let me tell you very seriously that everything is important. Everything Morrie says. We'll talk about it later when things aren't quite so public."

"What are you, a cop?"

"No, I'm a friend of Charlie McCall's."

"Yeah."

"And so are you."

"Yeah."

And Billy drank up and stood up. He and Martin moved toward the door, which opened to the pull of Daddy Big as they reached it, Daddy in his change apron and eyeshade, questing sweet blotto at eventide. Billy grabbed his shirtfront.

"You turned me in, you son of a bitch."

"What's got you, you gone nuts?"

"You told Bindy what I said about the snatch rumor."

"I asked about it. Bindy asked me where I heard it."

"And you finked on me, you fat weasel. And I don't know anything worth a goddamn pigeon fart."

"Then you got nothing to worry about."

"I worry about weasels. I never took you for a weasel."

"I don't like you either. Stay out of upstairs."

"I play tomorrow and you don't shut me out and don't try."

"I shut out people who need to be shut."

"Go easy, old man. There's three things you can't do in this world and all three of 'em are fight."

Daddy Big broke Billy's hold on his shirt and simultaneously, with a looping left out of nowhere, knocked him against the front door, which opened streetward. Billy fell on his back on

Becker's sidewalk, his fedora rolling into the gutter. Martin picked him up and then went for the hat.

"Not your day for judging talent," Martin said.

Billy put on his hat, blotted his lip. "He hits like he plays pool," he said.

"So, that's new. Something you learned," said Martin, brushing the dust off Billy's suit coat.

Martin walked with Billy up Broadway toward Clinton Avenue, thinking first he would go to Nick's cellar and watch the poker game but not play against his own money. Yet the notion of spectating at a poker game on such an evil day seemed almost evil in itself. His mind turned to thoughts of death: closing Scotty Streck's left eye, Charlie Boy maybe with a bullet in the head, dumped in the woods somewhere.

And passing the United Traction Company building at the corner of Columbia Street he saw Francis Phelan, again cocking his arm, just there, across the street, again ready to throw his smooth stone; and he remembered the bleeding and dying scab, his head laid open, face down on the floor of the trolley, one arm hanging over the top step. The scab had driven the trolley down Broadway from the North Albany barns, and when it reached Columbia Street a mob was waiting. Francis and two other young men heaved a kerosene-soaked sheet, twisted and knotted into a loose rope, over the overhead trolley wire and lit it with matches. The trolley could not pass the flaming obstacle and halted. The militiamen raised their rifles to the ready, fearful that the hostile crowd would assault the car, as it had the day before, and beat the driver unconscious. Militiamen on horseback pushed the mob back from the tracks, and one soldier hit Fiddler Quain with a rifle butt as Fiddler lit the sheet. But even as this was taking the full attention of the military, even before thoughts of reversing the trolley could be translated into action, other men threw a second twisted sheet over the trolley wire to the rear of the car and lit it, trapping the trolley and its strike-breaking passengers between two pillars of flame.

It was then that Francis uncocked his arm and that the smooth stone flew, and the scab fell and died. No way out. Death within the coordinates. And it was the shooting of the innocent onlookers which followed Francis's act that hastened the end of the strike. Violence enough. Martin saw two of the onlookers fall, just as he could still see the stone fly. The first was spun by the bullet and reeled backward and slid down the front of the railroad station wall. The second grabbed his stomach as the scab had grabbed his head, and he crumpled where he stood. Fiddler Quain lay on the granite blocks of Broadway after his clubbing, but the mob swirled around that horseman who hit him, an invasion of ants, and Fiddler was lifted up and swept away to safety and hiding. Like Franny, he was known but never prosecuted. The hands that carried the violence put honest men back to work. Broadway, then and now, full of men capable of violent deeds to achieve their ends.

"Listen, Billy," Martin said as they walked, "that business between you and Daddy Big, that's not really why the McCalls put you on the list. There's something else going on, and it's about Morrie Berman."

Billy stopped walking and faced Martin.

"What Morrie says could be important, since he knows people who could have taken Charlie."

"So do I. Everybody does on Broadway."

"Then what you or the others know is also important."

"What I know is my business. What Berman knows is his business. What the hell is this, Martin?"

"Patsy McCall is making it his business, too."

"How do you know that?"

104

"I talked to him this morning."

"Did he ask you to snoop around Morrie Berman?"

"No. He asked me to ask you to do that."

"Me? He wants me to be some kind of stoolie? What the hell's the matter with you, Martin?"

"I'm not aware that anything's the matter."

"I'm not one of the McCalls' political whores."

"Nobody said you were. I told him you wouldn't like the idea, but I also know you've been friendly with Charlie McCall all your life. Right now, he could be strapped to a bed someplace with a gun at his head. He could even be dead."

Billy made no response. Martin looked at him and saw puzzlement. Martin shaped the picture of Charlie Boy again in his mind but saw not Charlie but Edward Daugherty, tied to a bed by four towels, spread-eagled, his genitals uncovered. Why such a vision now? Martin had never seen his father in such a condition, nor was he in such a state even now at the nursing home. The old man was healthy, docile, no need to tie him to the bed. Naked prisoner. Naked father. It was Ham who saw Noah, his father, naked and drunk on wine, and Noah cursed Ham, while Shem and Japheth covered their father's nakedness and were blessed for it. Cursed for peering into the father's soul through the pores. Blessed for covering the secrets of the father's body with a blanket. Damn all who find me in my naked time.

Billy started to walk again toward Clinton Avenue. He spoke without looking at Martin, who kept pace with him. "Georgie the Syph knocked down an old woman and took four bucks out of her pocketbook. I came around the corner at James Street and saw him and I even knew the old woman, Marty Slyer the electrician's mother. They lived on Pearl Street. Georgie saw me and ran up Maiden Lane and the old lady told the cops I saw him. But I wouldn't rat even on a bum like Georgie. What I did the next time I saw him was kick him in the balls before he could say anything and take twenty off him and mail it to Mrs. Slyer. Georgie had to carry his balls around in a basket."

"That's a noble story, Billy, but it's just another version of the code of silence. What the underworld reveres. It doesn't have anything to do with morality or justice or honor or even friendship. It's a simplistic perversion of all those things."

"Whatever it is it don't make me a stool pigeon."

"All that's wanted is information."

"Maybe. Or maybe they want Morrie for something particular."

"No, I don't think so."

"How the hell do you know what they want, Martin?"

"Suit yourself in this, Billy. I was asked to put the question to you and I did."

"I don't get it, a man like you running errands for the McCalls. I don't figure you for that."

"What else can I tell you after I say I'm fond of Charlie, and I don't like kidnappers. I'm also part of that family."

"Yeah. We're all part of that family."

"I'll be around later to root for our money. Think about it."

"What exactly did Patsy say?"

"He said to hang around Berman and listen. That's all he said."

"That's all. Yeah."

And Billy crossed Clinton toward the alley beside Nick's haberdashery, where Nick, Footers O'Brien, and Morrie Berman were talking. Martin walked up the other side of the street, past the Pruyn Library, and crossed to The Grand Theater when he saw the Laughton film on the marquee. He looked back at the library corner and remembered the death of youth: his cousin's suicide in the wagon. Sudden behavior and pervasive silence. But sometimes living men tell no tales either. Francis Phelan suddenly gone and still no word why. *The Beachcomber.* Martin hadn't told Billy that his father was back in town. Duplicity and the code of silence. Who was honored by this? What higher morality was Martin preserving by keeping Billy ignorant of a fact so potentially significant to him? We are all in a conspiracy against the next man. Duplicity. And Billy Phelan saw through you, Martin: errand boy for the McCalls. Duplicity at every turn. Melissa back in town to remind you of how deep it goes. Oh yes, Martin Daugherty, you are one duplicitous son of a bitch.

In the drugstore next to The Grand, Martin phoned Patsy McCall.

"Do you have any news, Patsy?"

"No news."

"I made that contact we talked about, and it went just about the way I thought it would. He didn't like the idea. I don't think you can look for much information there."

"What the hell's the matter with him?"

"He's just got a feeling about that kind of thing. Some people do."

"That's all he's got a feeling for?"

"It gets sticky, Patsy. He's a good fellow, and he might well come up with something. He didn't say no entirely. But I thought you ought to know his reaction and maybe put somebody else on it if you think it's important."

"I'll take care of it," Patsy said curtly and hung up.

Martin called the *Times-Union* and got Emory. Yes, the lid was still on the Charlie story. "Everybody went along," Emory said, "including Dunsbach. I seared his ass all right. He wouldn't touch the story now with rubber gloves."

"Heroic, Em. I knew you could do it."

"Have you smoked out any kidnappers yet?"

"You know I don't smoke, Em. What happened with the A.L.P.?"

"I don't give a damn about that piss-ant stuff when I've got a story like this. Here. Talk to Viglucci."

Viglucci, the city editor, explained that some twelve hundred new voters had enrolled in the A.L.P., twice as many as necessary for Patsy McCall to control the young party. No, the desk hadn't reached Jake Berman, the phone constantly busy at the A.L.P. office. Martin volunteered to go there personally, being only two blocks away. Fine.

Jake Berman had been barely a specter all day for Martin, whose sympathy was all with the McCalls because of Charlie. But now Jake could surely use a little consolation. Martin had known Jake for years and liked him, a decent man, a lawyer for the poor, knew him when he was a city judge, appointed by McCall fiat as a sop to the Albany Jews. But that didn't last, for Jake refused to throw out a case against a gouging landlord, an untouchable who was a heavy contributor to the Democratic Party. Jake quit the bench and the party, and went back to practicing law.

In 1935, when the A.L.P. was founded to gain another line for Roosevelt's second run, Jake spearheaded the party locally and opened headquarters in his father's old tailor shop on Sheridan Avenue, just off North Pearl Street. Old Socialists and laboring men, who wanted nothing to do with the Democrats but liked F.D.R.'s New Deal, made the new party their own, and by 1936 the Albany branch had one hundred and eighty-four members. Patsy McCall tolerated it because it was a stepchild of the Democratic party, even though he had no use for Roosevelt, the snob son of a bitch. The Catholic Church grew restless with the New Party, however, as its ranks fattened with anti-Franco radicals and socialist intellectuals who spat on God. What's more, it promised the kind of growth that one day could be a power balance in local elections, and so Patsy decided it was time to pull the plug.

The word went out to the aldermen and ward leaders of the city's nineteen wards that some sixty voters in each ward should change their enrollment from Democrat to American Labor. As enrolled members, they would then be entitled to vote at A.L.P. meetings, and would vote as Patsy told them to. Jake Berman's few hundred regulars would be dwarfed by the influx, and Jake's chairmanship negated. In time, all in good time, Patsy's majority, of which Chickie Phelan was now one, would elect a new party chairman.

The garmentless tailor's dummy that had been in Berman's tailor shop for as long as Martin could remember was still visible behind the Lehman-for-Governor posters taped to the old store window. The shop had stood empty for several years after the death of old Ben Berman, a socialist since the turn of the century and a leader in the New York City garment industry's labor struggle until strikebreakers fractured his skull. He came to Albany to put his life and his head back together and eventually opened this shop, just off Pearl Street at the edge of an old Irish slum, Sheridan Hollow, where Lackey Quinlan once advertised in the paper to rent a house with running water, and curious applicants found he had built his shack over a narrow spot in the old Canal Street creek. This was the running water, and in it Lackey kept his goose and his gander.

Ben Berman worked as a tailor in the neighborhood, though his clients came from all parts of the city, until he lost most of his eyesight and could no longer sew. He died soon after that, and then his son Jacob rented the shop to another tailor, who ran it for several years. But the new man was inferior to Ben Berman with the needle, and the trade fell away. It remained for the A.L.P. to reopen the shop, and now it looked as if its days were again numbered.

Martin pushed open the door, remembering when Ben Berman made suits and coats for his own father, those days when the Daughertys lived under the money tree. Martin could vividly recall Edward Daugherty standing in this room trying on a tan, speckled suit with knickers and a belt in the back, mottled buttons, and a brown, nonmatching vest. Martin mused again on how he had inherited none of his father's foppery, never owned a tailor-made suit or coat, lived off the rack, satisfied with ready-made. A woman Martin did not know was coming down the inside stairs as he entered. She looked about forty, a matron in style. She was weeping and her hat looked crooked to Martin.

"Jake upstairs?"

She nodded, sniffled, wiped an eye. Martin yearned to console her with gentle fondling.

"Can I help you?" he asked her.

She laughed once and shook her head, then went out. Martin climbed the old stairs and found Jake Berman leaning back in a swivel chair, hands behind head, feet propped up on an open rolltop desk. Jake had a thick gray mustache and wore his hair long, like a serious musician. The elbow was out of his gray sweater, and he was tieless. The desk dominated the room, two rooms really, with the adjoining wall knocked out. Folding chairs cluttered both rooms, and at a long table two men younger than Jake sat tallying numbers on pink pads. The phone on Jake's desk was off the hook.

"Why don't you answer your phone?" Martin asked.

"I'm too busy," Jake said. He moved only his lips and eyes to say that. "What can I do for you?"

"I heard the results."

"You did. And did they surprise you?"

"Quite a heavy enrollment. I was told twelve hundred plus. Is that accurate?"

"Your information is as good as mine. Better. You get yours from McCall headquarters."

"I got mine from the city desk."

"Same thing really, isn't it, Martin?"

"I wouldn't say so. The McCalls do have some support there."

"Some?"

"I for one don't see myself a total McCaller."

"Yes, you write some risky things now and then, Martin. You're quite an independent-minded man in your way. But I didn't see you or anybody else reporting about the plan to take us over. Didn't anybody down on that reactionary rag know about it?"

"Did you?"

"I knew this morning," said Jake. "I knew when I saw it happening. Fat old Irishmen who loathe us, drunken bums from the gutter, little German hausfraus enrolling with us. Up until then, the subversion was a well-kept secret."

Jake's face was battered, his eyes asymmetric, one lower than the other, his mustache trimmed too high on one side. In anger, his lower lip tightened to the left. His face was as off balance as his father's battered and dusty samovar, which sat behind him on a table, a fractured sculpture with spigot, one handle, and one leg broken. Another fractured face for Martin in a matter of hours: Charlie when Scotty died; Patsy and Matt this morning; and now Jake, victim of the McCalls. Interlocking trouble. Binding ironies. Martin felt sympathy for them all, had a fondness for them all, gave allegiance to none. Yet, now he was being accused, for the second time in half an hour, of being in league with the McCall machine. And was he not? Oh, duplicitous man, are you not?

"I came for a statement, Jake. Do you have one?"

"Very brief. May the McCalls be boiled in dead men's piss."

A young man at the tabulating table, bald at twenty-five, threw down his pencil and stood up. "And you can tell the Irish in this town to go fuck a duck."

"That's two unprintable statements," said Martin. "Shall we try for three?"

"Always a joke, Martin. Everything is comic to you."

"Some things are comic, Jake. When a man tells me with high seriousness to go fuck a duck, even though I'm only half Irish, I'm amused somewhere."

The young man, in shirtsleeves, and with Ben Franklin spectacles poised halfway down his nose, came to the desk, hovering over Martin. "It's the religion, isn't it?" he said. "Political Jews stand as an affront to the McCalls and their priests, priests no better than the fascist-dog Catholics who kiss the boots of Franco and Mussolini."

Martin made a squiggle on his notepad.

"Quote it about the fascists," said the young man.

"Do you think the McCalls are fascists, Jake?" Martin asked.

"I know a Jew who's been with them almost since the beginning," said Jake. "He works for a few pennies more than he started for in nineteen twenty-two, sixteen years of penurious loyalty and he never asked for a raise, or threatened to quit over money. 'If I do,' he once said to me, 'you know what they'll tell me? The same they told Levy, the accountant. Quit, then, you Jew fuck.' He is a man in fear, a man without spirit."

"People who don't promote Jews, are they fascists, or are they anti-Semites?"

"The same thing. The fascists exist because of all those good people, like those sheep who enrolled with us today, all full of passive hate, waiting for the catalyst to activate it."

"Your point is clear, Jake, but I still want a statement."

"Print this. That I'm not dead, not even defeated, that I'll take the party's case to court, and that we'll win. If ever the right to free elections was violated, then it was violated today in Albany with this farcical maneuver."

"The McCalls own the courts, too," said the young man. "Even the Federal court."

"There are honest judges. We'll find one," Jake said.

"We won't yield to mob rule," the young man said.

"He's right," Jake said. "We will not. You know an Irish mob threw my grandfather out a third-story window in New York during the Civil War. They were protesting against their great enemy back then, the niggers, but they killed a pious old Jew. He tried to reason with them, with the mob. He thought they would listen to reason, for, after all, he was an intelligent man and had nothing to do with the war, or the niggers. He was merely living upstairs over the draft office. Nevertheless, they threw him down onto the street and let him lie there twitching, dying, for hours. They wouldn't let anyone pick him up or even help him, and so he died, simply because he lived over the draft office. It was a moment of monstrous ethnic truth in American history, my friend, the persecuted Irish throwing a persecuted Jew out the window in protest against drafting Irishmen into the Union Army to help liberate the persecuted Negro.

"But the enormous irony hasn't led to wisdom, only to self-preservation and the awareness of the truth of mobs. My father told me that story after another mob set fire to paper bags on our front porch, and, when my father came out to stomp out the flames, the bags broke and human excrement squirted everywhere. A brilliant stroke by the mob. They were waiting with their portable flaming cross to watch my father dance on the fire and the shit. Fire and shit, my friend, fire and shit. Needless to say, we moved soon thereafter."

"The Klan's an old friend of mine, too, Jake," Martin said. "They burned a cross in front of my house and fired a shot through our front window because of what I wrote in support of Al Smith. You can't blame the Klan on the Irish. Maybe the Irish were crazy, but they were also used as cannon fodder in the Civil War. I could match grandfathers with you. One of mine was killed at Antietam, fighting for the niggers."

Jake held a letter opener in his hand like a knife. He poked the point of it lightly at the exposed desk top. Then his arm went rigid. "Goddamn it, Martin, this is a stinking, lousy existence. Goddamn its stink! Goddamn all of it!" And with sudden force he drove the point of the letter opener into the desk top. The point stuck but the blade broke and pierced the muscle of his thumb.

"Perfect," he said, and held his hand in front of his face and watched it bleed. The young man ran to the bathroom for a towel. He wrapped the wound tightly as Jake slumped in his chair.

"Violence solves it all," Jake said. "I no longer feel the need to say anything."

"We'll talk another night," Martin said.

"I won't be less bitter."

"Maybe less bloody."

"And unbowed."

"There's something else, Jake, and you ought to know. It'll be in the paper tonight. Your son, Morrie, is named as a possible intermediary in a kidnapping."

"Repeat that, Martin."

"Bindy McCall's son, Charlie, was kidnapped this morning and the ransom demand is a quarter of a million. The McCalls are publishing a list of names in a simple code, names of men they view as potential go-betweens for the kidnappers to pick from. Morrie is one of twelve."

"God is just," said Jake's young aide. "The McCalls are now getting theirs back."

"Stupid, stupid to say such a thing," Jake snapped. "Know when to be angry."

"I just saw Morrie," Martin said, "getting ready to go into a card game."

"Naturally," said Jake.

"I may see him later. Do you have any message?"

"We no longer talk. I have three daughters, all gold, and I have Morris, a lead slug."

Martin suddenly pictured Jake with a flowing beard, knife in hand on Mount Moriah, cutting out the heart of his son.

"I just had a vision of you holding that letter opener," Martin said to Jake. "You look very much like an engraving of Abraham I've looked at for years in the family Bible. Your hair, your forehead."

"Abraham with the blade."

"And Isaac beneath it," said Martin. He could not bring himself to mention the dissection of Isaac. "The likeness of you to that drawing of Abraham is amazing."

As he said this Martin was withholding; for he now had a clear memory of the biblical engraving and it wasn't like Jake at all. Abraham's was a face of weakness, a face full of faith and anguish, but no bitterness, no defiance. And the knife did not touch Isaac. Abraham's beard then disappeared in the vision. Where he gripped the sacrificial knife, part of a finger was missing. Isaac bore the face of a goat. The vision changed. The goat became a bawling infant, then a bleating lamb. Martin shut his eyes to stop the pictures. He looked at the samovar.

"Isaac," Jake was saying. "God loves the Isaacs of the world. But he wouldn't have bothered to ask Abraham to sacrifice a son as worthless as my Morris."

"Now you even know what God asks," Martin said.

"I withdraw the remark."

With his gaze, Martin restored the samovar, new leg, new handle, new spigot. Steam came from it once again. He looked up to see the 1936 poster: Roosevelt, the Working Man's President. Out of the spigot came the hot blood of centuries.

7

Bump Oliver was a dapper little guy with a new haircut who played cards with his hat on. Billy met him when he sat down at the table in Nick Levine's cellar, just under the electric meter and kitty-corner from the old asbestos coal furnace which smudged up the cellar air but didn't heat it enough so you could take off your suit coat. New man on Broadway, Nick said of Bump when he introduced him to Billy; no more than that and who needs to know more?

And yet after Bump had dealt twice, Billy did want to know more. Because he sensed a cheater. Why? Don't ask Billy to be precise about such things. He has been listening to cheater stories for ten years, has even seen some in action and found out about it later, to his chagrin. He has watched Ace Reilly, a would-be cheater, practicing his second-card deal for hours in front of a mirror. Billy even tried that one himself to see how it went, but didn't like it, didn't have the patience or the vocation for it. Because cheaters, you see, already know how it's going to end, and what the hell good is that? Also, Billy saw a cheater caught once: a salesman who played in Corky Ronan's clubroom on Van Woert Street, and when Corky saw he was using a shiner, he grabbed the cheater's hand and showed everybody how he wore it, a little bit of a mirror under a long fingernail. Joe Dembski reached over and punched the cheater on the side of the neck, and the others were ready to move in for their licks, but Corky said never mind that, just take his money and he won't come back, and they let the cheater go. Why? Well, Corky's idea was that everybody's got a trade, and that's Billy's idea too, now.

So Billy has seen all this and has thought about it, and because he knows so well how things should be when everything is straight, he also thinks he knows when it's off center, even when it's only a cunt hair off. That's how sensitive Billy's apparatus is. Maybe it was the way Bump beveled the deck and crooked a finger around it, or maybe it was his eyes and the fact that he was new on Broadway. Whatever it was, even though Bump lost twelve straight hands, Billy didn't trust him.

The game was now five-card stud, quarter ante, no limit, and four flush beats a pair. The deal was walking and when it came to Bump, Billy gave him the full eyeball.

"Where you from, Bump?" he asked, just like a fellow who was looking for information.

"Troy," Bump said. "Albia. You know it?"

"Sure, I know it. Who the hell don't know Albia?"

"Well, I was asking. Lot of people know about Troy don't know Albia."

"I know Albia, for chrissake. I know Albia."

"That's terrific, really terrific. Congratulations."

Bump looked at Billy; Billy looked at Bump. The others in the game looked at them both: dizzy-talking bastards. But Billy wanted the cheater thinking about something besides cheating, wanted him edgy. Billy smiled at Bump. Bump didn't smile at Billy. Good.

Billy drew deuce, four, eight and folded. He was ahead $21, which was nice. He'd sat down with about $315 and change, which included his original $170, $20 from Peg, $40 from

Tod, another $20 from Red Tom, and $67 from the Harvey Hess Benevolent Association. All he'd spent was carfare and the drinks at Becker's. Roughly speaking he still needed about $455 to get straight with Martin, but he was winging it now, wasn't he, getting where he had to go? And was there ever any doubt? Don'tcha know Billy can always get a buck?

Morrie Berman won the hand with three nines. He was a bigger winner than Billy.

"Your luck's running," Billy said to him.

"Yeah," said Morrie. "Money coming in, name in the paper."

Billy had told him as soon as they met in front of Nick's that both their names were on the list. Morrie already knew. Max Rosen had called around supper to ask him to stay in town, keep himself on tap. Rosen was nice as pie, Morrie said. If you don't mind, Mr. Berman. Naturally I don't mind, Mr. Rosen, and if I can be of any help at all, just call me. What else do you tell a McCall flunky in a situation like this? Neither Billy nor Morrie mentioned the list to anybody else at Nick's. Billy listened carefully to what Morrie said. He didn't say a goddamn thing worth telling anybody.

"What's that about name in the paper?" Nick Levine asked. Nick was his own house player, cutting the game. Nick would cut a deuce out of a $40 pot. Nick also had a nose for gossip when it moved into his cellar.

"Aw nothin', just a thing," Morrie said.

"What thing?"

"Forget it."

"I'll get the paper."

"That's it, get the paper."

But Nick wasn't satisfied. He was a persistent little man with double-thick glasses and he owned more suits of clothes personally than anybody Billy knew, except maybe George Quinn. But then Nick owned a suit store and George didn't, and George looked a hell of a lot better in clothes than Nick. Some people don't know how to wear clothes.

Nick looked across the table at Morrie and gave him a long stare while all play stopped. "They pull you in?"

"No, nothing like that," Morrie said. "Look, play cards. I'll tell you later."

That satisfied Nick and he bet his kings.

Lemon Lewis was a pointy-headed bald man, which was how he got his nickname. Didn't have a hair on his body. Not even a goddamn eyelash. When Lemon, who worked for Bindy McCall, didn't say anything about Morrie's name in the paper, Billy knew he hadn't heard about the list. But Lemon wasn't that close to Bindy any more, not since he overdid it with kickbacks when he handled the gambling patronage. Bindy demoted Lemon for his greed and put him to work on the odds board in the Monte Carlo. Man with the chalk, just another mug.

Lemon was alongside Bump and when the deal reached Lemon, Billy asked for a new deck. If Bump, who would deal next, had been marking cards, beveling them, nicking edges, waiting for his time to handle them again, then the new deck would wipe out his work. Coming at Lemon's deal, the request would also not point to Bump. But it did rattle Lemon, which was always nice.

"New deck, and you're winning?" Lemon said.

"Double my luck," Billy said.

"You think maybe Lemon knows something?" Footers O'Brien asked, and everybody laughed but Lemon. No mechanic, Lemon. Last man in town you'd accuse of cheating. A hound dog around the rackets all his life and he never learned how the game was played.

"Lemon shuffles like my mother when she deals Go Fish to my ten-year-old nephew," Billy said.

Lemon dealt the new cards, delivering aces wired to Billy.

"Ace bets," said Lemon, and when Billy bet five dollars, Bump, Morrie, and Nick all folded. Footers, a retired vaude-villian who sang Jolson tunes at local ministrel shows, stayed with a king. Lemon stayed with a queen.

On the third card nobody improved. Billy drew an eight and bet again with the ace. Lemon raised and so Billy read him for queens wired, because Lemon rarely bluffed. Footers called with king and jack showing, so probably he had a pair too. Footers wouldn't chase a pair. Too good a player. But whatever either of them had, Billy had them beat.

On the fourth card, Billy paired the eights. Aces and eights now. Neither Lemon nor Footers looked like they improved. Very unlikely. Yet both called, even when Billy bet $20. We can beat your eights, Billy.

Footers's last card was a seven, which didn't help, and Lemon drew a spade, which gave him three spades up. The bet was still to Billy's eights, but before he could bet them, Lemon turned over his hole card and showed the four flush.

"Can you beat it, boys?" he asked, smiling sunbeams.

"Only with a stick," Footers said, and he folded his jacks.

"I bet forty dollars," Billy said.

His hand, showing, was ace, seven and the pair of eights.

"Well that's a hell of a how-do-you-do," Lemon said. "I turn my hand over and show you I got a four flush."

"Yes, you did that. And then I bet you forty dollars. You want to play five cards open, that's okay by me. But, Lemon, my word to you is still four-oh."

"You're bluffing, Phelan."

"You could find out."

"What do you think of a guy like this, Nick?" Lemon said.

"It's the game, Lemon. Who the hell ever told you to show your hole card before the bet?"

"He's bluffing. I know the sevens were all played. He's got a third eight? Aces," Lemon said, now doing his private calculating out loud. "Nick folded an ace, I got an ace. So you got the case ace? That's what you're telling me?"

"Forty dollars, Lemon."

Lemon went to the sandwich table, bit a bologna sandwich, and drew a glass of beer. He came back and studied Billy's hand. Still ace, seven and the eights.

Billy sat with his arms folded. Keeping cool. But folks, he was really feeling the sweet pressure, and had been, all through the hand: rising, rising. And he keeps winning on top of that. It was so great he was almost ready to cream. Goddamn, life is fun, ain't it Billy? Win or lose, you're in the mix. He ran his fingers over the table's green felt, fingered his pile of quarters, flipped through his stack of bills while he waited for the Lemon squash. Goddamn, it's good.

Bump watched him with a squinty eye.

Footers was smiling as he chewed his cigar, his nickel Headline. The Great Footers. Nobody like him. Drinking pal of Billy's for years, always good for a touch. Footers knew how to survive, too. Told Billy once how he came off a four-day drunk and woke up broke and dirty, needing a shave bad. Called in a neighbor's kid and gave him a nickel, the only cash Footers had. Sent him down to the Turk's grocery for a razor blade. The kid came back with it and Footers shaved. Then he washed and dried the blade and folded it back in its wrapper and called the kid again and told him, take this back to the Turk and tell him you didn't get it straight. Tell him Mr. O'Brien didn't want a razor blade, he wanted a cigar. And the kid came back with the cigar.

Billy looked at Footers and laughed at the memory. Footers smiled and shook his head over the mousehole in Lemon's character. Five minutes had passed since Lemon turned up the hole card.

"Thirty seconds, Lemon," Nick said. "I give you thirty seconds and then you call it or the pot's over."

Lemon sat down and bit the bologna. He looked Billy in the eye as his time ticked away.

"You said it too fast when you bet," Lemon said with a mouthful. "You probably got it."

"I'll be glad to show you," Billy said.

"Yeah, well you're good, you lucky bastard."

"Ah," said Billy, pulling in the pot at last. "My mother thanks you, my sister thanks you, my nephew thanks you, and above all, Lemon, I, William Francis Irish Catholic Democrat Phelan, I too thank you."

And Billy shoved his hole card face down into the discards.

Lemon sulked, but life went on. Bump Oliver dealt and Billy came up with kings wired. Very lovely. Also Billy heard for the first time the unmistakable whipsaw snap of a real mechanic at work dealing seconds. Billy watched Bump deal, admiringly. Billy appreciated talent wherever he saw it. Nobody else seemed to notice, but the whipsaw was as loud as a brass band to Billy's ear. It was not Billy's music, however. He did not mind the music cheaters made, so long as they didn't make it all over him. He caught Bump's eye, smiled, and then folded the kings.

"No thanks," was all he said to Bump, but it was plenty. Bump stopped looking at Billy and folded his own hand after the next card. He played two more hands and dropped out of the game. The cheater lost money. Never took a nickel from anybody, thanks to doughty Billy. Nobody knew Bump was really a wicked fellow at heart. Nobody knew either, how Billy absolutely neutralized him.

Billy, you're a goddamned patent-leather wonder.

Martin arrived at the card game in time to see Lemon Lewis throw the deck across the room and hear Nick tell him, "Pick 'em up or get out. Do it again, I don't want your action." Lemon, the world's only loser, picked up the cards and sat down, bent his shiny bald head over a new hand and continued, sullenly, to lose. Billy looked like a winner to Martin, but Morrie Berman had the heavyweight stack of cash.

"You've been doing all right, then," Martin said, pulling a chair up behind Billy.

"Seem to be doing fine." Half a glass of beer sat beside Billy's winnings, his eyes at least six beers heavier than when Martin had last seen him.

"You coachin' this fella, Martin?" Nick said.

"Doesn't look to me as if he needs much coaching."

"He's got the luck of the fuckin' Irish," Lemon said.

"Be careful what you say about the Irish," Footers said. "There's Jews in this game."

"So what? I'm a Jew."

"You're not a Jew, Lemon. You're an asshole."

"Up yours, too," Lemon said, and he checked his hole card.

"Lemon, with repartee like that you belong on the stage," Footers said, and he looked at his watch. "And there's one leaving in ten minutes."

"Play cards," Nick said.

"The bet," said Morrie, "is eighty dollars."

"Eighty," Nick said.

Morrie smiled and looked nothing like Isaac. He had a theatrical quality Martin found derivative—a touch of Valentino, a bit of George Raft, but very like Ricardo Cortez: dark, slick, sleek-haired Latin stud, as if Morrie had studied the type to energize his own image as a Broadway cocksmith and would-be gigolo, a heavy gambler, an engaging young pimp with one of the smartest whores on Broadway, name of Marsha. Marsha was still in business but had split with Morrie five years back and worked alone now. Pimping is enough to weight down a paternal brow, but Jake's imputation of lead sluggery implied a far broader absence of quality in Morrie, and Martin could not see it.

What he saw was Morrie's suavity, and an ominous reserve in that muscular smile which George Raft, at his most evil, could never have managed; for Raft was too intellectually soft, too ready for simple solutions. Morrie, like Cortez, and unlike the pliant, innocent Isaac, conveyed with that controlled smile that he understood thoroughly that life was shaped by will, wit, brains, a reverence for power, a sense of the comic; that things were never simple; and that the end of behavior was not action but comprehension on which to base action. George Raft, you are a champion, but how would you ever arrive at such a conclusion?

"K-K-K-Katy, he's bettin' me eighty," sang Footers, and he folded. That left Nick, Billy, and Morrie with money to win. The pot fattened, and Nick cut it for the house.

The cellar door opened and a kid, twenty-two maybe, stepped in and was met by Nick's doorman, the hefty Bud Bradt, an All-Albany fullback for Philip Schuyler High in the late twenties. The players looked up, saw the kid getting the okay from Bud, and went back to their cards. Then the kid came down the eight steps, stood with his back to the door that led to Nick's furnace and coal bin, and, taking a small pistol from his sock, told the players: "Okay, it's a holdup."

"Cowboy," Morrie said, and he reached for his cash.

"Don't touch that, mister," the kid said. "That's what I came for," and he threw a cloth bag on top of the pot. "Put your watches and rings in that."

"This isn't a healthy thing to do in Albany, young man," Footers said to him. "They've got rules in this town."

"Do what I say, Pop. Off with the jewelry and out with the wallets. Empty your pockets and then move over against that wall." He pointed with his small pistol toward the bologna sandwiches.

The kid looked barely twenty to Martin, if that. Yet here he was committed to an irrevocably bold act. Psychopathic?

Suicidal? Early criminal? Breadwinner desperate for cash? An aberrant gesture in the young, in any case. The kid's shoulders were spotted with rain, a drizzle that had begun as Martin arrived. The kid wore a black fedora with brim down, and rubbers. A holdup man in shiny rubbers with large tongues that protected his shoelaces from the damp night. What's wrong with this picture?

"Come on, move," the kid said, in a louder voice. And Martin felt his body readying to stand and obey, shed wallet, watch, and gold wedding band bought and inscribed in Galway: *Martin and Maire, Together*. Never another like that. Give it up? Well, there are priorities beyond the staunchest sentiment. And yet, and yet. Martin contained his impulse, for the other players still stared at the kid and his .22 target pistol. Gentlemen, do you realize that psychopaths snap under stress? Are you snapping, young crazy? Is blood in the cards tonight? Martin envisioned a bleeding corpus and trembled at the possibilities.

And then Billy reached for the kid's swag bag, picked it off the money pile, and threw it back at the gunny boy. Billy grabbed a fistful of cash from the pot and stuffed it into his coat. The kid stepped behind Bump Oliver's chair and shoved the pistol into the light. "Hey," he said to Billy, yelling. But Billy went back for a second handful of bills.

"That pea-shooter you got there wouldn't even poison me," he said.

Martin's thought was: Billy's snapped; the kid will kill him. But the kid could not move, his response to Billy lost, perhaps, inside his rubbers. The kid's holding position deteriorated entirely with the arrival of a sucker punch to the back of his neck by Bud Bradt, a man of heft, yes, but also of stealth, who had been edging toward the kid from the rear and then made a sudden leap to deliver his massive dose of fist to the sucker spot, sending the kid sprawling over the empty chair, gun hand sliding through the money, gun clattering to the floor on the far side of the table. Lemon pulled the kid off the table, punched his face, and threw him to the floor. Then he and Morrie kicked the kid body in dual celebration of the vanquishing until Nick said, "Shit, that's enough." Bud Bradt took over, kicked the kid once more, and then lifted him by collar and leg up the stairs, a bleeding carcass.

"Don't leave him in my alley," Nick said.

Bud Bradt came right back and Nick said, "Where'd you put him?"

"In the gutter between two cars."

"Good," said Nick. "Maybe they'll run over him."

"I would guess," said Martin, "that that would look very like a murder to somebody. And that's not only illegal, it also requires explanations."

"Yeah," said Nick, crestfallen. "Put him up on the sidewalk."

Martin went outside with Bud in time to see the kid hoisting himself up from the gutter with the help of the bumper of a parked car. The kid drew up to full height, full pain, and a fully bloodied face. He looked toward the alley and saw Martin and Bud, and then, with strength rising up from the secret reservoir fear draws upon, he turned from them and ran with a punishing limp across Clinton Avenue, down Quackenbush Street, down toward the waterworks and the New York Central tracks, and was gone then, fitfully gone into the darkness.

"Didn't kick him enough," Bud said. "The son of a bitch can still run. But he'll think twice before he does that again."

"Or shoot somebody first to make his point."

"Yeah, there's that."

Footers had come up behind them in time to see the kid

limp into the blackness. "I was in a crap game once," Footers said, "and a fellow went broke and put a pistol on the table to cover his bet. Five guys faded him."

Martin saw the kid limping into the beginning of his manhood, victim of crazy need, but insufficient control of his craziness. Martin had been delighted to see the kid suckerpunched five minutes earlier, salvation of the Galway wedding band. Now he felt only compassion for a victim, lugubrious emotions having to do with pity at pain, foreboding over concussions, lungs punctured by broken ribs, internal ruptures, and other leaky avenues to death or lesser grievings. Victims, villains were interchangeable. Have it both ways, lads. Weep for Judas at the last gasp. We knew he'd come to the end of his rope. He couldn't beat the fate the Big Boy knew was on him, poor bastard.

"I don't know what the hell to do with this pot," Nick was saying as they reentered the cellar. He was still picking quarters off the floor.

"Give it to Billy," Morrie said. "He deserves it."

"You're a genuine hero," Martin said to Billy. "Like the quarterback who makes the touchdown with a broken leg. There's a heroic edge to such behavior. You think bullets don't kill the single-minded."

"Weird day," Billy said. "I took a knife away from a looney in the Grand Lunch a few hours ago."

The others stopped talking.

"This kid was poking near my belly," and Billy showed them and told them about the coffee game.

"But you had a weapon in the coffee," Martin said. "Tonight you had nothing. You know a twenty-two slug can damage you just as permanently as five rounds from a machine gun. Or is your education lacking in this?"

"I didn't think like that," Billy said. "I just wasn't ready to hand over a night's work to that drippy little bastard. His gun didn't even look real. Looked like a handful of candy. Like one of them popguns my nephew has that shoots corks. Worst I'm gonna get is a cork in the ear, that's how it went. But the money counted, Martin. I owe people, and I was hot for that pot, too. I had kings and nines, ready to fill up."

"Billy should get a chunk of that pot, Nick," Morrie said.

"He got two handfuls," Nick said.

"That was his own dough going back home," Morrie said. "What about the rest? And Bud ought to get something. Without them guys, I'd have personally lost one hell of a bundle."

"Everybody oughta split the pot," Lemon said. "Nobody had a winning hand."

"Especially you," Footers said.

"You folded, Lemon, forget it," Morrie said.

"Fuck you guys," Lemon said.

"Why you gommy, stupid shit," Morrie said. "You might be dead if it wasn't for Billy and Bud. Your head is up your ass."

"While it's up there, Lemon," Footers said, "see if you can see Judge Crater anywhere. He's been gone a long time."

"The only three had the power in that last hand," said Morrie, "was Billy, me, and you, Nick. Everybody else was out of it. So it's a three-way split. I say Billy gets half my share and Bud the other half."

"I got enough," Billy said.

"I'll take it," said Bud.

"It's about forty apiece, what's left, three ways. One-twenty and some silver here." Nick counted out the split, forty to each, and pocketed his own share.

"You really keeping your whole forty, Nick?" Morrie asked, divvying his share between Billy and Bud. "After what those boys did for you and your joint?"

"Whataya got in mind now?"

"The house buys them steaks at Becker's."

"I don't fight that," Billy said.

"I ate," Nick said.

"So eat again, or send money."

Nick snapped a five on the table to Morrie, who looked at it, looked at Nick, didn't pick it up. Nick peeled off another five.

"I give ten to the meal. Eat up. But is the game dead here? What the hell, everybody gonna eat? Nobody gonna play cards?"

"Dead for me," Morrie said, picking up the fivers. And clearly, Billy and Martin were pointed elsewhere when Nick took a good look, and Footers was drawing himself another beer.

"I do believe I'll pass, Nick, me boy," Footers said. "That last one was a tough act to follow."

"I'm still playing," Lemon said, sitting alone at the table.

"You're playing with yourself," Footers said. "As usual."

"Tomorrow night, nine-thirty," Nick said. "Same time, same station."

"Steak time, boys," Morrie said.

Billy found Nick's toilet and pissed before they left. While the old beer sudsed up in the bowl, he consolidated his cash. Out of the coat pocket came the handfuls of bills. He counted it all. Nice. He'd pulled more out of the pot than he put in. He wrapped it all around the rest of the wad. He still needed $275 to pay off Martin, his bankroll now up to $514.

It mounts up. No question about that. Put your mind to it and it mounts up.

8

No man who wore socks in Albany felt better in the nighttime than Billy Phelan, walking with a couple of pals along his own Broadway from Nick's card game to Union Station to get the papers, including the paper that was going to make him famous tonight. Maybe he feels so good that he's getting a little crazy about not being afraid. Martin was right. A .22 in the eye gives you a hell of a headache.

But now Billy looks around and sees this Broadway of his and knows he's not crazy, because he knows it all and it all makes sense. He has known it this way since 1913 when he was six and his father took him in the rowboat and they rowed down the middle of the street. The Hudson had backed up over its banks and they were rowing down to Keeler's Hotel to rescue his grandfather, who had had a fight with Billy's grandmother and hadn't been home for a month and was caught now, stranded at the hotel with the big trunk he was taking to New York. He was an engineer on the Central and due back to his train, but he had no intention of carting the trunk on his back through two and three feet of water from Keeler's to the station. And so his son, Francis, became the hero, the man who would rescue Grandpa. Francis put Billy in the boat at the station and right now Billy can see the spot where he stepped off the curb into that boat, where Steuben Street intersects Broadway. The water was up to the curb there, and toward State Street it became deeper and deeper.

Billy got into the boat, one of a dozen rowing around on Broadway, and his father rowed them down the center of the street, down the canyon of buildings, wearing his cap and the heavy knit sweater with the collar that Billy remembers. Never a coat; a sweater and gloves always enough for that man. He rowed Billy half a block and then said: They'll fix this stuff one of these days.

I don't want them to fix it, Billy said.

They've got to, said his father, because they can't let this kind of thing go on.

Billy, sitting in the back of the boat like the captain, said, I hope they never fix it. Then they got Grandpa and his trunk. Grandpa sat with Billy on his lap, and the trunk standing up in the middle of the boat.

A damn shame, Grandpa said, to put up with this, but I suppose you like it, young fellow. And Billy said he liked it better than snow. They rowed Grandpa to the station, where he got his train and went away.

Now 1913 was gone, too, but Billy was again gliding down Broadway in a craft of his own making, and he relished the sight. There was Albany's river of bright white lights, the lights on in the Famous Lunch, still open, and the dark, smoky reds of Brockley's and Becker's neon tubes, and the tubes also shaping the point over the door of the American Hotel, and the window of Louie's pool room lit up, where somebody was still getting some action, and the light on in the Waldorf restaurant, where the pimps worked out of and where you could get a baked apple right now if you needed one, and the lights of the Cadillac Cafeteria with the pretty great custard pie, and the lights on in the upper rooms of the Cadillac Hotel, where the Greek card game was going on and where Broadway Frances was probably turning a customer upside down and inside out, pretty, tough, busy, knobby lady and Billy's old friend, and the lights in the stairway to the Monte Carlo, where the action would go on until everybody ran out of money or steam, and the lights, too, in Chief Humphrey's private detective office, the Chief working late on somebody's busted marriage, and the light in Joe Mangione's rooms upstairs over his fruit store, and light in the back of Red's barbershop coming through a crack in the door, and Billy knew that Red and others were in there playing blackjack. And look there, too, buddy boy: The lights are on in Bill's Magic Shop, where Bill is staying late, hoping to sell a deck of cards or a pair of dice or a punch board or a magic wand to some nighthawk in search of transport, and the lights are on, too, in Bradt's drug store, where Billy does all his cundrum business.

The lights are on because it's not quite half past eleven on Broadway and some movies are still not out and plenty of people are waiting for the westbound train just now pulling into Union Station, bound for Cleveland and Chicago and carrying the New York papers. Lights are on in Gleason's Grill, which was a soda fountain before beer came back, and lights are shining in the other direction, up toward Orange Street and Little Harlem, like Broadway but only a block long, with the colored crap and card games going strong now, and the Hotel Taft doing its colored business on white sheets, and Prime and Gisburg's candy store still open, with beer by the bottle and a game in the back and people talking politics there, McCall nigger politics, even at this hour, because that is where the power Democrats gather in Little Harlem.

There is Helen's Lunch, dark now, which feeds the colored hungry and Martha's colored bar all lit up and full of all-night wild music (Play it, Fatha), where Martha wets down the colored thirsty but not *just* the colored. Lights burn in the Carterer Mission, where the colored bums get the same treat-

ment and food the white bums get; and in the colored rooming house run by Mrs. Colored O'Mara, where Slopie Dodds
has his rooms and where he keeps his crutches when he's
wearing his leg.

There is light still in the triangular sign of the Railroad
YMCA, keeping the lamp lit for the conductors and brakemen
and engineers who terminate in Albany tonight and want a
clean pillow. And next door a light is on in the Public Bath,
closed now but where Billy watched his sister, Peg, learn to
swim, ducked by Uncle Chick. Peg, older than Billy by
eight years, was terrified when she went under. Billy was
already a swimmer then, learned in the Basin and in the
Hudson when Peg was afraid to go near it. Billy learned everything by himself, everything worth learning. He'd been swimming all that summer when his mother told him to stay away
from the river. That August he climbed the Livingston Avenue
railroad bridge and dove in—forty feet high, was it?—wearing a straw hat to protect his head. The next summer Billy
dove off that trestle without the hat and came up with a fish
in his mouth and a mermaid biting his big toe.

Look down Broadway.

Here comes a Pine Hills trolley, and here are the cars
coming in to pick up the train people, and there are the
Yellow cabs and the gypsies waiting for their long-distance
action.

And here comes Mike the Wop ahead of all the passengers,
Mike always one of the first off the train because he knows
the kids are waiting. Thirty kids anyway. Oughta be in bed,
you scurvy little rug-rats. But they know Mike is due.

Mike comes out wearing his candy butcher's apron full of
change. He has no use for change because he is thick with
folding money and bound for the action at the Monte Carlo,
and after that he may contract for a bit of the old interrelat-
edness with Broadway Frances or one of her peers, but for now

he is the God Almighty Hero of the Albany rug-rats who scream: Here he comes. And of course Mike sees them as soon as he moves across the concourse of the station, the great, glorious, New York Central monument to power, and, feeling perhaps as potent as Vanderbilt, Mike expansively lets his great, pasta-filled stomach precede him toward the door to Broadway.

He then pushes open the station's storm door and enters onto that segment of Broadway Billy and his friends are just now approaching from the north.

Billy pauses and says, Hey, Mike.

Mike turns and is distracted only momentarily from the performance at hand but does say, Eh, Billy, and turns back then to the rug-rats and spins out the change onto the sidewalk under the canopy: dollar, two, five, ten, twenty. Who knows how much change Mike the Wop strews before the rug-rats of Broadway? He gives, they receive. They scramble and pick it up, take it home, and buy the milk and beer.

A man, a grown man, a bum, a wino, a lost derelict from the sewers and gutters of elsewhere, passes and sees Mike's generosity and reaches down for a dime.

Get lost, bum, says Mike, and when the bum does not, Mike raises a foot and pushes the bum over, into the street, where he falls and rolls and is almost run over by a Yellow cab just leaving for Loudonville with a customer and four valises, and is also almost decapitated by the Number Four Pine Hills trolley.

The bum rises, walks on, the dime in his grip.

Mike supervises as the rug-rats clean up every visible nickel and penny, sift in the soft dirt of the gutters for dimes that rolled into the glop. And some will be back, scrounging at dawn for coins that eluded everyone last night. Now they take their cache and disentangle themselves from one another. They run, seethe into the night, and evaporate off Broadway.

Billy watches them go, watches, too, as Mike crosses the street to walk beneath the brightest of the bright lights, one of the many maestros of Broadway power, now heading into the center of the garden in search of other earthly delights.

The station was still alive with travelers, with the queers buzzing in and out of the men's room, and the night crowd hot for the papers. When Billy had bought the *Times-Union*, found the ad, decoded what they all knew was there to begin with, then Martin said to Morrie: "I saw your father tonight and told him about this."

"Heh," said Morrie. "What'd he say?"

"Ah, a few things."

"Nothing good, bet your ass on that, the old son of a bitch."

"It wasn't exactly flattering, but he was interested."

"Who's that?" Billy asked, looking up from the news-
.paper.

"My old man," Morrie said.

"He's a son of a bitch?"

"In spades."

"What'd he do?"

"Nothing. He's just a son of a bitch. He always was."

Well, you got an old man, is what Billy did not say out loud.

They stood in the rotunda, in front of the busy Union News stand with the belt-high stacks of Albany papers, the knee-high stacks of New York *Newses* and *Daily Mirrors*, the ankle-high stacks of *Herald Tribs* and *Timeses* and *Suns*. Billy was translating Honey Curry's name from the code. E-d-w-a-r-d C-u-r-r-e-y. They spelled it wrong.

"Honey Curry," Billy said. "Where the hell is *he* these days?"

Martin passed on that, and Morrie said, "Who knows where that son of a bitch is?"

Billy laughed out loud. "Remember when they had the excursion. The Sheridan Avenue Gang. And Curry went wild and hit Healy, the cop, with a crock of butter and knocked him right off the boat and Healy goddamn near drowned. Curry lit out and wound up in Boston and Maloy met him there, downtown, and they're cuttin' it up and Curry's afraid of his shadow. Then a broad walks by, a hooker, and looks at Curry and says to him, Hi ya, honey, how ya doin'? and Curry grabs her with both hands and shoves her up against a tree and shakes the hell out of her. How come you know my name? he says to her."

"That's Curry," said Morrie.

"Where's Maloy? I hear he's in Jersey. Newark, is it?" Billy asked.

"Could be," said Morrie.

"Goddamn," Billy said. "That's where I heard it."

"What?"

"The rumor they were going to kidnap Bindy last summer. We were up in Tabby Bender's saloon. You and me. Remember?"

"No. When was that?" said Morrie.

"Goddamn it, don't anybody remember what I remember? We were sitting at the bar, you and me, and Maloy was with Curry, and Maloy asks if I heard about the Bindy kidnap thing and I didn't. We talked about it, Maloy and Curry shootin' the shit and comin' up to the bar for drinks. And then Maloy tells me, We're gonna take this joint. Now, you remember?"

"I remember *that*," Morrie said. "Screwballs."

"Right," said Billy. "Maloy says, Get out now if you want; we're gonna clean him out. And I told him, I'm comfortable.

Clean him out. Take the pictures off the walls. What the hell do I care? And you and me kept drinking."

"Right," Morrie said. "We never moved."

"Right, and they go out and they're gone ten minutes and back they come with handkerchiefs on their faces. Goddamn wouldn't of fooled my nephew, in the same suits and hats. And they cleaned out the whole damper, every nickel. And when they were gone, I said to George Kindlon, the bartender, Let's have a drink, George, and I pushed a fiver at him. I don't think I can change it, he said, and we all busted up because George didn't give a rat's ass, he didn't own the joint. It was Tabby's problem, not George's."

"Right," Morrie said, "and George give us the drink free."

"Yeah," said Billy. "But it was Maloy and Curry really got us the free drink."

"That's it. Maloy and Curry bought that one," and Morrie laughed.

"Son of a bitch," Billy said.

"Right," said Morrie.

Billy pictured Morrie kicking the holdup kid. Vicious mouth on him then, really vicious, yet likable even if he used to be a pimp. He had a good girl in Marsha. Marsha Witherspoon, what the hell kind of a name is that? Billy screwed her before she even went professional. She was a bum screw. Maybe that's why Morrie dumped her, couldn't make a buck with her. But he didn't take up any other whores. Morrie would always let Billy have twenty, even fifty if he needed it. Morrie was with Maloy the night Billy almost lost a match to Doc Fay two years ago. Billy played safe till his ass fell off to win that one, and when he won and had the cash, Morrie and Maloy came over and Maloy said, You didn't have to worry, Billy. If he'd of won the game, we'd of taken the fuckin' money away from him and give it to you anyway. Crazy Maloy. And Morrie was tickled when Maloy said that, and he told Billy, Billy, you couldn't have lost tonight even if you threw the match. Morrie was two years older than Billy and he was a Jew and a smart Jew and Billy liked him. This was funny because Billy didn't like or even know that many Jews. But then Billy thought of Morrie as a gambler, not as a Jew. Morrie was a hustler who knew how to make a buck. He was all right. One of Billy's own kind.

While Billy, Martin, and Morrie ate midnight steaks in Becker's back room, tables for ladies but no ladies, George Quinn came in and found Billy, took him away from the table and whispered: "You hear that Charlie McCall's been kidnapped?"

"I heard that, George."

"Do you know your name's in the paper in some kind of mixed-up spelling?"

"I know that, too."

"The cops were just at the house looking for you."

"Me? What for?"

"They didn't say. Peg talked to them. She asked if you were in trouble and they said no, but that's all they'd tell her."

"Who was it?"

"Bo Linder and somebody else in the car, maybe Jimmy Bergan. That's his partner."

"You see Bo?"

"He came to the door and told Peg for you to call the detective office."

"He didn't say why."

"He said what I told you."

"Right, George. Peg said you wanted to talk to me about a book."

"There's a fellow named Muller works over in Huyck's mill and writes a hell of a good-sized book. I figured you might sit in while I talked to him about taking his layoff. Kind of break the ice a little. I don't know him at all."

"All right, George, I'll do that. When you meeting him?"

"Tonight, one-thirty, quarter to two, when he gets off work. He's coming here."

"I'll probably be here. If I go anyplace, I'll try to be back by then."

"Are you in trouble, Billy? Did you get mixed up with something?"

"No, George. I really don't know what the hell they want."

"You need money? Peg said you took a lickin' today."

"I'm all right on that."

"I can rustle up some if you need it. What do you need?"

"Don't worry about it, George. You need it yourself. I'll be all right. I just got lucky in a card game."

"You're sure you're not in trouble?"

"If I was in trouble, I'd be the first to know."

"All you got to do is ask, whatever it is. And I mean that, even on the money if you're in a jackpot. We'll find it."

"You're a sweetheart, George. Have a drink, relax. I gotta finish my steak."

"Isn't that Jake Berman's kid there?"

"Right, Morrie."

"His name's in the paper, too."

"Right."

"Jake's father made me the first suit of clothes I ever had made."

At the bar a man's voice said, "That's right, I said I hope they don't catch them, whoever they are."

The bar went quiet and Red Tom said, "That's just about enough of that talk," and he took the man's beer away. Billy recognized the talker, name of Rivera, spic like Angie's husband, a pimp. Red Tom poured Rivera's beer in the sink and shoved his change closer to him on the bar. "I don't want your business," Red Tom said. But Rivera wouldn't move. Red

140

Tom came around the bar and grabbed his arm. Rivera resisted. Red Tom reached for the change and shoved it into his pocket. Then he lifted him with one arm, like a sack of garbage, lifted him off the bar stool and walked him out the door.

"The McCalls got everybody scared to do pee-pee," Rivera said over his shoulder. "They think they can treat people like dogs."

"Who's that guy?" George Quinn asked.

"He's a bughouse pimp. Gotta be bugs," Billy said.

Red Tom closed the front door and moved in behind the bar.

"That kind of talk stays out in the street," he said to all in earshot, looking at no one in particular. He pointed twice toward the door with one finger. "Out in the street," he said.

When he'd finished his steak, Morrie Berman stood up and announced he was going off to get laid. Billy thought of tagging along with him but rejected the idea. He envisioned Angie in bed up at the Kenmore, waiting. He would go and see her. He was tired of gambling, tired of these people here. Maybe later he could come back and play some blackjack if the game was still running. Do that when he left Angie. If he left Angie. All right, he would see her, then leave her be and come down and play some blackjack. Billy still owed money. First things first.

"I got a date, Martin," Billy said, pushing away from the table.

"That sounds healthful. Bon voyage."

"I'll keep you posted on the bankroll. We're doing all right."

"I know we are. You've decided not to go along with Patsy's suggestion?"

"I listened all night. He didn't say a goddamn thing."

"What about the Bindy kidnap rumor? He doesn't seem to remember it, but you do. Isn't that odd?"

"That don't mean anything."

"Are you sure?"

"Aaahh," Billy said, and he waved off the possibility and went out onto Broadway and turned up Columbia Street, past the old Satin Slipper, a hot place when Butch McHale ran it during Prohibition and now cut up into furnished rooms. He crossed James Street and was halfway to North Pearl when the car pulled alongside him, Bo Linder at the wheel, Jimmy Bergan with him. Billy. Bo. Been looking for you. Oh yeah?

"Bindy wants to talk to you."

"Bindy? About what?"

"You ask him that."

"Where is he?"

"Up at Patsy's house."

"Patsy who?"

"Patsy who my ass."

"When's he want to see me?"

"Two hours ago."

"If this's got something to do with Charlie, I don't know anything."

"Tell Bindy that. Get in."

"No thanks."

"Get in, Billy."

"You pulling me in? Charging me with something?"

"I can get particular."

"I'm under arrest, I'll get in. Otherwise, I'll take a cab. I know where Pasty lives."

"All right, take a cab. We'll follow so the driver don't get lost."

Billy walked to Pearl Street and at the corner looked up at

the Kenmore, maybe at Angie's room. She liked the front so she could look down and see people on Pearl Street after she and Billy had loved all possible juices out of one another. Billy didn't see Angie in any window. She'd be asleep now, wouldn't go on the town alone. Twelve-thirty now, hell of a time to visit the McCalls.

Two cabs stood in front of the Kenmore. Billy whistled and the front one made a U-turn and Billy got in. Bo Linder was idling at the corner, Bo the cop, a good kid when he was a kid. Good second baseman for The Little Potatoes, Hard to Peel. But what can you do with somebody who grows up to be a mean cop? Never was mean on second base. After he went on the force, Bo walked into Phil Slattery's joint and shot Phil's dog when it growled at him. Dog should've bit him on the ass.

"Conalee Street," Billy told the cabbie.

Billy had never learned to pronounce Colonie Street the usual way. But people understood anyway. The driver moved north on Pearl Street, and Bo Linder swung out of Columbia Street and made it a parade.

9

illy didn't hate Colonie Street entirely, for it would have meant hating his mother, his greatest friends, Toddy Dunn, for one, even his ancestors. It would have meant hating the city the Irish had claimed as their own from vantage points of streets like Colonie. It was the street where he was born and had lived until adolescence, when he went off to room by himself. It was the street his sister, Peg, left with their mother when Peg married George Quinn and took a bigger and newer house in the North End.

Billy told the taxi driver to leave him off at the corner of North Pearl, and he walked up the hill toward Patsy McCall's house. He passed the old Burns house, where the ancient Joe Burns always sat in the window, ten years in the window at least. Old Joe lived with his son, Kid, the sexton of St. Joseph's Church for years until Father Mooney put him through undertakers' school; and next door to them the Dillons: Floyd, a conductor on the Central, who put Billy and Peg and their mother in a Pullman with only coach tickets when they went to New York to see the ocean for the first time. Across the street was the vacant lot where the Brothers School used to stand, and next to that the Daugherty house, gone, and then the other house: That house Billy did not now look at directly but saw always in his memory and hated, truly did hate that much of the old street.

And it was an old street even when Billy was born on it. It ran westward along the river flats from the Basin, that sheltered harbor that formed the mouth of the Erie Canal, and rose up the northernmost of the three steep ridges on which Albany was built: Arbor Hill. It rose for half a mile, crossed Ten Broeck, the street where the lumber barons had built their brownstones, and, still rising, ran another half mile westward to all but bump the Dudley Observatory, where scientific men of the city catalogued the stars (8241 measured and recorded for the International Catalogue as of 1883) from the top of the same hill on which Mike Mulvaney grazed and daily counted his two dozen goats.

The street took its name from The Colonie itself, that vast medieval demesne colonized in 1630 by an Amsterdam pearl merchant named Kiliaen Van Rensselaer, who was also known as the First Patroon, the absentee landlord who bought from five tribes of Indians some seven hundred thousand acres of land, twenty-four miles long and forty-eight miles wide, out of which a modest seven thousand acres would eventually be expropriated by the subsequent Yankee overlords to create the city of Albany.

Each power-wielding descendant of Van Rensselaer to assume the feudal mantle of the Patroonship during the next two centuries would maintain exploitative supremacy over thousands of farm renters on the enormous manor called, first, Rensselaerswyck, and later, The Colonie. Each Patroon would make his home in the Manor House, which rose handsomely out of a riverside meadow just north of the city on the bank of a stream that is still called Patroon Creek. Mickey McManus from Van Woert Street went rabbit hunting one day near The Patroon's creek and shot a cow. Few can now remember that meadow or even where the Manor House stood precisely. It closed forever in 1875, when the widow of the Last Patroon died there, and it was later moved to make room for the Delaware and Hudson railroad tracks, dismantled brick by brick and reassembled in Williamstown as a fraternity house.

But long before that, North Albany, where Billy Phelan and Martin Daugherty both now lived, and Arbor Hill, where the McCalls and Billy's aunts and uncles still lived, had been seeded in part with the homes of settlers who worked as servants and as farm and field hands for the Patroon. Billy Phelan's great-grandfather, Johnny Phelan, a notably belligerent under-sheriff, was given the safekeeping of the Manor House as his personal charge after four rebellious prisoners barricaded themselves in their cell at the penitentiary and, with a stolen keg of gunpowder, threatened to blow themselves up unless the food improved. Johnny Phelan sneaked a fire hose to the door of their cell, opened the door suddenly, and drenched their powder with a swift blast. Then he leaped over their barricade and clubbed them one by one into civility.

Martin Daugherty's grandmother, Hanorah Sweeney, had been the pastry cook in the Patroon's kitchen and was famed for her soda bread and fruitcakes, which, everyone said, always danced off their platters and onto the finicky palates of the Patroon and his table companions, among them the Prince of Wales, George Washington's grandnephew, and Sam Houston.

Arbor Hill and North Albany continued to grow as the railroads came in, along with the foundries, the stove works, the tobacco factory and the famous Lumber District, which started at the Basin and ran northward two and a half miles between the river and the canal. Processing Adirondack logs into lumber was Albany's biggest business at mid-century, and the city fathers proclaimed that Albany was now the white pine distribution center of the world.

The North End and Arbor Hill grew dense with the homes of lumber handlers, moulders, railroad men, and canalers, and in the winter, when the river and the canal froze, many of them cut ice, fifteen thousand men and boys cutting three million tons from the Hudson in six weeks at century's end.

They all clustered on streets such as Colonie to live among their own kind, and the solidarity became an obvious political asset. Not the first to notice this, but the first to ride it to local eminence, was the fat, bearded, Irish-born owner of the Beverwyck brewery, Michael Nolan, who in 1878 was elected mayor of the city. Coming only three years after the death of the Last Patroon's widow, this clearly signaled a climactic change in city rule: the Dutch and Yankees fading, the American Irish, with the help of Jesus, and by dint of numbering forty per cent of the city's population, waxing strong. And eight years ahead of Boston in putting an Irishman in City Hall.

Nolan had lived on Millionaire's Row, on the east side of Ten Broeck, two and a half blocks from Patsy McCall's home on Colonie Street. Patsy, who could have lived like a millionaire but didn't, was in the Irish descendance of political power from Nolan as surely as the Last Patroon had descended from the first; and was a descendant in style as well as power. When Nolan was elected, he swathed his brewery wagons and dray horses in red, white, and blue bunting and saw to it that Beverwyck beer was sold in every saloon in town. Nolan's example was not wasted on the McCalls. Gubernatorial hopeful Tom Dewey revealed that in October 1938, Stanwix, the McCall beer, was sold in 243 of the city's 249 taverns.

Billy Phelan knew the Patroon only as a dead word, Nolan not at all. But in the filtered regions of his cunning Irish brain, he knew the McCalls stood for power far beyond his capacity to imagine.

They were up from below. And when you're up, you let no

147

man pull you down. You roll your wagons over the faces of the enemy.

And who is the enemy?

It's well you might ask.

Billy pushed the door bell.

Bindy McCall opened the door, smiled, and pulled Billy by the arm, gently, into the house, the first time Billy had entered Patsy's home. The front hall, leading upstairs and also into both front and back parlors, reminded Billy of the hated house across the street, probably built from the same blueprints.

Bindy held Billy's arm and led him into the front parlor with its thick oriental rug, its heavy drapes and drawn shades, where a scowling male ancestor of the McCalls looked down insistently on Billy: a powerful face above a neck stretched by a high collar and string tie, a face not unlike Patsy's, who sat beneath it at a card table, shirtless, reclining in his blue bathrobe in a leather armchair; pads and pencils on the table beside a telephone. An old player piano dominated the room, where Patsy no doubt played and sang the ditties he was famous for, "Paddy McGinty's Goat," for one.

Billy had heard him sing that at the Phoenix Club in the North End on a Sunday years ago when the political notables of North Albany turned out for an election rally. Billy went just to watch the spectacle and barely spoke to anyone, never said, Hello Patsy, as he could have, as thousands did whenever the great leader hove into range. Hello Patsy. Billy just listened and never forgot the song and later learned it himself: *Patrick McGinty, an Irishman of note, fell heir to a fortune and he bought himself a goat.*

A panorama of a Civil War battle, one of Patsy's well-known interests, hung in a gilded frame over the piano. A pair of brass donkeys as bookends, and with Dickens and Jefferson, a biography of Jim Jeffries, and canvasses of Fifth and Eighth Ward voters sandwiched between the butt ends of the animals, sat on top of the piano. On an old oak sofa across from Patsy sat a man Billy didn't know. Bindy introduced him as Max Rosen, Matt McCall's law partner.

"You're a tough man to find," Bindy said. "We've been looking for you."

"I wasn't hiding. Just playing cards."

"We heard about the holdup and what you did. You're a tough guy, Billy."

"How'd you hear about it? It just happened."

"Word gets around. We also heard what you did in the Grand Lunch with that crazy kid."

"You heard that, too?"

"That, too," Bindy said.

"Listen, Bin," said Billy, "I'm really sorry about Charlie."

"Are you?"

"Sure I am. You got any word on him yet?"

"We got a little. That's why we wanted to talk to you."

"Me? What've I got to do with anything?"

"Relax. You want a beer?"

"Sure, I'll have a beer with you, Bin."

Bindy, shirtsleeves rolled above the elbow, soup stain on shirtfront, no tie, wearing eyeglasses and house slippers, looked like somebody else to Billy, not Bindy McCall, the dapper boss of the street. He looked tired, too, and Patsy the same. Patsy stared at Billy. Max Rosen, in his suit coat, tie up tight to a fresh collar, also stared. Billy in the middle, a new game. He was glad to see Bindy come back with the beer bottle and glass: Stanwix.

"I heard you took a beating today with the nags," Bindy said, pouring Billy's beer.

"You hear what I had for breakfast?"

"No, but I could find out."

"I ate alone, no witnesses."

"There's other ways."

"Yeah." And Billy took a drink.

"You know where your old man is?" Patsy asked.

"My old man?"

"Yours."

"No. I don't know."

"I heard he was in town," said Patsy.

"My father in Albany? Where?"

"I didn't hear that. Somebody saw him downtown today."

"Goddamn," Billy said.

"You wanna see him?" asked Patsy.

"Sure I wanna see him. I haven't saw him in twenty years. Twenty-two years."

"I'll see if I can track him down."

"That'd be terriffic, Mr. McCall."

"Call me Patsy."

"Patsy. That's a terrific thing if you can do that."

"Maybe you can do something for us."

"Maybe I can."

"You heard that kidnap rumor about me," Bindy said, sitting on a folding chair across the card table from Patsy. The card table Billy worked at was in better shape.

"I heard that last summer."

"From who?"

"Jesus, I don't remember, Bin. One of those things you hear at a bar when you're half in the bag, you don't remember. I didn't give it the time of day. Then I remembered it today."

"And got hot at Louie Dugan for telling me about it."

"I didn't expect to have it repeated."

150

"We heard the same rumor last year and traced it to a couple of local fellows. And maybe, just maybe, that ties in to Charlie. Do you follow me?"

"I follow."

"Neither of these fellows are in town and we don't know just where they are. But they got a friend who's in town, and that's why you're here."

"I'm the friend?"

"No, you're a friend of the friend. The friend is Morrie Berman."

The noise Billy made then was a noncommittal grunt. Maloy and Curry, Berman's pals. On the list, Curry.

"We understand you know Mr. Berman well," Max Rosen said.

"We play cards together."

"We understand you know him better than that," Rosen said.

"I know him a long time."

"Yeah, yeah, we know all about it," said Patsy, "and we also know you didn't give Pop O'Rourke's man his ten dollars today."

"I told Pop why."

"We know what you told him," said Patsy, "and we know your brother-in-law, Georgie Quinn, is writing numbers and don't have the okay for the size books he's taking on."

"Georgie talked to Pop about that, too."

"And Pop told him he could write a little, but now he's backing the play himself. He's ambitious, your brother-in-law."

"What is all this, Bindy? What are we talking about? You know the color of my shorts. What's it for?" Billy felt comfortable only with Bindy, but Bindy said nothing.

"Do you know the Berman family, Mr. Phelan?" Max Rosen asked.

"I know Morrie's old man's in politics, that's all."

"Do you like Morrie Berman?" Rosen asked.

"I like him like I like a lot of guys. I got nothing against him. He's the guy had the idea to buy me a steak tonight. Nice."

"Do you like Charlie?" Patsy asked.

"Do I like him? Sure I like him. I grew up with him. Charlie was always a good friend of mine, and I don't say that just here. I bullshit nobody on this."

Bindy poured more beer into Billy's glass and smiled at him.

"All right, Billy," Bindy said, "we figure we know your feelings. We wouldn't have okayed you for that Saratoga job if we didn't trust you. We know you a long time. And you remember after the Paul Whiteman thing, we gave you that other job, too."

"The Chicago Club?"

"That's right."

"I thought that came from Lemon Lewis. I didn't think you even knew about that."

"We knew. We do Albany people."

"Then it's two I owe you."

"Just one," Bindy said. "We trusted you then, we trust you now. But that don't mean forever."

"Who the hell am I not to trust? What do I know?"

"We don't know what you know," Patsy said.

"It's what you might come to know in the next few days that's important," Max Rosen said. "We're interested in Mr. Berman, in everything he says and does. Everything."

"Morrie doesn't tell me secrets," Billy said.

"We don't expect that," said Max. "If he's involved in the kidnapping, and we're by no means saying that he is, then he's hardly likely to talk about it at all. But you must know, Mr. Phelan, that men sometimes betray themselves indirectly. They reveal what's on their mind merely by random comment.

152

Berman might, for instance, mention the men involved in a context other than criminal. Do you follow me.?"

"No."

"You're not stupid," Patsy said, an edge to his voice. He leaned forward in his chair and looked through Billy's head.

"Nobody ever said I was," Billy said, looking back through Patsy's head.

"Billy," said Bindy in a soothing tone, "we're playing in every joint where we can get a bet down. I tell you one thing. Some people wouldn't even put it past Berman's old man to be in on this."

"That's ridiculous," Max Rosen said. "Jake Berman isn't capable of such behavior. I've known him all my life."

"I don't accuse him," Bindy said, "but he don't like us. I just make the point that we suspect everybody."

"People might even suspect you, with your name in the paper," Patsy said.

Billy snorted. "Me?"

"People talk."

"Don't pay attention if you hear that," Bindy said. "We know you're clean. We wanted you and Berman in the same boat. He don't know why you're on the list, but now you and him got that in common."

"You think that'll make him talk to me?"

"It could. What'd he say tonight?"

"We played cards and he kicked the holdup guy a little. He said he talked to Mr. Rosen here, and he said he didn't get along with his old man. We talked about a drink that we had one time."

"Who did he talk about?" Bindy asked. "Who?"

"Tabby Bender. George Kindlon, who tended bar for Tabby."

"Who else?"

"That's all I remember."

"Edward Curry is on the list. Did he mention him?"

"I mentioned Curry, that his name was spelled wrong. And I told a story about him."

"What story?"

"About the whore in Boston called him honey and he asked her, How come you know my name. You think Curry's mixed up in this?"

"What did Berman say when you told the story?" Bindy asked.

"He laughed."

"You didn't talk about nobody else? Nobody? Think."

"I talked about a lot of things but not to Berman."

"Did he say anything about Hubert Maloy?"

"No."

Bindy leaned back in his chair and looked at Patsy. Billy looked at the brothers, from one to the other, and wondered how he would get out of the Maloy lie. He wondered why he'd even bothered to lie. It meant nothing. He saw the faces of strangers he'd known all his life staring him down. In between them, the face of the McCall ancestor was no longer scowling down from the wall but was only stern and knowing, a face flowing with power and knowledge in every line. There was a world of behavior in this room Billy did not grasp with the clarity he had in pool and poker, or at the crap table. Billy knew jazz and betting and booking horses and baseball. He knew how to stay at arm's length from the family and how to make out. He resisted knowing more than these things. If you knew what the McCalls knew, you'd be a politician. If you knew what George Quinn knew, you'd be a family man. They had their rewards but Billy did not covet them. Tie you up in knots, pin you down, put you in the box. He could learn anything, study it. He could have been in politics years ago. Who couldn't on Colonie Street? But he chose other ways of staying alive. There never was a politician Billy could really talk to, and never a hustler he couldn't.

"All right, Billy," Bindy said, standing up. "I think we've made our point. Call us any time." He wrote two phone numbers on the pad and handed the sheet to Billy.

"You come up with anything that means something to Charlie," Patsy said, "you got one hell of a future in this town."

"What if I don't run into Berman again?"

"You don't run into him, then you find him and stay with him," Patsy said. "If you need money for that, call us."

"Berman's a big boy. He goes where he wants."

"You're a big boy, too," Patsy said.

"What Patsy says about your future," Bindy said, "that goes triple for me. For a starter we clear up your debt with Martin Daugherty. And you never worry about anything again. Your family the same."

"What if Berman catches on? He's too smart to pump."

"If you're sure he's on to it, drop it."

"We'll get word to you."

When Billy stood up, Max Rosen put a paternal hand on his shoulder. "Don't worry about anything, Mr. Phelan. Do what you can. It's an unusual situation."

"Yeah, all of that," Billy said.

Bindy shook hands and Patsy gave him a nod, and then Billy was in the hallway looking at the bannister, pretty much like the one he used to slide down in the shithouse across the street until his Aunt Sate caught him and pulled his ear and sent him home. He went out the door and closed it behind him. He stood on the McCall stoop, looking up the street at the Dolan house, remembering the Dolan kid who was kidnapped off this street when Billy was little. An uncle did it. They found the kid in the Pine Bush, safe, and brought him home and put him in the window so everybody could see that he was all right. The kid was only four. Everybody wanted to hang the uncle, but he only went to jail.

Billy walked toward Pearl Street, heading back downtown. He remembered Georgie Fox, marked lousy for what he did to Daddy Big. All anybody on Broadway needed to hear was that Billy was finking on Morrie, and they'd put him in the same box with Georgie. Who'd trust him after that? Who'd tell him a secret? Who'd lend him a quarter? He wouldn't have a friend on the whole fucking street. It'd be the dead end of Billy's world, all he ever lived for, and the McCalls were asking him to risk that. Asking hell, telling him. Call us any time.

When he was half way to Clinton Avenue, Bo Linder pulled up and asked if everything was all right. Billy said it was, and Bo said, "That's good, Billy, now keep your nose clean." And Billy just looked at the son of a bitch and finally nodded, not at all sure he knew how to do that any more.

When Billy got to Becker's and sat down in the booth beside him (across from Bart Muller), George Quinn was eating a ham sandwich and telling Muller of the old days when he ran dances in Baumann's Dancing Academy and hired King Jazz and his orchestra to play, and McEnelly's Singing Orchestra, and ran dances, too, up in Sacandaga Park and brought in Zita's orchestra, and danced himself at all of them, of course. "They put pins in our heels for the prize waltz," George said. "Anybody bent the pin was out. I won many a prize up on my toes and I got the loving cups to prove it."

"No need to prove it," Muller said.

"We danced on the boat to Kingston sometimes, and the night boat to New York, but mostly we took the ferry from Maiden Lane for a nickel and it went up to Al-Tro Park,

Al-Tro Park on the Hudson; they even wrote a song about that place, and what a wonder of a place it was. Were you ever up there?"

"Many times," Muller said.

"We'd take the boat back down to Maiden Lane, or sometimes we'd walk back downtown to save the nickel. One night, three fellows on the other side of the street kept up with me and Giddy O'Laughlin all the way to Clinton Avenue. We didn't know who they were till they crossed Broadway, and one was Legs Diamond. Somebody was gonna throw Legs off the roof of the Hendrick Hudson Hotel that night, but he gave 'em the slip."

"Why are you talking about Legs Diamond?" Billy asked George.

"I'm not talking about Legs Diamond, I'm talking about going to dances. Bart lives in Rensselaer. We both went to dances at the pavilion out at Snyder's Lake."

"George," said Billy, "did you come in here to reminisce or what?"

"We've just been cuttin' it up, me and Bart," George said, "and the business is on, anyway. I'm interested in Bart's book. I'm branching out and Bart knows that. He just took over the night-shift book over at Huyck's mill, and now he's looking for somebody to lay off with. Am I right, Bart?"

"That's right, George."

"Then you made the deal," Billy said.

"I guess we did," said George.

"I'll give you a buzz on it," Muller said. "But I got to get home or the wife worries."

"We'll talk on the phone, Bart," George said. "I was glad to meet you."

"Mutual," said Muller, and he nodded at Billy and left.

George sat back and finished his tea and wiped his lips with his white linen napkin and folded it carefully.

"I don't know what the hell that was all about," Billy said. "Why'd you want me here?"

"Just to break the ice."

"Break the ice? There was no ice. You never shut up."

"I didn't want to push too hard the first time. We'll iron out the details when he calls."

"Calls? He's not gonna call. You made no impression on him. You didn't talk about money."

"He didn't bring it up."

"He came to see you, didn't he? Why the hell does he want to talk about Snyder's Lake, for chrissake? He's writing a book and he wants a layoff and he wants protection. You didn't give him a goddamn thing to make him think you even know what the hell a number is."

"He knows."

"He does like hell. How could he? You didn't talk about having the okay or that you got cash to guarantee his payoffs. You didn't say how late he could call in a play or tell him he wouldn't have to worry getting stuck with a number because you'll give him the last call and get rid of it for him. You didn't tell him doodley bejesus. George, what the hell are you doing in the rackets? You ought to be selling golf clubs."

"Who died and left you so smart?"

"I'm not smart, George, or I'd be rich. But I hustle. You don't know how to hustle."

"I'm not in debt up to my ass."

"You ain't rich either. And let me tell you something else. You don't even have the okay."

"Says who?"

"Says Patsy McCall. I was talking to him, and he says you never got the okay to back numbers. All you got the okay for was to lay off. Twenty per cent, no more."

"Pop O'Rourke knows what I'm doing."

"Patsy said Pop *didn't* know."

"I'll call Pop in the morning. I'll straighten it out. How come you talked to Patsy?"

"It was about another thing."

"Something about your name in the paper?"

"Something about that, yeah."

"Oh, it's a secret. You got secrets with Patsy McCall. Excuse me, let me out. Your company is too rich for my blood."

"Look, George, don't strain your juice. I don't keep secrets I don't have to keep. You know what's going on with Charlie McCall, and you ought to know by this time I'm on your side. For chrissake, don't you know that?"

"Mmmmmm," said George.

"You don't *want* to know what I know, George. Believe me."

"All right, Billy, but you got a nasty tongue."

"Yeah. Have a drink. I buy."

"No, I just had tea."

"Have a drink, for chrissake. Do you good."

"I don't want a drink. I'll take the nickel. What did Patsy say about me? Was he mad?"

"He didn't sound happy. He mentioned you by name."

"I don't want to get in any jackpots with Patsy. I'll call Pop first thing in the morning. I never had a cross word with the McCalls all my life. I give fifteen dollars to John Kelleher for Patsy's first campaign as assessor and Kelleher only asked me for five."

"You'll fix it. Probably you just got to pay more dues."

"I'm not making anything yet. I'm losing money."

"It's goin' around, that problem."

"But I can't afford more."

"You can't afford to stay in business?"

"Pop understands I'm not in the chips yet."

"How does he understand that? You expect him to check your books?"

"No, I don't expect nothing like that."

"Then how the hell does he know your action? All he knows is you're moving into heavier stuff. And you got to pay heavier dues for that. George, you been in this racket fifteen years, and you been in this town all your life. You know how it works."

"I'll pay if Patsy said I got to pay. But Patsy understands a guy being down on his luck."

"Don't cry the blues to them. Don't beg for anything. If they say pay, just pay and shut up about it."

"I don't beg from anybody."

"Tell 'em your story straight and don't weep no tears. I'm telling you be tough, George."

"I know what I'm doing. I know how it works."

"All right. You want that drink?"

"I'll take a rain check."

George went out onto Broadway, and Billy went to the bar for a tall beer, thinking how George couldn't get off the dime. A banty rooster and don't underrate him when he fights. But he don't fight easy enough. Been around tough guys and politicians all his life and he don't know how to blow his nose right. But Billy has to admit George ain't doing bad for a fifty-year-old geezer. Got the house and Peg and a great kid in Danny. Billy's fifty, he'll be what? Alone? Racking balls like Daddy Big? On the chalk like Lemon Lewis? Nineteen years to find out.

"Your lady friend Angie called again, Billy," Red Tom said, as he slid Billy a new, tall, free one. "She says it's urgent."

"I know her urgent."

"And she says it's not what you think. Important, she says."

"Important."

"She sounded like she meant it."

"I'll check her out, Tommy. Have one on me."

"Save your money, Billy. Winter's coming."

"Billy knows where the heat is."

"Up in Angie's room?"

"Some there, yeah. Definitely some up there."

10

'll screw you as long as my equipment lasts, Billy once told
Angie, but I won't marry you. She repeated the line for
Billy after he rolled off her. He sat up, lit a cigarette, and
then fixed a scotch with tap water. He put on his white boxer
shorts, hiding the ragged scar on the left cheek of his behind.
He got that when he was ten, sliding into a second base made
from a flattened tin oil can. Almost made him half-assed. But
Doc Lennon sewed it up after he poured two bottles of iodine
into the slice, which still gives Billy the screaming meemies
when he thinks about it. Then Billy's mother bathed the
wound and fussed at it for weeks, and the teamwork let Billy
grow up with a complete tail.

"Why you bringing that up now?" Billy asked. "You
thinking about marriage again?"

"I'm always thinking about marriage, with you."

"Drop it, Ange. I'll never be any good in that husband
racket."

"And you couldn't, wouldn't marry a divorcee."

"The hell with that stuff."

"I'm only teasing, Billy. I love to tease you."

Angie stood up and slipped back into her nightgown, sheer
white silk with white lace trim where her cleavage would've
been if she had any. She was a long, lean, dark-haired Latin-

162

esque girl of twenty-five who looked thirty when she talked because she was smart but who grew wispy with a turn of emotion and fled into the look of adolescence. She read sad poetry and went to sad movies in order to cry, for crying at trouble, she told Billy, was almost as good as weeping with love. There was so little love in the world, she said, that people needed substitutes. It's why lonely old people keep pets, she said. Billy was Angie's pet. I can't imagine anyone who didn't sometime want to do away with themselves because of love, she once said to Billy, for chrissake. Billy, she said, stroking him, tickling the back of his neck, if you ever died I'd make sure they put flowers on your grave forever, just like they do for Valentino. This, of course, is just what Billy needs.

But Angie was part of his life now, and had been since her husband slapped her around in the Clubhouse at Saratoga. Billy was watching from the bar when they started their screaming over the car keys. Give 'em to me, you bitch, he said. I haven't got 'em, Angie said. You got 'em, he said. You just wanna hang around here makin' moon eyes at all the studs. Billy was her only stud then, and when her husband was around, she never even gave Billy a nod. So she walked away from the son of a bitch when he said that, and he spun her around by the arm and slapped her twice. Billy wanted to hit him till his teeth fell out, but all he could do was watch. Angie took the whipping and didn't say a word, which beat the bastard. He slammed out of the Clubhouse and left their car in the lot and walked back to the hotel. And found the car keys in his own coat pocket when he was halfway there. Billy bought Angie a drink and smooched her on the cheek where she'd been hit and put her in a taxi and bet twenty on a horse named Smacker in the last race and it showed eight dollars.

Angie came to Albany every other month after that, for a weekend at least and sometimes a week. She'd call Billy and

163

he'd see her and once in a while she'd give him money, which made him feel like a gigolo, but of course that wasn't what Billy was. He only took it when he needed it. Angie called Billy her little wheel of excitement. When I was a kid I used to sit on the stoop and wait for it to roll down the street to me, she said. But it never showed up till I met you.

Why'd ya marry that bum? Billy asked her once, and she said, Because he was like my father and I loved my father, but you're right, he is a bum, he's not like my father at all. He's a bum, he's a bum, and he's got his women, too. He came home one night with the smell of oral sex on his face. Angie never called him on it. She just packed a bag and came to Albany. But he was good in bed, Angie said, he was very good. Angie never told Billy he was very good in bed, but then he didn't hear any complaints out of her either. What got Billy about Angie was the way she was alone so much. Billy was almost never alone. I can stand being alone, Angie told him. Being with him is like being alone. It won't kill you.

Billy looked down on the lights of Pearl Street. No traffic.

"You got aspirin?" he asked Angie. "I got a headache."

"The closet shelf on the left, a small bag," she said. "Why have you got a headache? You never get headaches."

"Whataya mean I never get headaches? Everybody gets headaches. How the hell do you know I never get headaches?"

"All right, you get headaches," Angie said, and she fell back into bed and crossed her feet.

In the closet, Billy looked at her picture hat, black with two white flowers. Billy snatched the hat off the shelf and waved it at her. "When you got a face like you got, you don't need any flowers on your hat." He put the hat back on the shelf and felt for the aspirin and found them. Then he saw her black linen suit with the plaid scarf, and the gray wool suit with the darker gray silk lapels. Goddamn Angie knew how to dress. Like a model. Too goddamn smart. A college dame. Thinks like a man.

"You're too goddamn smart," he said, as he went to the sink.

"What does that mean?"

"The hell with it."

"Billy, come here. Come and sit down."

"Gimme a rest."

"Not that. Just come and sit."

Billy washed his aspirin down and went and sat. She stroked his face and then dropped her hand and eyes and said, "I've got something sad to tell you."

"Your cat got run over."

"Something like that. I had an abortion."

"Yeah?"

"It was ours."

Billy smoked a little and then looked at her. Her eyes were on him now.

"When?"

"About three weeks ago."

"Why didn't you ring me in on it?"

"What would you have done?"

"I don't know. Helped you."

"Helped get it done? A good Catholic boy like you?"

"I mean with your head. It must've been lousy for you."

"You never want to know things like that. Anything that involves you. You really didn't want to know, did you?"

"Half of it's my kid."

"Not a kid, a fetus. And it's gone. Nobody's now."

"Goddamn it, I had a right to know."

"You had a *right*?"

"You bet your ass. What the hell, I don't have a say in my own son?"

"Of course it was a boy. You're really classic, Billy."

"Whatever the hell it was."

Billy looked at his hand and saw the cigarette shaking. Goddamn ton of goddamn bricks. He'd wanted to talk about the Berman business and about his father being back in town. Angie had good sense. He wanted to ask her about money, maybe borrow some, but they got into the sack too fast. You can't ask for money after you've been in the sack with a woman. Now, with this business, he couldn't ask her anything. How do so many things happen all of a sudden? He thought of making nineteen straight passes at Slicky Joyce's in Mechanicville. Almost broke the Greek bankrolling the game. How do nineteen straight passes happen? He stubbed out his cigarette and walked across the room to put on his pants.

"Why are you putting on your pants?"

"I got chilly."

"No. You're ashamed of the part of you that made me pregnant and now you want to cover yourself and hide."

"You know everything about me. My headaches, why I put on my pants. Goddamn it cut it *out!*" Billy screamed. "You don't know the first goddamn thing that's going on with me. You think I'm a goddamn moron like your goddamn dummy husband?"

"All right, Billy. Don't get violent."

"Violent? You kill my kid without even asking me about it. Who made you the butcher?"

"Don't get like this, Billy. I'm sorry I started it this way."

"Started?"

"I'm pregnant."

"Oh, Christ Jesus, what is this game?"

"I wanted to see if you wanted the baby."

"Hell no, I don't want no baby."

"So now it's different."

Billy put on his shirt, unable to speak. He folded his tie

and put it in the pocket of his coat, which hung on a black bentwood chair. He sat on the chair and stared at Angie.

"I can take care of it," she said. "I already slept with Joe when I found I had it, just so I could tell him it was his. But I'd never raise it with him. All he wants to raise is money. But I would keep it and give it all the nannies and private schools a kid'd ever need. The only thing it wouldn't have is a real father."

She stood up. "Or I could put it up for adoption."

"No," Billy said.

She came across the room and stroked his face. "Or we could raise it together, somehow. Any way you wanted. I don't mean marriage. I'll go away and have it, and you can come and see us when you want to. The only problem is that if my husband figured it out, he'd probably have all three of us killed. But I don't care, do you?"

"No. Of course not. What the hell do I care?"

Billy walked away from her and sat in the armchair and looked at her standing there barefoot in front of him, the shadow of her crotch winking through the silk nightgown.

"Or you can claim it any time you want, and we could go off then. I've got plenty of my own money. I wouldn't need alimony."

Billy shook his head. "I don't buy it. All this shotgun stuff can go to hell."

"Then you want me to get rid of it?"

"No, I don't want that. I think you'oughta have it."

"But you don't want anything to do with it?"

"I'll do something."

"What?"

"I'll go see it."

"Like a cocker spaniel? Why shouldn't I get rid of it?"

"By myself, I don't want to hurt nobody. If you do it, it's you and I can't say don't. I don't even want to know about it."

"That's as far as you go?"

"If you have it, I'll say it's mine."

"You'll do that?"

"I'll do that, yeah."

"Even if Joe says he'll shoot you?"

"He shoots me, he's got big trouble."

"I didn't expect this."

"I'd do it for any kid. You let him into the action, he's got to know who his old man is."

"It's for the kid, not me?"

"Maybe some is for you."

"Birth certificate, baptism, that whole business?"

"Whatever you want."

"I really didn't think you'd do this. You never committed yourself to me on anything. You never even answered my letters."

"Letters? What the hell am I gonna do, write you letters and have you fix up my spelling?"

"I wouldn't do that. Oh God, I love you. You're such a life-bringer, Billy. You're the real man for me, but you're the wrong clay."

"Clay?"

"You can't be molded. Sex won't do it and money won't. Even the idea of a kid wouldn't. But you did say you'd go along with me. That's really something."

"What do you mean the *idea* of a kid?"

"There's no kid."

She was rocking from foot to foot, half-twisting her body, playing with the ends of her hair.

"You did get rid of it."

"I was never pregnant." She smiled at Billy.

"Then what, what the hell, what?"

"I needed to know what you felt, Billy. You really think I'm dumb enough to let you knock me up? It's just that we never talk about things that really matter. This was the first time we ever talked about anything important that wasn't money or my goddamn husband. I know almost nothing about your life. All I know is I love you more now than I did when you walked in the door. I knew I wanted you even before I met you."

Billy was shaking his head. "Imagine that," he said. "You conned me right out of my jock."

"Yes, I know."

"What a sucker."

"Yes, it was lovely. You were wonderful. Now will you take me out for a sandwich? I missed dinner waiting for you."

"Sure. But first get busy with the douche bag. And I'm gonna watch. I'm not going through this noise again."

"Ah, Romeo," Angie said, massaging Billy's crotch.

11

Martin, thinking of his father, of Charlie Boy, of Noah, all spread-eagled on their beds, of Melissa spread-eagled naked in fatigue on the floor of her suite at the Hampton Hotel, failed to sleep. He faced downward and leftward into the pillow, a trick he played on the fluids of his brain that generally brought sleep, but not now. And so he faced upward, rightward. He closed his eyes, fixating on a point just above his nose, behind the frontal bone, trying to drive out thoughts as they appeared.

But this also failed, and he saw the lonely, driven figure entering the wholly darkened tunnel, so narrow no man could survive the train should it come roaring through before he reached the far exit. He would be crushed by the wheels or squeezed to juice and pulp against the wall. The figure reached the trestle that spanned the bottomless canyon and began to inch across it on hands and knees, fearful of falling, fearful the train would come from beyond the forest curve and bear down on him at mid-trestle. No chance then for backward flight, no chance to sidestep, only to hang from trestle's edge by fingertips. Would vertigo then claim him? Would his fingers hold him?

He sat up and lit the bedside lamp and began to count the ceiling panels again, eleven horizontal, twelve vertical. He multiplied. One hundred and thirty-two panels, including fragments. He counted the sides of the dresser, the number of edges on the six drawers: twenty-four. He counted the edges on the decorative trim on Mary Daugherty's closet. He totaled the edge count: two-seventy-eight. He counted the edges on the ceiling molding. He counted the backs, fronts, and sides of books on his dresser. He lost track of the total.

He could never contain the numbers, nor did he want to. He usually counted sidewalk cracks when he walked, telephone poles when he drove. He remembered no totals except the eighteen steps to the city room, twelve to the upstairs of this house, and remembered these only after years of repetition. If he miscounted either staircase, he would recount carefully on the return trip. He once viewed the counting as a private way of demarcating his place in the world, numbering all boundaries, four counts to the edge of a drawer, four to the perimeter of a tile, an act of personal coherence. On the day he awoke and drawer edges were worth three, tile perimeters five, he would know the rules of his civilization had been superseded.

He switched off the lamp, closed his eyes, and found a staircase. He climbed it and at the turning saw the hag squirming on the wide step, caught in an enormous cobweb which covered all of her except her legs. Beneath her thighs, two dozen white baby shoes were in constant motion, being hatched.

I don't like what everybody is doing to me, she said.

The hag reached a hand out to Martin, who fled up the stairs in terror, a wisp of cobweb caught on his sleeve.

He plucked himself from the scene without moving and felt panic in his heartbeat. He said the Our Father, the Hail Mary, the Confiteor. Deliver us from evil. Blessed is the fruit of thy womb. *Mea maxima culpa.* He had not prayed in twenty-five years except for knee-jerk recitations at funerals, and did not

171

now believe in these or any other prayers. Yet as he prayed, his pulse slowly slackened, his eyes stayed closed. And as he moved into sleep, he knew that despite his infidel ways, the remnants of tattered faith still had power over his mind.

He knew his mind had no interest in the genuineness of faith, that it fed on the imagery of any conflict that touched the deepest layers of his history. Years ago, he'd dreamed repeatedly of hexagons, rhomboids, and threes, and still had no idea why. He understood almost none of the fragmented pictures his mind created, but he knew now for the first time that it was possible to trick the apparatus. He had done it. He was moving into a peaceful sleep, his first since the departure of Peter. And as he did, he understood the message the images had sent him. He would go to Harmanus Bleecker Hall and watch Melissa impersonate his mother on stage. Then, all in good time, he would find a way to make love to Melissa again, in the way a one-legged man carves a crutch from the fallen tree that crushed his leg.

The fountain cherub, small boy in full pee, greeted Martin as he walked through the Hall's foyer. Psssss. *The Golden Bowlful,* by Henry Pease Lotz. Martin remembered seeing Bert Lytell here, the Barrymores and Mrs. Fiske strutting on this cultural altar. He saw the young Jolson here, and the great Isadora, and when he was only thirteen he saw a play called *The Ten-Ton Door,* in which a man strapped to that huge door was exploded across the stage by a great blast, an epic moment.

"So you made it," said Agnes, the hennaed gum chewer in the Hall's box office. "We expected you last night."

"I was up in Troy last night," Martin said, "walking the duck."

"The duck?"

Martin smiled and looked at his ticket, B–108 center, and

then he entered the Hall, a quarter century after the premiere that never was. Edward Sheldon's *Romance* premiered here in 1913 instead of *The Flaming Corsage*, and Sheldon's reputation blossomed. But when the priests and Grundys killed Edward Daugherty's play, calling it the work of a scandalous, vice-ridden man, they made Edward a pariah in the theater for years to come.

In 1928, a bad year for some, Melissa set out to convert the play to a talking picture in which she would star as the mistress, her long-standing dream. She wanted Von Stroheim to direct, appreciative of his sexual candor, but the studios found both the play and the scandal dated, and dated, too, Melissa, the idea of you as a young mistress.

Aging but undauntable, Melissa turned up then with something not so old: Edward Daugherty's journal from the years just before and just after the scandal, full of the drama and eroticism of the famous event, in case, chums, you can't find enough in the play. Still, no studio was interested, for Melissa was a fading emblem of a waning era, her voice adjudged too quirky for talkies, her imperious and litigious ways (when in doubt she sued) too much of a liability for the moguls.

And so *The Flaming Corsage* continued unproduced either as play or film until the Daugherty renaissance, which began with an obscure New York mounting of his 1902 work, *The Car Barns*. George Jean Nathan saw that production and wrote that here was a writer many cuts above Gillette, Belasco, Fitch, and others, more significantly Irish-American than Boucicault or Sheldon, for he is tapping deeper currents, and superior to any of the raffish Marxist didacticists currently cluttering up the boards. Was this neglected writer an American O'Casey or Pirandello? Another O'Neill? No, said Nathan, he's merely original, which serious men should find sufficient.

The Car Barns revival was followed by *The Masks of*

Pyramis, Edward Daugherty's one venture into symbolism. It provoked a great public yawn and slowed the renaissance. *The Baron of Ten Broeck Street* followed within a year, a play with the capitalist as villain and tragic figure, the protagonist patterned after Katrina Daugherty's father, an Albany lumber baron. Reaction to the play was positive, but the renaissance might have halted there had not Melissa's need to see herself transfigured on stage been so unyielding.

Six more years would pass before *The Flaming Corsage* entered its new age. By then, three decades after its inspiration, it had become a wholly new play, its old sin now the stuff of myth, its antique realism now an exquisite parody of bitter love and foolish death. The New York production was a spectacular success. Melissa made her comeback, and Edward Daugherty strode into the dimension he had sought for a lifetime as an artist. But he strode with a partial mind. He beamed at the telling when Martin brought the news, but minutes later he had forgotten that he had ever written that play, or any other. What would please him most, he said, squirming in his leather armchair in the old house on Main Street, would be a hot cup of tea, son, with lemon if you'd be so kind, and a sugar cookie.

The theater was already two-thirds full and more were still arriving to see the famed beauty in the infamous play about Albany. Martin positioned himself at the head of an aisle, holding his battered hat in hand, standing out of the way as the playgoers seated themselves. Joe Morrissey nodded to him, ex-assemblyman, tight as a teacup, who lived near Sacred Heart; when the pastor asked him to donate his house to the nuns, old Joe sold the place immediately and moved out of the parish. And there, moving down front, Tip Mooney, the roofer, with the adopted daughter everybody chucklingly says is his mistress. Taboo. Ooo-ooo. The zest for it. And here, as the houselights dim, stands the fellow out for redemption. I'm just as big a sinner as you, Dad. Playboy of the North End, but keeping it in the family. Here to see everybody's favorite honeycomb, who, as Marlene, the reporter, wrote, is out to prove she can plumb the depths of the human heart with her acting, even as she keeps the human spirit all aglow with her dancing, and the human imagination fevered merely by her well-known sensual presence, etc.

The lights went all the way down, the curtain rose and the Daugherty living room on Colonie Street was magically reconstituted from thirty years past, even to the Edison phonograph and its cylinders, the Tiffany butterfly lamp from Van Heusen Charles, the Hudson River landscape on the far wall, and all the other meticulously copied details demanded by the author; for those possessions were inseparable from the woman who sits there among them: the simulated Katrina, remarkably reincarnated by Melissa in a blondish gray wig, unswept into a perfect Katrina crown, her glasses on, her lavender shawl over her legs as she sits in the black rocker, book open in her lap, hands crossed upon it.

"Where will you go?" she asks the young man standing by the bay window.

And the young man, in whom Martin does not recognize anything of his disordered self of 1908, replies, "Someplace where they don't snigger when my name is mentioned."

"Will you go to Paris?"

"Perhaps. I don't know."

"It must be dreary there without Baudelaire and Rimbaud."

"They have that tower now."

"Your father will want to know where you are."

"Perhaps I'll go to Versailles and see where the king kept Marie Antoinette."

"Yes, do that. Send your father a postcard."

And Melissa put her book aside and stood up, sweeping her hand up behind her neck, tapping the wig, smoothing the rattled mind. The gesture was not Katrina's but Melissa's,

175

which generated confusion in Martin. He felt impatient with the play, half fearful of seeing the development a few scenes hence when his father would enter with the awful dialogue of duplicity and defeat, to be met by the witty near-madness of Katrina.

Now the dialogue of mother and son moved the play on toward that moment, but Martin closed out all the talk and watched the silent movement of Melissa, not at all like Katrina, and remembered her in her voluptuary state, drenched in sweat, oozing his semen. The Olmecs built a monument of a sacred jaguar mating with a lustful woman. A male offspring of such a mating would have been half-jaguar, half-boy, a divine creature. The boy-animal of Martin's morning vision, perhaps? Is your mind telling you, Martin, that you're the divine progeny of a sacred mating? But which one? Your father's with your mother? Your father's with Melissa? Your own with Melissa?

The corruption he felt after his time with Melissa came back now with full power: the simoniac being paid off with venereal gifts. He stayed with her three days, she securing her purchase with a lust that soared beyond his own. That body, now walking across the stage, he saw walking the length of the sitting room in The Hampton to stand naked by the window and peer through the curtains at the movement on Broadway and State Street below. He stood beside her and with a compulsion grown weary, slid his hand between her thighs as a gesture. They looked down together, connected to the traffic of other men and women in transit toward and away from their lust. He would stay in the room with her another day, until she said, Now I want a woman. And then Martin went away.

Through the years since then he insisted he would never touch her sexually again. But perceiving now that a second infusion of pain distracts the brain and reduces the pain of the

176

first and more grievous wound, he would, yes, make love to Melissa as soon as possible. He might ask her to wear the blond wig. That would appeal to her twist. He might even call her Katrina. She could call him Edward.

They would pretend it was 1887 and that this was a true wedding of sacred figures. He would tell her of the Olmecs, and of the divine progeny. He would tell her his dream of the divine animal at bedside and suggest that it was perhaps himself in a new stage of being. As they made their fierce and fraudulent love, they would become jaguar and lustful partner entwined. Both would know that a new Martin Daugherty would be the offspring of this divine mating.

The quest to love yourself is a moral quest.

How simple this psychic game is, once you know the rules.

12

All of a sudden Doc Fay was playing like a champ in Daddy Big's round robin. Billy had been ahead sixteen points and then old Doc ran twenty-six and left Billy nothing on the table. The Doc blew his streak on the last ball of a rack. Didn't leave himself in a position where he could sink it and also make the cue ball break the new rack. And so he called safe and sank the ball, and it was respotted at the peak of the new rack, the full rack now facing Billy.

The Doc also left the cue ball way up the table, snug against the back cushion. Toughest possible shot for Billy. Or anybody. Billy, natch, had to call another safe shot—make contact with a ball, and make sure one ball, any ball, also touched a cushion. If he failed to do this, it would be his third scratch in a row, and he'd lose fifteen points, plus a point for the lastest scratch. Billy did have the out of breaking the rack instead of playing safe, as a way of beating the third scratch. But when he looked at the full rack he couldn't bring himself to break it. It would seem cowardly. What's more, it'd set Doc up for another fat run, and they'd all know Billy Phelan would never do a thing like that.

He bent over the table and remembered bringing Danny into this pool room one afternoon. The kid stood up straight to shoot. Get your head down, put your eye at the level of the ball, Billy told him. How the hell can you see what you're hitting when you ain't even looking at it? Get that head down and stroke that cue, firm up your bridge, don't let them fingers wobble. The kid leaned over and sank a few. Great kid. Stay out of pool rooms, kid, or all you'll ever have is fun.

Billy tapped the cue ball gently. He was thrilled at how lightly he hit it. Just right. The ball moved slowly toward the rear right corner of the pack. It touched the pack and separated two balls. No ball touched a cushion.

Scratch.

Scratch number three, in a row.

Billy loses fifteen, plus one for this scratch.

Billy is down twenty-seven points and the Doc is hot. Billy doubts he could catch the Doc now even if he wanted to.

Billy hits the table with his fist, hits the floor with the heel of his cue and curses that last goddamn safe shot, thrilled.

Billy is acting. He has just begun to throw his first match.

The lights in the pool room went out just as the Doc lined up for the next shot. I'll get candles, said Daddy Big. Don't nobody touch them balls. Which balls are they, Daddy? Footers asked in a falsetto. Billy remembered Footers just before the lights went out, licking a green lollipop, and Harvey Hess, his thumbs stuck in his vest, nodding his approval at the Doctor burying Billy. Daddy Big liked that development too, the string of his change apron tight on his gut, like a tick tied in the middle. Behind Billy stood Morrie Berman, who was again backing Billy. Morrie had given Billy fifty to bet on himself with the Doc, and also took all side bets on his boy. Billy heard Morrie softly muttering unhhh, eeeng, every time the Doc sank one.

Maybe a hundred men were standing and sitting around the table when the lights went. Billy saw Martin come in late and stand at the back of the crowd, behind the chairs Daddy Big had set up. Daddy Big lit four candles. They flickered on the cigar counter, on the edge of a pool table covered with a tarpaulin, on a shelf near the toilet. Many of the men were smoking in the half-darkness, their cigars and cigarettes glowing and fading, their faces moving in and out of shadows. Here was the obscure collective power. What'll they do if I fink? Will I see my father? Some of the shadowy men left the room when the lights went out. Most of those with chairs stayed put, but then some of them, too, went down to the street, needing, in the absence of light, at least an open sky.

"Tough shot you had," Morrie said to Billy.

"The toughest."

"You'll pick up. You got what it takes."

"That Doctor's hot as ten-cent pussy."

"You'll take him."

"Sure," said Billy.

But he won't, or else how can he do what he's got to do, if he's got to do it? Wrong-Way Corrigan starts out for California and winds up in Ireland. I guess I got lost, he says, and people say, Yeah, oh yeah, he got lost. Ain't he some sweet son of a bitch?

13

Through the front window of Louie's, Martin saw that the lights were out on Broadway and in the station. He saluted Billy across the candlelight and went down to the street, which was dark in all directions. He walked to the corner of Columbia Street and looked up. Pearl Street was also dark, candles already dancing in two windows up the block. He walked back and into Becker's and headed for the phone, past customers drinking by the light of the old kerosene lamp that had sat on the back bar for years, unused. Now it illuminated Red Tom's mustache. The test of a real mustache is whether it can be seen from behind. Red Tom's therefore is not real.

The city desk told him that lights were out all over the city and parts of Colonie, Watervliet and Cohoes. All hospitals had been called an hour earlier and told a power failure was possible, and not to schedule any operations unless they had their own generators. Nursing homes were also alerted. But the power company said it hadn't made the calls. Who had? Nobody knew.

Martin went back to the bar and ordered a Grandad on ice and looked at the photo behind the bar. A new star shone on the chest of Scotty Streck, brighter than all others. In the kerosene lamplight the men in the photo moved backward in time. They were all smiling and all younger than their pictures. They were boys and young men under the shirt-sleeved, summer sun. None of them was dead or would ever die.

"Lights are out all over town," Martin told Red Tom.

"Is that a fact? I was listening to the radio when they went. Dewey was on, talking about Albany."

"Albany? What was he saying?"

"He mentioned Patsy, and that was all I heard."

"Did he mention Charlie Boy?"

"Not that I heard."

Martin gulped his drink and went outside. People were clustered under the canopy at the station, all cabs were gone, and a West Albany trolley was stalled between Maiden Lane and Steuben Street. Martin could see it in the headlights of cars. The night was a deep, moonless black, with only a few stars visible. It was as if rural darkness had descended upon the city. Faces were unrecognizable three feet away. Albany had never been so dark in Martin's memory. There were gas lamps in his boyhood, then the first few electric lights, now the power poles everywhere. But tonight was the lightless time in which highwaymen had performed, the dark night of the century gone, his father's childhood darkness on new streets cut out of the raw hills and the grassy flats. A woman with a bundle came by, half running toward Clinton Avenue, pursued by the night. Alongside Martin, a match flared and he turned to see Morrie Berman lighting a cigar.

"What news do you hear?"

"Only that they're out all over town."

"I mean about the McCall kid. You fellows at the paper turn up any news?"

"I heard there was another ransom note."

"Is that so?"

"Signed by Charlie Boy. I didn't see it, but from what I gather there'll be another go-between list in the paper tonight."

"They didn't like us on the first list?"

"So it seems."

"You hear anything else?"

Dark shapes moved in behind Morrie, and Martin withheld his answer. The shapes hovered.

"Let's take a walk," Martin said and he took a step toward Steuben Street. Morrie stepped along and they moved south on Broadway, candles in the Waldorf, a bunch of men on the street in front of the Monte Carlo. They stepped around the men in the light of a passing auto. Martin did not want to speak until they had turned the corner onto Steuben. They passed Hagaman's Bakery and Joe's Bookshop on Steuben Street, where Martin knew his father's early novel, *The Mosquito Lovers*, and the volume of his collected plays were sitting in faded dust jackets in the window, and had been for months, ever since the success of *The Flaming Corsage*.

"So what's the secret?" Morrie asked.

"No secret, but I don't want to broadcast it. I know you're a friend of Maloy and the news is they're looking for him. And Curry."

"Why tell me? They got a lot of friends."

"You asked for news. They've both been out of town a week."

"So that ties them in?"

"No, but even their families don't know where they are."

"Hell, I saw Maloy two or three days ago on Broadway. They're apt to be anywhere. Maloy's crazy and Curry's a moron. But they wouldn't mix up in a thing like this, not in their own town."

"Nevertheless, they're looking for them."

"They'll turn up. What else do you hear?"

"The note said they'd starve Charlie Boy till the ransom was paid."

"Tough stuff."

"Very."

Up toward Pearl Street, a window shattered and a burglar alarm rang and rang. Martin saw a silhouette running toward him and Morrie. The runner brushed Martin's elbow, stepping off the curb as they touched, but Martin could not see the face.

"Somebody did all right," said Morrie. "Ain't that a jewelry store there?"

"Right," said Martin. "Just about where Henry James's grandmother used to live."

"Who?"

"An old-timer."

And on the other corner, DeWitt Clinton lived. And across the street, Bret Harte was born. And up Columbia was one of Melville's homes, and on Clinton Square another. An old man had answered when Martin knocked on the door of the Columbia Street house and said, yeauh, he seemed to remember the name Melville but that was next door and they tore that house down and built a new one. Melville, he said. I heard he moved to Troy. Don't know what become of him after that.

Martin and Morrie neared Pearl Street, the glimmerings of light from the cars giving them a fragmented view of the broken window in Wilson's Jewelry Store. When they saw the window, they crossed Pearl. Martin looked down toward State and saw a torchlight parade coming north in support of the nomination of Millard Fillmore. The John G. Myers department store collapsed into itself, killing thirteen and making men bald from flying plaster dust. Henry James, suffused in the brilliance of a sunny summer morning, walked out of his grandmother's house, opened the front gate, and floated like a flowered balloon into ethereal regions. Martin walked in the phosphorescent footsteps of his father and his grandfather.

"Where the hell are we walking?" Morrie asked.

"Just around," said Martin. "You want to go back down?"

"I guess it's all right."

They walked to Clinton Square, where two more trolleys were stalled on the bend. A siren screamed and stopped, back near Steuben and Pearl. Martin and Morrie, their eyes grown accustomed to the darkness, watched the shadowy action in front of the Palace Theater, hundreds waiting to go back inside and see the rest of *Boys' Town* with Spencer Tracy as Father Flanagan, the miracle man. There is no such thing as a bad boy.

"They got some kind of light in the Grand Lunch," Morrie said. "You want some coffee?"

"No, you go ahead. I want to watch the panic."

"What panic?"

"There's got to be panic someplace with this much darkness."

"Whatever you say. See you down below."

In the Sudetenland only last week when Hitler arrived, at nightfall there was an epidemic of suicide.

In France in 1918, Martin had heard a man scream from the darkness beyond a farmhouse where a shell had just hit. Help me, oh God, oh heavenly God, help me, the man yelled, and then he wailed his pain. Martin nudged a corporal and they crawled toward the voice and found an American soldier pinned between two dead cows. The top cow was bloated from inhaling the explosion. Martin and the corporal could not move the bloated cow so they pulled the squeezed man by his arms, and the top half of him came away in their grip. He stopped screaming.

Martin crossed Pearl and went into the K. of C. and called the city desk by candlelight. Viglucci said there was still no explanation for the blackout, but up at Harmanus Bleecker Hall the audience had panicked when the lights went. People shoved one another and Tip Mooney was knocked down and trampled.

Punishment.

"This bum's a Cuban and so's one of the broads," said Morrie as Billy and Martin followed him down two slate steps to the basement doorway beneath the high stoop. Morrie rapped and the pimp peered out in his puce shirt, his hair brilliantined, his shoes pointed and shiny, both ends of him gleaming in the harsh backlight. The lights of the city had come back on an hour earlier.

"Hey, Mo-ree," the pimp said. "Whatchou lookin' for?"

"Pussy," said Morrie.

"You in the right place."

The pimp, the same man Red Tom threw out of Becker's, had a face as pointy as his shoes and resembled Martin's long-snouted animal child. Why should the likes of him concretize a Daugherty abstraction? But why not? Ooze to ooze, slime to slime. Brothers under the sheets.

Two young women sat at the kitchen table drinking sarsa-parilla out of jelly glasses. Knives, forks, glasses, and dishes sat in the sink. The stub of a candle stood in a pool of dry wax on a saucer. The pimp introduced the girls as Fela and Margie. Fela, obviously *La Cubana*, was dark, with hair to her kidneys. Margie had carroty red hair, redder by blood weight than Mary Daugherty's crop. Both wore brassieres, Woolworth couture, a size too small, shorts to mid-thigh, with cuffs, and high heels.

"They got shorts on," Morrie said. "Last time I saw a whore in shorts was Mame Fay's."

"I know Mame," said the pimp. "She's got influence up in Troy."

"She used to recruit salesgirls in the grocery marts," Billy said. "She tried to hawk a friend of mine."

"She'd give talks in the high schools if they let her," said Morrie.

"Young stuff is what Mame likes," Margie said.

"Yeah," said Morrie, licking his lips.

"Talk is gettin' hot, *hombres*. Young stuff right in front of you. Who's ready?"

"Don't rush me," said Morrie.

Billy pulled up a chair between Fela and Margie and looked them over. Martin felt a thirst rising.

"You have any beer?"

"Twenty-five cents, *hombre*."

"I'm a sport," said Martin, and the pimp cracked a quart of Stanwix.

"Those broads up at Mame's," Morrie said, "took their tops off when we come in. I'm the best, one of 'em says to us, so take me. If you're the best, says the other, how come your boyfriend screwed me? You? says the other. He'd screw a dead dog with the clap, but he wouldn't screw you. And then they went at it. Best whore fight I ever saw. Bit one another, blood all over the joint, one of their heads split open. Me and Maloy laughed our tits off."

"We don't fight," Margie said. "We like one another."

"That's nice," said Morrie, and he put his hand inside her brassiere. "Soft." He laughed, found a chair, and sat down.

"Maloy," said Billy. "What the hell is he doing in Newark?"

"Who said he was in Newark?" Morrie asked.

"I thought you did."

"He ain't in Newark."

"Where is he?"

"He's someplace else."

"How do you know he ain't in Newark. I heard he was in Newark."

"What the hell'd he be in Newark for?"

"Why not Newark?"

"He don't know nobody in Newark."

"This is a famous guy," the pimp told the girls, putting his hand on Morrie's shoulder. "His name's in the paper this morning. They say that's all about the kidnapping, right Mo-ree?"

"Billy's name's in there, too."

"Very big men in Albany if the McCalls put your name in there," said the pimp.

"You don't like the McCalls," Billy said. "They threw you out of Becker's for bad-mouthing them."

"I never like them," said the pimp. "They make me a janitor at the public bath, then fire me."

"What'd they do that for?"

"For nothing. A little thing. Look at the ladies and pull the old rope. They catch me and tell me I'm all finish. Little thing like that."

"It ain't against the law to pull your rope," Morrie said. "It's against the law to get caught."

"It sure ain't against the law here," Margie said.

"Yeah, you boys come here to talk or screw?" Fela the Cubana said.

"Screw," said Morrie, "and you got it, lady. Let's go." He stood up and tongued her ear and she knocked a jelly glass off the table. He took her down the hallway and into a bedroom.

"Hey, Mo-ree," said the pimp, "she's the best blow-job in town." Then he told Martin and Billy: "Margie's good too."

"Is that right?" Billy asked Margie. "Are you good?"

"I ain't had a complaint all week."

Billy washed a glass in the sink with soap and water and poured himself a beer. The pimp came over to Martin.

"What do you like, Mister? Little blow from the best?"

"I'm just along for the ride. I'll stay with the drink."

Martin washed a glass and poured a beer. He stared at the door of the broom closet, then opened the door and saw the notebook for *The Flaming Corsage* hanging from a nail on a short piece of cord. It was inscribed on the cover: *To my beloved son, who played a whore's trick on his father.* Martin closed the closet door and sipped his beer, which tasted like the juice of rotted lemons. He spat into the sink.

Martin dried his mouth and studied Margie, who removed her brassiere for him. Her nipples lay at the bottom of the curves, projecting somewhat obliquely. Martin considered the nipple fetishists of history. Plutarch, Spinoza, Schubert, Cardinal Wolsey. The doorbells of ecstasy, Curzio Malaparte called them. Billy reached across the table and lifted one of Margie's breasts. People preparing for sexual conflict. The pimp slavered and picked his nose with his thumb.

How had Martin's father prepared for sex? On spindly legs, he stood in his shorts in his bedroom, reading Blake on the dresser top. The shorts seemed unusually long. Perhaps he had short thighs. He looked sexually disinterested, but that was unquestionably deceptive. His teeth carried stains from pipe-smoking. He had a recurring ingrown toenail, clipped with a V, a protruding bone on the right elbow from an old fracture. These things were antisexual.

How would Martin's son ever know anything of his own sexuality? Gone to the priests at thirteen, blanketed with repressive prayer and sacramental censure. How could the tigers of chastity be wiser than the horses of coition?

Ten years ago, a phone call had come for Martin after he'd

completed a sexual romp with his wife. The caller, a Boston lawyer, had heard that the notebook of The Flaming Corsage was in Martin's possession. Was that true?

Yes.

Was it for sale, or would it be preserved in the trove of Daugherty papers?

The latter, of course.

Well, you may take my name and address, and should you change your mind I want you to know that I will pay a handsome price for that notebook. Like the play made from it, it has a deep significance for my client.

What significance is that?

My client, said the lawyer, was your father's mistress.

"All right," Morrie said, emerging from the bedroom. "Little bit of all right."

"That was quick," Billy said. "You like it?"

"Short but sweet," Morrie said. "How much?"

"Buck and a half," said the pimp.

Morrie snapped a dollar off his roll and fished for the fifty cents. Margie put on her brassiere. Fela picked up the sarsaparilla bottle and looked for a glass.

"Only a buck and a half?" Billy said.

"That's all," said the pimp.

"It must be some great stuff for a buck and a half."

"Go try it."

Fela tipped up the bottle and gargled with sarsaparilla. She spat it into the sink and eyed Billy. The pimp took Morrie's dollar and change. Martin opened the broom closet and found a dust pan hanging from a nail.

"How the hell can it be any good for a buck and a half?" Billy asked.

"Hey, I ought to know," said the pimp with a rattish smile of cuspids. "She's my sister."

Billy hit him on the chin. The pimp sped backward and

knocked over a chair, shook his head and leaped at Billy's throat. Billy shook him off, and the pimp reached for the butcher knife in the sink, but Martin reached it first and threw it out the open window into the alley. Billy hit the pimp again, a graze of the head, but the pimp found Billy's throat again and held on. Martin pulled at the pimp as the whores scrambled away from the table. Morrie pushed past Martin and bashed the pimp with the sarsaparilla bottle. The pimp slid to the floor and lay still. The whores came out of the bedroom carrying their dresses and handbags.

"He looks dead," Billy said.

"Who gives a goddamn?" Morrie said, and he tipped over the kitchen table, opened the dish closet and threw the dishes on the floor. Billy tipped over the garbage pail and threw a chair at the kitchen window. The whores went out the back door.

"Son of a bitch, pimping for his own sister," said Billy.

"She wasn't bad," said Morrie as he swept the contents of the refrigerator onto the floor. "She's got nice teeth."

Martin salvaged a new cold bottle of Stanwix and poured himself a glass. He opened the broom closet so Morrie could empty it. Billy went into the bedroom where Morrie had been with Fela and tore up the bed clothes, then kicked the footboard until the bed fell apart. On the bedside table stood a metal lamp of a nautical F.D.R. at the wheel of the Ship of State, standing above the caption: "Our Leader." Billy threw the lamp through the bedroom window. Martin straightened up two kitchen chairs, sat on one and used the other as a table for his beer, which no longer tasted like rotten lemons. Billy came back and nudged the inert pimp with his foot.

"I think you killed him," he said to Morrie.

"No," said Martin. "He moved his fingers."

"He's all right then," Morrie said. "You ain't dead if you can move your fingers."

"I knew a guy couldn't move his toes," Billy said, winded

but calming. "His feet turned to stone. First his feet then the rest of him. Only guy I ever knew whose feet turned to stone and then the rest of him."

Transgressors of good fame are punished for their deeds, was what occurred to Martin. He stood up and opened his fly, then urinated on the pimp's feet. Simoniacs among us.

"What'd you make of Morrie's answer about Maloy?" Billy asked.

"I thought he was evasive," Martin said.

"I think he's lying."

"Why would he lie?"

"You tell me," Billy said. "Must be he doesn't want Maloy connected to Newark."

"Maybe he's not connected."

"No. He was lying. I saw it in his face."

They listened to the dismal blues Slopie Dodds was making at the piano. Martin squinted in the dim light of Martha's Place, where they'd come for a nightcap after leaving Morrie. The smoke was dense in the low-ceilinged bar, which was full of Negroes. There were four white men in the place, Martin and Billy, a stranger at the far end of the bar, and Daddy Big, a nightly Negrophile after he reached his drunken beyond. Daddy was oblivious now of everything except hustling Martha, a handsome tan woman in her forties with shoulder-length conked hair, small lips, and a gold-capped canine tooth. Martha was not about to be hustled, but Daddy Big did not accept this, steeped as he was in his professional wisdom that everybody is hustleable once you find the weak spot.

Slopie ended his blues and, as Martha moved to another customer, Daddy Big swung around on his stool and said, "Play me the white man's song, Slopie." Slopie grinned and trilled an intro, a ricky-tick throwback, and Daddy Big sang from his barstool the song he said he had learned from a jailhouse nigger who'd sung it in World War One: *I don't care what it costs, I'll suffer all the loss. It's worth twice the money just to be the boss. 'Cause I got a white man workin' for me now.* The song merged with "The Broadway Rag," into which Slopie passed without comment. Daddy Big opened his arms to the room and said as the ragtime bounced off the walls, "I love all niggers." Looking then to the black faces for reciprocation and getting none, he discovered Billy at the corner table, near the neon-lighted window.

"What're you doing here, Phelan?" he asked. "You ain't a nigger." The words were crooked with whiskey.

"I'm an Irish Catholic," Billy said. "Same thing to some people."

A few who heard this smiled. Daddy Big hurled himself off the barstool and staggered toward Billy, stopping his own forward motion by grabbing the back of a chair with both hands.

"You got your tail whipped tonight."

"Doc was hot," Billy said. "A good player got hot."

"Bet your ass he's a good player. Bet your ass. He'll whip you every time out."

"Then why didn't he whip me the last two matches we played?"

"He'll whip you from now on. He's got your number. All you know how to shoot is safe and you blew that tonight. You ain't got nothin' left, if you ever had anything." Daddy waved his left hand in front of his face like a man shooing flies. He lurched for the door with one word: "Bum," and went out cross-footed, leaving the door ajar. Martin closed it as Daddy Big careened in the direction of Union Station.

"He's got a mean mouth," Martin said.

"Yeah," said Billy. "He's a prick now. Prison got him twisted. But he used to be a nice guy, and at pool he was a champ. Nobody in Albany could beat him. I learned a whole lot watching him sucker chumps who thought they knew something about the game."

The white man from the end of the bar stopped beside Billy. "That guy talks like he wants to wind up dead in the alley. He keeps that up in here, he'll get what he's after."

"He's a cousin of the McCalls," Billy told the man. "Nobody'll touch him."

"Is that so?" The man was chastened. "I didn't know that."

"That pimp," Billy said to Martin when the stranger left, "I don't know why he didn't stay down. I hit him right on the button. They used to stay down when I hit 'em like that."

"Do you suppose he'll try to get even?"

"He'd get worse. You don't come back at Morrie."

"Then you think Morrie's dangerous?"

"Anybody pals around with Maloy and Curry's dangerous." Billy thought about that. "But I like Morrie," he said. "And I like Maloy. Curry's nuts, but Morrie's all right. He saved my ass there."

Slopie finished his ragtime number, a *tour de force* that won applause. Billy signaled to Martha to buy Slopie a drink.

"Can I tell you something, Martin?"

"Anything."

"Positively on the q.t."

"Do you trust me?"

"Yeah, I do. For a straight guy, you know a lot. Why'd you piss on that guy's feet?"

"He seemed worth that kind of attention. I don't meet too many like that. What did you want to tell me?"

"I threw that match tonight."

"Hey," said Martin. "What for?"

"So I wouldn't owe Berman."

"I don't think I follow that."

"He lent me fifty to bet on myself. If I win, then I got money through him, right? But if I lose, I owe him nothing.

I already give him back the fifty and we were even. Then the son of a bitch saves my ass."

"So you were going to talk to Patsy about him then?"

"I don't know."

"I could tell them what you want to say. I don't have your qualms."

"They'd know I pumped him and then didn't tell them."

"Then tell them."

"But that puts me full on the tit. Bindy and Patsy paying my debts. Paying you. Me on the tit like Daddy Big. That bastard calls me a bum, but he'd chew catshit if Bindy said it was strawberries."

The stranger who said Daddy Big wanted to die came back into Martha's. "Somebody better call an ambulance," he said. "That drunk guy is outside bleedin' all over the street."

Martha went for the phone, and Billy and Martin ran down the block. Daddy Big lay on his back, his face bloodied badly, staring at the black sky with bugged eyes and puffed cheeks, his skin purple where it wasn't smeared with blood. Two of his front teeth were bent inward and the faint squeal of a terrified mouse came out of his mouth. Billy rolled him face down and with two fingers pulled out his upper plate, then grabbed him around the waist with both arms and lifted him, head down, to release the vomit in his throat. Billy sat down on the sidewalk, knees up, and held Daddy across his lap, face down, tail in the air. Billy slapped his back and pressed both knees into his stomach until his vomiting stopped. Daddy looked up.

"You son of a bitch," Billy said. "Are you all right?"

"Blllgggggggghhh," Daddy said, gasping.

"Then get your ass up."

Billy rolled him off his lap, stood up and pulled the drunken Daddy to his feet. Customers from Martha's stood behind the two men, along with half a dozen passersby. Billy leaned

Daddy against the wall of the Railroad Y.M.C.A. and Martha blotted his face with a wet towel, revealing a split forehead and a badly scraped nose, cheek, and chin. A prowl car arrived and two patrolmen helped Daddy into the back seat.

"Where'll you take him?" Martin asked.

"Home. He does this regular," one policeman said.

"You should have him looked at up at the emergency room. He might have aspirated. Inhaled some vomit."

"Nngggggnnnhhh," said Daddy Big.

The policeman frowned at Martin and got behind the wheel.

"He don't have any teeth," Billy said. Billy found the teeth on the edge of the curb, where a dog was licking the vomit. Billy reached in through the car window and put the teeth in Daddy Big's shirt pocket. As the crowd moved back toward Martha's, Martin saw another car pull up behind the police car, Poop Powell at the wheel.

"Hey, Phelan," Poop called, and both Billy and Martin then saw Bindy McCall in the front seat alongside Poop. Martin patted Billy gently on the shoulder.

"You do lead a full life, Billy," he said.

Martin sat in Martha's window looking at Billy standing in the middle of Broadway, his back to traffic, talking into Bindy's window. The neon sign, which spelled Martha's name backward, gave off a humming, crackling sound, flaming gas contained, controlled. Martin drank his beer and considered the combustibility of men. Billy on fire going through the emotions of whoring for Bindy when he understood nothing about how it was done. It was not done out of need. It rose out of the talent for assuming the position before whoremongers. Billy lacked such talent. He was so innocent of whoring he could worry over lead slugs.

Slopie played "Lullaby of Broadway," a seductive tune.

Slopie was now playing in a world never meant to be, a world he couldn't have imagined when he had both his legs and Bessie on his arm. Yet, he'd arrived here in Martha's, where Billy and Martin had also arrived. The music brought back *Gold Diggers* of some year gone. Winnie Shaw singing and dancing the "Lullaby." Come and dance, said the hoofers, cajoling her, and she danced with them through all those early mornings. Broadway Baby couldn't sleep till break of dawn, and so she danced, but fled them finally. Please let me rest, she pleaded from her balcony refuge. Dick Powell kissed her through the balcony door, all the hoofers pleading, beckoning. Dance with us, Baby. And they pushed open the door. She backed away from them, back, back, and ooooh, over the railing she went. There goes Broadway Baby, falling, poor Baby, falling, falling, and gone. Good night, Baby.

Spud, the paper boy, came into Martha's with a stack of *Times-Unions* under his right arm, glasses sliding down his nose, cap on, his car running outside behind Bindy's, with doors open, hundreds more papers on the back seat.

"Paper," Martin said. He gave Spud the nickel and turned to the classifieds, found the second code ad. Footers O'Brien was the top name, then Benny Goldberg, who wrote a big numbers book in Albany and whose brother was shot in his Schenectady roadhouse for having five jacks in a house deck. Martin lost patience translating the names in the dim light and turned to the front page. No story on Charlie Boy, but the Vatican was probing a new sale of indulgences in the U.S. And across the top a promotion headline screamed: "Coming Sunday in the *Times-Union*: How and Why We Piss."

Billy went straight to the men's room when he came back into Martha's and washed off Daddy Big's stink. Then he ordered a double scotch and sat down.

"So I told him about Newark," he said.

"You did? Was he pleased?"

"He wanted more, but I told him straight. I can't do this no more, Bin. I ain't cut out to be a squealer."

"Did he accept that?"

"I don't think so."

"Why don't you think so?"

"Because he says to me, All right, hotshot, you're all by yourself, and he rolls up the window."

14

Martin, ducking his head, entered the city room at pristine morning. Across the freshly oiled floor, free now from the sea of used paper, shinbone high, that would cover it nine or ten hours hence, he walked softly, playing the intruder, hoping to catch a rat in action. The room was empty except for the clacking, which never deterred the *Times-Union*'s rats. It was their lullaby. They got to be a size, came along a pipe from out back, and ran over the heads of the working stiffs. Benson Hunt, the rewrite man, the star, moved his desk back two feet and never took off his hat again after a three-pounder lost its footing on the pipe and tumbled into his lap. Benson screamed and tipped himself over, breaking a pint of gin in his coat. Martin had no such worries, for no pipes traversed the space over his desk, and he never packed gin. But he too wore his hat to keep his scalp free of the fine rain of lead filings that filtered through the porous ceiling from the composing room overhead.

Martin paused at the sports desk to read a final edition with the story on the blackout. Some sort of sabotage, perhaps, went one theory; though the power company and the police had no culprits. The darkness blacked out, through most of Albany County, the speech by Thomas E. Dewey, aaaahhh, largely an attack on the McCall machine. Sublime. The speech was reported separately. Political monopoly in Albany. Vicious mess of corruption in the shadow of the Capitol. Vice not fit to discuss on the radio. Politics for profit. Packed grand juries. Tax assessments used to punish enemies. Vote fraud rampant. The arrest only today of several men, one for registering twenty-one times.

Martin clicked on the drop light over his own desk and prepared to write a column for the Sunday paper, his first since the kidnapping. In the days since Charlie Boy had been taken, Martin stayed busy chronicling the event as he came to know it, for use when the story finally did break. He had filled his regular space in the paper with extra columns he kept in overset for just such distracted times.

Now he wrote about Billy's two-ninety-nine game and about Scotty dropping dead. Without malice toward Scotty, he discussed the hex, and Billy's response to it. He viewed Billy as a strong man, indifferent to luck, a gamester who accepted the rules and played by them, but who also played above them. He wrote of Billy's disdain of money and viewed Billy as a healthy man without need for artifice or mysticism, a serious fellow who put play in its proper place: an adjunct to breathing and eating.

By comparison, Martin wrote, I find myself an embarrassed ecclesiarch, a foolish believer in luck, fate, magicians, and divine animals. It would serve me right if I died and went to heaven and found out it was a storefront run by Hungarian palm readers. In the meantime, he concluded, I aspire to the condition of Billy Phelan, and will try to be done mollycoddling my personal spooks.

It took him half an hour to write the column. He put it in the overnight folder in a drawer of the city desk, ready for noontime scrutiny by Matt Viglucci, the city editor.

In his mailbox, he found a letter on Ten Eyck Hotel stationery, delivered by hand. Dearest Martin, I missed you at the theater. Do come and call. We have so much to talk about and I have a "gift" for you. Yours always, Melissa.

A gift, oh yes. Another ticket to lotus land? Or was there mystery lurking in those quotation marks? What son eats the body of his father in the womb of his mother? The priest, of course, devouring the host in the Holy Church. But what son is it that eats the body of his father's sin in the womb of his father's mistress? Suggested answer: the plenary self-indulger.

Paper rustled behind him as he stood amid the clackety lullaby. He turned noiselessly to see a large, relaxed rat walking across the scatter of early editions and old wire copy left by the nightside on top of the copy desk. The rat stopped at a paste pot on the desk and nibbled at the hardened outer crust. The pot moved, the rat inched forward, and then, with dexterous forefeet, it lifted the dauber an inch and pushed its own nose into the center of the pot, into the cool, fresh, soft, sweet stickiness of the paste.

Breakfast.

Martin counted eighteen steps going out of the building and waved at Rory Walsh, the early man in the sports department, schoolboy football specialist coming out of Steve White's twenty-four-hour bar. Old man Ridley stood in front of his newsroom, burning yesterday's policy slips in the gutter. The window seats of the Capitol Hotel restaurant, reserved for *T-U* folk, were empty. Martin's stomach rolled at the thought of the lobster tail special, three for fifty-five cents. He stopped at Green's stationery store and bought wrapping paper, ribbon, and a card for the present he would give Melissa, tit for tat. The horseroom upstairs over Green's was already open for business. Across the street, Keeler's tempted, as always, and his stomach rolled again. He had slept badly and left the house without waking Mary, without eating. Should he indulge? He did.

Perhaps his decision was colored by his having eaten here in 1928 with Melissa, two breakfasts and one dinner in three days, the only times they left the hotel room, fortifying their bodies with what he considered the equal of the best food on earth, reconstituting themselves for the return to their bed of second-generation concubinage.

He now ordered eggs Benedict, hard rolls and salt sticks, iced butter, marmalade, hashed browns, steaming coffee in the silver pot. A grumpy Jewish waiter in black jacket and long white apron, shuffling on flat feet, served the meal impeccably. Two thirty-five with tip. Gorgeous. He felt stylish, and buoyed by nostalgia. Ready for the lady.

She was registered in a twelfth-floor suite, and he approached it along the carpeted hallway, certain he would rouse her from sleep. He knocked loudly four times before she opened the door, each rap an explosion in the silent corridor.

"I came for my gift," he said.

"You fool. Why didn't you call? Haven't you any thought for a lady's condition at such an hour?"

"Your condition looks fetchingly normal to me. Dressed for bed."

"I must look wretched."

She left the door open and crossed the suite's sitting room, barefoot in a white calf-length negligee, and disappeared into the bedroom. Martin entered and the door swung closed. He put his hat on the coffee table and sat in the love seat. An etching of a step-gabled Dutch house hung on one wall, a Maxfield Parrish print on another wall—Daybreak, everybody's favorite picture fifteen years ago. The naked nymph bent over the reclining beauty waking from sleep, the mountain lake and the trees of Arcadia framing the morning confrontation, the brightening sky dappling the mountains and lighting incipient joy. Beneath it on the sideboard Martin saw his father's notebook. It lay flat, a ledger eighteen inches

202

long with canvas and leather cover and binding, and bearing the India ink marking his father had made to identify it by date.

Here was a contrast of low and high art by master achievers: Parrish setting out to entrap popular taste, Edward Daugherty laboring with the death throes of his soul to produce a play that reflected his supreme independence of the crowd. The ledger contained the notation of the history of a masterpiece as well as the revelations of a notorious disgrace. *Daybreak*, with all its dynamic symmetry, made Martin want to throttle Parrish for foisting on the millions the notion that life was tidy, life was golden. Still, the hint of Lesbos had its place on any wall of Melissa's suite, as Edward and Martin Daugherty both knew.

Looking at the ledger, it occurred to him to take it and leave. He had often mused on burglary as a means of retrieving it. He turned his eyes from it only because Melissa re-entered the room in a baby blue satin robe and matching pom-pommed mules. She had brushed her silvering chestnut hair, colored the cream of her cheeks with a subtle touch of rouge, lifted her eyes from sleep with pale green eye shadow, and powdered away the gleam of her shining morning brow. Her beauty, though controlled by chemistry, was a miracle at forty-nine, given the terror of personal and professional oblivion with which she had lived most of the last decade. Even her wrinkles were now seemly, allowing her to relinquish at last that girlish beauty with which she had lived far too long, keeping her on the cover of *Photoplay*, but sabotaging all her efforts to become a serious actress. For who could believe an anguished spirit lurked behind a face as elegant and proud of itself as Melissa's? No one could, until her role as the cloistered Marina (Katrina) of *The Flaming Corsage* forced a reappraisal of her talent by the critics: Here is a totally new Melissa Spencer . . . acts as if born to the stage . . . confounds

203

critics who said her voice would fail in talkies . . . most fully articulated female presence on the Broadway stage this year, etc.

She went straight to the telephone and ordered breakfast for two: cantaloupe, camembert, croissants, and champagne. Of course. Then she flounced into an armchair across from Martin, framed by *Daybreak* and a cut-glass vase full of white roses opening to the morning with the shining sublimity of their final blooming, only hours left in their life.

"Are you well?" she asked.

"I may be recuperating, but I'm not sure."

"That sounds dreadful, as if you're living in some awful sanitarium."

"That's not far off. I've been on a morose spiritual jag for years, and it's worse these past few days."

"Is it your father? How is he?"

"It's that, but it's not that simple. And he's quite senile but otherwise healthy. It's my son going off to the priesthood, and it's a friend just kidnapped by hoodlums."

"A kidnapping! How fascinating!"

"Oh, Christ, Melissa."

"Well, isn't it fascinating?"

"Everything isn't fascinating. Some things are serious."

"Oh, poo."

"Tell me about you. I suspect you're well. I read your notices."

"It is rather a ducky time."

"You look very fit. For anything."

"Don't be forward now, lovey. It's much too early."

"I've known you, my dear, to throw away the clock."

"Me? Not me, Martin. You must be remembering one of your casual women."

"I could've sworn it was you. That week the taboos came tumbling down. The Hampton, was it?"

"Don't be awful now. Don't. I get shivery about that. Tell me about the play. Did you like it?"

"You were quite splendid. But then you're always quite splendid. And I did find that wig becoming."

"Did I look like her to you? I did try."

"At times. But she was never quite as sensually animated as you played her."

"She must have had her moments."

"I think," said Martin, and he pictured his mother coming down the back stoop naked, walking past the small garbage pail, wearing only her sunbonnet hat and her white shoes and carrying her calico handbag, "that all she ever had was her repressions." Walking into the waiting arms of Francis Phelan? Did they ever make love after that intimacy?

"So sad," said Melissa.

"Very sad. But that's not one of your problems, I've noticed."

"Avoiding things never made any sense to me, none whatever."

"You've done it all."

"I wouldn't go as far as to say that, lovey."

"But it must be difficult to surprise you." Martin resented her use of "lovey." It sounded vaguely cockney, and insufficiently intimate for what they'd had together.

"Surprises are always welcome," said Melissa, "but they're only the interest on the principal, and it's the principal I'm most fond of."

"I have a bit of a surprise for you," Martin said.

"How delicious," said Melissa. "When do I get it?"

"Don't be forward now."

When breakfast came she insisted he sit on the sofa as they had at the Hampton, and she dropped pieces of melon into his mouth, a scene, he presumed, she had copied from a Valentino or Gilbert film. She lifted champagne to his lips, gave him wafer-thin slices of camembert and croissant, and more and more champagne. He thought he had eaten his fill at Keeler's, but satiation too has its limitations, and he accepted all that she offered.

He kissed her when both their mouths were full, shared his champagne with her. He kissed her again when their mouths were empty, stroking the breast of her robe lightly. And then he leaned away.

"What is this gift you have for me?" he said.

"Can't you guess?"

"I've imagined a thing or two."

"I hope you didn't see it," she said, rising from the sofa and crossing the room. She held up the ledger, giving him a full view of the cover with another of his father's date markings: February 1908 to April 1909.

"I didn't mean to leave it here in full view, but you caught me unawares, coming in like that. You didn't see it before, did you?"

"No, no, I didn't. You say you're returning it?"

"It's yours," she said, coming toward him with it. "I took all I needed for my memoirs."

"I thought you wanted it for the film."

"It's not necessary now. They have more than enough in the play, if they really want to do it. They don't deserve any more than that. So it's yours."

"Then I must return your money."

"Of course you must *not. Absolutely* you must not."

He had charged her eight hundred dollars for the ledger, an arbitrary price from nowhere, for how could he possibly have set a true dollar value on one of his father's notebooks? He'd said eight hundred for reasons no more explicable than his dream of rhomboids. An odd figure, she said. Oddness, he told her, is my profession.

They had been talking then on the roof garden of the

Hampton, where she had taken a suite while she found a way to take possession of the ledger, whose contents she had, at moments, watched being written. The Albany sky was the darkest of blues, swept by millions of stars, the moon silvering the river and the rooftops of buildings on the Rensselaer side. From where Martin and Melissa sat, the Yacht Club, the night boat landing, the Dunn bridge, and much of lower Broadway were blocked from view by a tall, ghostly structure with window openings but no windows, with an unfinished, jagged, and roofless top. This was the "Spite Building," built by a bitter cleric who felt the Hampton had wronged him. And when the hotel opened its roof garden to enormous crowds, the cleric erected this uninhabitable tower of vengeance. It fronted on Beaver Street and nestled back to back with the hotel, and it rose, finally, above the glamorous rooftop cafe, blocking the view and insulting the lofty crowds with its crude bricks and its grotesque eyeless sockets, where squads of verminous pigeons roosted.

Martin and Melissa dined and danced and drank together, abandoning the Hampton roof eventually for the privacy of Melissa's suite. And when the morning came, Martin walked the few blocks to the newspaper, took the ledger from the bottom drawer of his desk, where he'd put it the day before, and brought it back to Melissa. In return he accepted the mysterious eight hundred, and also accepted two and a half more days of lascivious riches from this calculating, venal, and voluptuous incarnation of his psychic downfall.

Melissa now placed the ledger on his lap and sat beside him. He opened it to a page from 1908 and read the words written in his father's upright script, which looked like a wheat field on a windless day.

The hero will not be a writer. Profession left vague? No. He will be Irish-American foundry owner who came up hard way in commerce, through opportunity and hard work, well educated, from family whose social pretensions were wiped out by influx of '49. Marries daughter of aristocratic Dutch-English family (any near-autobiographical data must be transformed) and secret life of failed marriage is revealed. Wife's aspirations for money and position, not for themselves but out of halcyon yearning, become clear; and these are ineradicable and dementing. Sexually dutiful but her wound in Delavan Hotel fire eradicates even that; early traumas only suggested, yet evident. Eventually she retreats, marriage begins to wither.

Martin turned the pages well forward, stopped, smiled, and read out loud: " 'Clarissa. Valley of veneration. Cave of nuances. Isosceles jungle. Lair of the snake. Grave of the stalker.' " He paused to look at her.

"I know that page by heart," she said.

" 'Grave of the stalker,' " Martin said. "He could be a silly man. I see an erected Hawkshaw. Tell me. Did you ever go round the clock with him for three days as you did with me?"

"That's a very impertinent question. Do you really think I'd tell you?"

"I thought one day you might compare notes on us. I fantasized your reply."

"And naturally you win that contest."

"I didn't think of it as a contest. More a contrast of styles."

"Let me say, and end it here, that exuberance runs in your family."

"Up exuberance," he said, and drank his champagne.

She refilled his glass and raised hers.

"And here," she said, "a toast to my gifts."

"And rare and splendid they are. Up your gifts."

"I was speaking of my gifts to you."

"Gifts, you say. Is there more than one?" And he touched the ledger.

"One more."

"Which one is that?"

"The one and only," she said, and stood up before him and opened her robe to reveal no negligee, only that indelibly remembered torso, with its somewhat graying isosceles jungle trimmed and shaved with supreme care in the contour of a heart.

"It's a bit late in the year," she said, "but will you be my valentine?"

Martin opened his belt, the front buttons of his trousers, the three buttons of the shorts he'd put on clean this morning, and presented to her the second generation stalker, full grown now, oh yes, wrapped in white tissue paper, tied with green ribbon, and tagged with a small card bearing the greeting: Happy Anniversary.

As he made love to Melissa he studied that portion of her neck and breast where his mother had been scarred by the point of a flaming, flying stick in the fire that killed fifteen people, most of them Irish servant girls. Melissa bore no such marks. Her mark was her face, and he kissed it lavishly, loathing both himself and her, loving her with passionate confusion, pitying her the gift of such a face, for it had been her torment. What man could ever think he alone possessed a beauty so famed, so excessive. Who could own Botticelli's Primavera?

His mother's scar had been a white oval with a scalloped circumference where the stitching had drawn her wound together. He closed his eyes as he kissed Melissa, and behind him the white scar grew by itself, a floating ovoid that became witness to his act. The scar swelled, and Martin thought of the flaming ball of tow that had marked the elder Henry James, playing in Albany Academy park, the park on which Katrina's Elk Street home fronted. The young James, then only thirteen, had been flying hot-air balloons, which rose skyward when the flaming tow balls were placed beneath them. One James balloon ascended from the park and when the flaming tow ball fell to earth, someone kicked it and arced it into the hayloft of a livery stable across Washington Avenue. The conscientious James ran to the stable to put out the fire, but his pants leg had been splashed by turpentine from soaking the tow, and it ignited like the tail of a comet. The burns led to amputation, creating a mystic philosopher from an incipient outdoorsman, and changing the future of American culture. Serendipitous movement from Edward to Melissa to Henry to Martin. Bright flaming people in a roundelay of accidental life that alters the world.

The scar grew behind Martin, its center becoming the most brilliant of all possible whites. Martin saw to it that the animal-child was seated on the chair beside the hotel bed in a typical spectator's position.

The animal-child watched the cleansing siege of the taboo, unaware the maternal flame was flirting blindly with his presence. The divine figure saw too late the advent of love's flaming embrace, and he ignited with a rasping, crackling brilliance. He tried to scream but the sound caught in his immaterial throat, and he was suddenly ashes, a spume of sooty flakes flying upward. To heaven? To hell?

Martin ejaculated with an onrush of benediction.

Aware that Melissa had been shorted on the significance of the moment, Martin manipulated her vigorously into a writhing, low-level ecstasy. This, she sadly admitted, was the only estate she could inhabit since her hysterectomy four years before. When her ovaries were taken from her, something else went with them. Oh, she could approach climax, almost peak. But there was a point beyond which nothing would take her. She had tried. Oh, how she had tried. Poor little one. And now she gave what could be given, took what must be taken. Her explanation sounded vaguely biblical to Martin, as if she read Saint Augustine hopefully every time the nuances flooded her cave.

Yet Martin could not escape the notion that his presence here at this altar of hand-me-down flesh was in some way therapistic, that he was expected to remantle the wings of Melissa's passion, that his time with her a decade ago had been as maleficent for her as it had for him, that she was searching in his flaming ashes for a new display of her own lost fireworks. They're not really all gone, are they, Daddy?

He rubbed, oh, how he rubbed. She tried, oh, how she tried.

But when she exploded it was only with exhaustion, to save her heart's wearying ventricle.

They dressed and rested and poured new champagne, and Melissa ate a piece of melon standing up. Martin sat on the sofa trying to understand the meaning of what he had just gone through. He was unable to grasp the significance of so many people suddenly webbed in the same small compass of events. He dismissed coincidence as a mindless explanation of anything. Was it his mind discovering patterns that had always existed but that he, in his self-absorption, had never noticed? But how? He was a fairly perceptive man. More than that, he was foresightful. Even now he had the impulse to call the newspaper, for what reason he did not know. Emory would not be in yet, and he had no reason to speak with anyone else.

He went to Melissa's bedroom and sat on the rumpled bed, still damp with drops of love and loathing, and asked the hotel operator to ring the *Times-Union*. When Madge, the crone, answered, all he could think to ask was whether anyone had left him a message. "Yes," said Madge, "some bozo named Franny Phelan called. He's in jail and wants you to bail him out."

Martin went back to the couch.

"Did you ever hear my father speak of having a gift of foresight, or anything comparable?" he asked Melissa.

"I remember he was superstitious," she said. "He used to throw salt over his shoulder when it spilled and he had a lucky pair of pants. They were green with small checks. I can still see them. He almost never wore them except when he needed money, and he swore that when he put them on, money started to trickle in. We were standing in the middle of Fourteenth Street one afternoon and he was wearing a blue suit and he didn't have enough money to buy our lunch at Luchow's. 'Nobody knows I need money,' he said. 'How could they? I don't have my green pants on.' We went to his rooms and he put the pants on, and the next day he got a bank draft in the mail for eleven hundred dollars from a producer."

Martin felt a lazy rapture come over him looking at Melissa, the golden bird of paradise. Yet, he resented the intimacy such a story reflected, and the pain it caused his mother in her grave. It was the first time he'd ever heard of clairvoyance in anyone else in the family. But Martin quickly decided his father, through telepathy with the producer, learned of the money on the way and put on the green pants as a way of turning the vision into something magical but not quite serious. It was not the same gift as his own. No.

"You're going now, aren't you?" Melissa said.

"I had a call at the paper. An old neighbor of mine's in jail and wants my help."

"I could tell by your face you were going to leave me."

"What is it? Do you want to talk? I don't have to go right this minute."

"I don't see you in ten years and you pop in and use me like a Klondike whore."

"Use you? Klondike?" Martin's fingers still ached from the reciprocal friction.

"You drink my champagne and eat my food and exploit my body and leave me alone with my energy. You use me." She hurled a croissant at him. It missed him and bounced off a lampshade.

"You crazy bitch," he said. "You're as crazy as my mother."

He pulled her robe off her shoulders, pinning her arms to her side. Then he dragged her to the floor and undid his trousers.

How do I use thee? Let me count the ways. As a sacred vessel to be violated. As a thief of Holy Writ. As the transcendent trinity: Melissa-Katrina-Marina, which my father discovered and loved; which I now love. As my father immortalized them all, like the figures on the Grecian urn, so do I now perceive them in all their lambent lunacy. Seeing with my father's eyes and knowing how he was victimized by glory and self-absorption, I now forgive the man his exorbitant expectations, his indifference, his absence. Once forgiven, it is a short walk to forgive myself for failing to penetrate such passionate complexity as his. Forgiving myself, I can again begin to love myself. All this, thanks to the use of the fair Melissa.

As he pronged the dying fire, Martin sensed the presence of his parents in the room, not as flaming balls of tow this time, but as a happy couple, holding hands and watching him do diddle with Melissa for them, just as he had once done proud piddle for them in his personal pot. Clearly, they saw him as the redeemer of all their misalliances, the conqueror of incoherence, the spirit of synthesis in an anarchic family. Martin, in the consanguineous saddle, was their link with love past and future, a figure of generational communion, the father of a son en route to the priesthood, the functioning father of the senile Edward. More than that he had, here, obviously become his own father. He was Edward, son of Emmett Daugherty, father of Martin Daugherty, grandfather of Peter Daugherty, and progenitor of the unchartable Daugherty line to come. Lost son of a lost father, he was now fatherhood incarnate.

Perceiving this, he spent himself in Melissa's ravine of purification.

"You are my yum-yum," she said to him, wholly flattened, the corners of her mouth yanked downward by unseen powers at the center of the earth. She stroked the fluids at the center of herself and sucked the mixture off her middle finger, evoking in Martin a ten-year-old memory of the same act performed at the Hampton. Moved profoundly both by the act and the memory, he loathed himself for his own psychic mendacity, for trying to persuade himself he had other than venereal reasons for jingling everybody's favorite triangle.

Hypocrite!

Lecher!

My boy!

15

Billy found Martin in the news coop of police head-quarters playing knock rummy with Ned Curtin, the *Times-Union's* police reporter. Martin saw Billy and nodded. Then he drew a card and knocked. Ned Curtin slid a dime to him across the desk.

"How come he called you?" Billy said when Martin came out to meet him. They walked together up the stairs, Billy still smelling the pine disinfectant he always associated with this building. Billy had been here only once, five years ago, for dealing cards on Orange Street. He'd been hired by a punk who said he had Bindy's okay to run the game, but didn't, so they pulled everybody in and held them an hour here and then let the players go. But they kept the punk, who had to pay up and do a night in jail.

"I saw him Thursday down in Spanish George's," Martin said, "and I told him to call me if he needed anything."

"You didn't tell me you saw him."

"He didn't want me to. When you see him, you'll know why."

"Why'd you call me now?"

"It'll be in the paper tonight, or maybe even this afternoon, who he is and used to be. You had to know before that."

They sat down on a long, wooden bench in the empty court-

215

room. A white-haired man in shirtsleeves came in from the room behind the judge's bench and sniffed at them, then went out again.

"Did you ever know why he left home?" Billy asked.

"I know the gossip. He drank, then the baby died. The one fed the other."

"I was nine."

"Do you remember him well? You could at nine."

"I don't know if I remember his face from seeing it, or from the picture. There's one home in a box of snapshots, about nineteen fifteen, the year before he left. He's standing on our old stoop on Colonie street."

"He was all done with baseball then. I can remember how he looked. He doesn't look like that any more."

With a magnifying glass, Billy had studied how his father wore his sweater, the same one he wore in the rowboat, and maybe the same cap. He studied the cut of his jaw, the shape of his eyes, and his smile, the lips open and twisted a little to the left. It was a good smile, a strong smile. But Billy's mother said it was a weak thing to leave us and drink so much. A man shouldn't be weak like that, she said. But, oh my, how he cried, she said. How we all cried.

"Here," said Martin, nudging Billy. Through an open door they saw men entering the hallway behind the courtroom. One guard in blue shirt and policeman's cap walked ahead of the prisoner, and one behind him. Billy was not prepared for this sight. It was Pete the Tramp without a hat, without the spiky mustache, without the comedy. When tramps came to the house and asked for a meal, Billy's mother always fed them, and gave them coffee with milk. Now he knew why. Billy and Martin followed the procession. The tramp dragged his feet, slouched, shuffled on fallen arches, or maybe on stumps with toes frozen and gone. Billy kept his father's dirty

216

gray hair in sight. He did not remember hair on his father, he remembered a cap.

The white-haired man who had sniffed at them turned from the large ledger in which he was writing. Billy remembered seeing the man only last month at Foley's pit in Troy, handling fighting cocks for Patsy McCall. His name was Kelly and he was a hell of a handler.

"What's this?" Kelly said, pen in hand.

"Bail. Francis Phelan," said the first policeman.

"Ah, you're the one," Kelly said, putting down his pen and sticking out his right hand to Francis. "Congratulations. Twenty-one, was it?" And everyone laughed.

"So they say," Francis said.

Billy saw his father's smile and recognized the curve of the lips, but the teeth were brown in front, and there were no teeth at all behind them. The mouth was a dark cavity. The smile was dead.

"Somebody got bail money?" Kelly asked.

"Here," said Billy, and he weaved his way through the men. He counted out four hundred dollars and Kelly took it to the next room and put it in a box in the open safe. Billy looked at his father and received a stare of indifference.

"You a bail bondsman? I don't remember you," Kelly said, his pen poised over the receipt book.

"No," Billy said. "Family."

Kelly handed Billy a receipt, and one of the policemen gave Francis a small white envelope with his belongings. Then both guards left the corridor. Billy, Martin, and Francis stood looking at one another until Martin said, "Let's go," and led the way out the door. He stopped at the top of the stairs.

"Martin, thanks for fixing it up," Francis said.

"Not at all. I told you to call me."

"You know a lawyer who'll take me on?"

"I do. Marcus Gorman, the best in town. I already talked to him."

Francis looked at Billy and nodded his head. "You're Billy, ain't you?"

"Yeah," said Billy.

"Thanks for that dough."

"My pleasure."

Francis nodded again. "How you been?"

"Not bad," Billy said. "How about yourself?"

"Well, I ain't in jail." And Francis cackled a throaty laugh, showing his brown teeth and the cavity of his mouth, and fell into a cough that twisted his whole body.

Billy offered him a Camel.

He took it.

They went down the stairs and out the front door onto Eagle Street, confronting a golden October afternoon, the bright sun warming the day with Indian summer's final passion. Men were walking the street in shirtsleeves, and women's dresses still had the look of August about them. The black mood that had fallen on Billy when he first saw his father faded into a new and more hopeful coloration under a sky so full of white, woolly clouds.

The bail almost wiped out Billy's bankroll, but he still had sixty-two dollars and change. It was enough to get the old man a new outfit: shoes, suit, shirt, and tie. Make him look like an American citizen again.

When Martin told Billy about the bail, Billy had immediately said, I got it, I'll go for it. I know it's your money, Martin, but I'll get more. I don't want that money, Martin had said. Forget I ever won that bet. No, I don't forget that, Billy said. What do you do when you lose? You pay.

"I gotta get something in my stomach," Francis said. "I ain't et in two days."

"Didn't they feed you out there in the can?" Billy asked.

"Nothin'd stay down. I still ain't right."

"We can go home. I'll call Peg at the office and have her whip up a meal. She cooks good."

"No," Francis said. "No thanks, no. No."

"Then what do you want?" asked Billy.

"Garlic soup," Francis said. "You know an Italian place? They always got garlic."

"Garlic soup?"

"Lombardo's," Martin said. "First-rate place."

"I don't want no meal," said Francis. "Just garlic soup. Fixes up the stomach. A Mexican bum taught me that in Texas."

"They'll make whatever you want at Lombardo's," said Martin. "But listen, I've got appointments. I'll leave you all to solve the garlic problem."

"No, stick around," Francis said.

"I've got work to do, Fran."

"Nah, nah, nah," said Francis and he grabbed Martin's arm and started to walk with him. "Nah, nah. Stick around a while. It ain't gonna kill you to be seen with an old bum."

"Some of my best friends are bums," said Martin. "The newspaper specializes in them."

"So stick around, stick around."

Billy followed the two men as they all walked down Eagle Street, his father's slouch not so pronounced now, but his shuffle clearly the gimp's gait, left leg dragging. Billy remembered somebody in the family saying Francis was lame, very lame, when he came back to Albany in thirty-five. Whatever it was, he's still got a little of it.

They turned down Hudson Avenue and walked toward the Italian neighborhood, through the farmers' market with its half a hundred trucks, and a scattering of horses and wagons. This had been the city produce market since the days before Francis was born, when everything here was horses and wagons. Billy was maybe six or seven when he gripped his father's hand as they walked among the animals here, smelling the fresh and decaying produce, the fresh and decaying manure, a fluid stench Billy remembered now as clearly as he'd remembered the pine disinfectant. They walked past a spavined animal in its traces, chomping at the feed bag, mashing its leavings with its hind feet, and Billy looked at his father's right hand, the back of it bulging with blue veins and scars Billy did not remember. Then he saw the first two joints were gone from the first finger. Billy pictured them curving around the hand-sewn and soap-rubbed seams of a baseball when his father was instructing him in the ways of an outcurve.

"What happened to your finger?" Billy asked. They were three abreast and he was beside his father.

"What finger?"

"The one that ain't there."

"Oh, that. Some wine bum went nuts and chopped it off. Tried to cut my feet off with a cleaver, but all he got was a piece of the finger."

"Why'd he come after you?"

"He wanted my shoes. I had good-lookin' shoes on and he didn't have none."

"What'd you do to him?"

"I think he went in the river. Somebody told me that."

"When was all this?"

"Hell, I don't know. Ten, twelve years ago. Colorado, I think. Or maybe Idaho."

"You got around some."

"Yowsah. Trains go everywhere."

"Lunch is on me," Billy said.

"Okay by me, Bill."

Bill. That didn't sound right to Billy. People who didn't know him called him Bill. But that's the way it is. He don't know me at all. It then occurred to Billy that he'd known for a day and a half that his father was in town and that he'd made no effort to find him. No effort. None.

"I was never here," Francis said when they walked into the bar of Lombardo's restaurant. "How long's it been here?"

"Must be twenty years," Martin said. "You shouldn't stay away so long."

"Got great Italian roast beef, best in town," Billy said.

"No beef, just soup," Francis said.

They sat in a booth in the bar area, Martin seating himself first, Francis sliding in beside him. At the bar, three young men with black hair and pure white shirts were talking to the bartender. The bar mirror was spotless, and so were the white floor tiles. Only thing old man Lombardo don't have in the joint is dirt. Billy, in his gray gabardine, new last month, and a fresh silk shirt, felt clean to the skin. His father looked dirtier now than he had on the street.

Francis told the chubby waitress the way to make the soup. Boil two garlic cloves in water for five minutes. That's all? No salt, no oregano? No, nothing but the garlic, said Francis.

"You want something to drink?" the waitress asked.

"A double scotch," Billy said.

"I'll have a glass of port," said Martin.

"In that case, muscatel, large," said Francis.

Martin gave Francis the phone number of Marcus Gorman and explained why the best trial lawyer in town might take his case: because the McCalls, up against the wall from the Dewey attack, would be looking for scapegoats, and who'd care if a drifter and runaway husband took the fall? And Gorman would take any case that needled the McCalls, because they had dumped him as their candidate for Congress after a photo of him vacationing in Europe with Legs Diamond appeared in the local papers.

"The McCall people still owe me money," Francis said. "I

221

could pay the lawyer something. I only collected fifty of the hundred and five I got coming."

"Hundred and five," Billy said. "That ain't a bad day's work at the polls."

"I didn't work the whole day," Francis said.

"I doubt they'll pay you that," Martin said. "They'll be afraid of a setup now."

"If they don't, I'll sing to the troopers and take some of them two-bit sonsabitches to jail with me."

"So we both got our problems with the McCalls," Billy said.

"What's your problem?"

"Did you know Bindy's son, Charlie, was snatched?"

"I heard that out in jail."

"So Bindy and Patsy want me to shadow a guy they think might be mixed up in it. Spy on him, pump him, then tell them what he says."

"What's wrong with that?"

"The guy's a friend of mine."

"Yeah, Bill, but don't forget the McCalls got the power. You do a favor for a guy in power, chances are he'll do you one back. That's why I think they won't do nothin' to me after what I done for them."

"I look at it different," Billy said.

"Did anybody hit on you, or anything like that?"

"Not yet, but I'm waiting."

The waitress brought the drinks and Francis drank half of his wine in one draught. He motioned to her for another and fished in his pocket for the white envelope. He took a crisp five dollar bill from it and put it on the table.

"Not a chance," Billy said. "I told you this was on me."

"You said lunch."

"That's everything."

Francis held the fiver up. "The troopers found I had ten of

222

these and they said, How come a bum like you has fifty bucks in new bills? They was old ones, I said. I just sent 'em out to the Chink's to get 'em washed and ironed." He laughed and showed his cavity.

"You didn't ask about my mother," Billy said.

"No, I didn't. How is she?"

"She's fine."

"Good."

"You didn't ask about my sister, either."

"No. How is *she*?"

"She's fine."

"I'm glad they're all right."

"You really don't give a shit about them, or me either, do you?"

"Keep it cool now, Billy," Martin said.

"I'm not anybody you know any more," Francis said. "It ain't personal. I always liked the family."

"That's why you left us?"

"I been leavin' home ever since I was a kid. Martin knows some of that. And I woulda been long gone even before that if only they'da let me. I wanted to go west and work on the railroad but Ma always said the railroad killed my father. He was a boss gandy dancer, and an engine knocked him fifty feet. But what the hell, he couldn'ta been payin' attention. Maybe he was gettin' deef, I don't know. You can't blame the railroad if a man backs his ass into a steam engine. But Ma did and wouldn't let me go."

"Did you hate my mother?"

"Hate her? No. I liked her fine. She was a great girl. We had good times, good years. But I was one of them guys never shoulda got married. And after I dropped the kid, I knew nobody'd ever forgive me, that it was gonna be hell from then on. So I ran."

"You dropped Gerald? I never knew that."

"No?"

"No. Whataya mean dropped?"

"You didn't know?"

"I told you I didn't."

"Somebody knew."

"Peg never knew it, either. Nobody knows it."

"Somebody knows it. Your mother knows it."

"The hell she does."

"She saw it happen."

"She saw it? She never told none of us if she did."

"Nobody?"

"Not even me and Peg, I'm telling you."

"She musta told somebody. Her brother, or her screwball sisters."

"They all talked about you and still do, but nobody ever mentioned that, and they don't keep secrets."

"That's the goddamn truth."

Francis drank the rest of his wine. When the waitress set a new glass in front of him, he immediately drank half of that and stared at the empty seat beside Billy."

"She never told," he said. "Imagine that." He glugged more wine as tears came to his eyes. "She was a great girl. She was always a great girl." Tears fell off his chin into the muscatel.

"Why don't you come home and see her?" Billy said. "Whatever you did, she forgave you for it a long time ago."

"I can't," Francis said and finished the wine. "You tell her I'll come back some day when I can do something for her. And for your sister. And you, too."

"Do what?"

"I don't know. Something. Maybe I'll come by of a Sunday and bring a turkey."

"Who the fuck wants a turkey?" Billy said.

"Yeah," said Francis. "Who does?"

"Come on home and see them, even if you don't stay.

That's something you can do. Never mind the turkey."

"No, Bill, I can't do that. You don't understand that I can't do it. Not now. Not yet."

"You better do it soon. You ain't gonna live forever, the way you look."

"I'll do it one of these days. I promise you that."

"Why should I believe your promises?"

"No reason you should, I guess."

Francis shoved the empty wine glass away and pushed himself sideways out of the booth.

"I gotta get outa here. Tell her I don't want the soup. I gotta get me down to George's and get the rest of my money."

"You're goin'?" Billy said. "You're leavin'?"

"Gotta keep movin'. My bones don't know nothin' about sittin' still."

"You'll get in touch with Gorman yourself, then?" Martin said.

"I'll do that," Francis said. "Righty so."

"That bail money," Billy said. "Don't worry about it. You wanna skip, just skip and forget it. It don't mean anything to me."

"I ain't figurin' to skip," Francis said. "But okay, thanks."

"It doesn't make any sense to skip," Martin said. "You won't do any time with Gorman taking your case. Nobody wants to go to court with him. He turns them all into clowns."

"I'll remember that," Francis said. "Now I gotta move. You understand, Martin."

"I was gonna buy you some new clothes," Billy said.

"Hell, they'd just get dirtied up, the way I bounce around. These clothes ain't so bad."

When he got no response to that, he took a step toward the door and stopped. "You tell the folks I said hello and that I'm glad they're feelin' good."

"I'll pass the word," Billy said.

"Wish you'd let me pay for the drinks. I got the cash." He was halfway into another step and didn't know where to put his hands. He held them in front of his stomach.

Billy just stared at him. Martin spoke up.

"No need for that, Fran. Billy said it was his treat."

"Well, I enjoyed it," Francis said. "Be seein' ya around."

"Around," Billy said.

Billy and Martin sipped their drinks and said nothing.

"He thinks it's all right to fink," Billy said finally, staring at the empty seat.

"I heard what he said."

"He's nothin' like I thought he'd be."

"Who could be, Billy?"

"How could he tell me to rat on a friend?"

"He doesn't understand your situation. He knows better. When he got in trouble in the trolley strike . . . you know about that?"

"He killed a guy."

"Not too many knew, and it never got in the papers who did it. Three of us helped him look for round stones that morning. Patsy McCall, your Uncle Chick, and myself. We were twelve, fourteen, like that, and your father was seven or eight years older and on strike. But we hated the scabs as much as he did and we all had stones of our own. Any one of us might have done what he did, but your father had that ballplayer's arm. He had the fastest throw from third to first I ever saw, and I include Heine Groh. We were down on Broadway in front of the Railroad Y, standing at the back of the crowd. People collected there because they thought the strike talks were going on in the Traction Company building across the street.

"Just then the scabs and the soldiers came along with a trolley and tried to drive it straight through that crowd. It was a bad mistake. There were hundreds ready for them, women too. The women were warriors in the street during that strike. Well, the crowd trapped the trolley between two fires and it couldn't move either way, and that's when the stones flew. Everybody was throwing them, and then Francis threw his. It flew out of his fist like a bullet and caught the scab driver on the head. People turned to see who threw it, but your father was already on the run down Broadway and around the corner of Columbia toward the tracks. The soldiers fired on the crowd, and I saw two men hit. We ran then, too, nobody chasing us, and we saw Francis way off and followed him, and when he saw it was us, he waited. We all thought somebody must've seen him make the throw, so we started running again and went up to the filtration plant in North Albany, about three miles. Your grandfather, Iron Joe Farrell, was caretaker up there then, and he hid Francis in a room full of sinks and test tubes for two hours.

"We all hung around the place while Iron Joe went back up to Broadway and hitched a ride downtown to find out what was up. He learned from a cop he knew that the soldiers were looking for a young man wearing a cap. The cops didn't care about catching your father, of course. They were all with the strikers. But the Traction Company bosses forced them into a manhunt, and so we all knew your father couldn't go back to Colonie Street for a while. Chick went home and packed your father a suitcase and brought it back. Francis said he might head west to play ball somewhere, and if he got a job in a few months, he'd write and tell us.

"He cried then. We all did, over the way he had to go, especially Chick, who worshipped your father. Even Patsy cried a little bit. I remember he wiped his eyes dry with a trainman's blue handkerchief. And then your father walked across the tracks and hopped a slow freight going north to Troy, which was the wrong direction, but that's what he did. And Iron Joe said solemnly that none of us should ever say what we knew, and he told us to go home.

"On the way home, Chick said we should take a blood oath not to talk. Patsy and I said that was okay with us but we didn't know where to get the blood. Patsy wanted to steal a kid from old man Bailey's herd, but Chick said that was against the Seventh Commandment and he suggested Bid Finnerty's one-eyed cat, which everybody on Colonie Street hated as a hoodoo anyway. It took us an hour to find the cat, and then Patsy coaxed it with a fish head and brained it with a billy club so it'd lay still. Chick sliced it open and pulled out its heart and made the sign of the cross in blood on the palms of each of our hands. And I made the oath. We swear by the heart of Bid Finnerty's cat that we won't say what we know about Francis Phelan as long as we live, and that we won't wash this sacrificial blood off our hands until it's time to eat supper.

"The blood was all gone in half an hour, the way we sweated that day. As far as I know, none of us ever said anything until your father came back to town by himself months later, when the baseball season was over in Dayton. He called my father from out there to find out whether it was safe for him to come home to Colonie Street. And it was. And he came home and stayed fifteen years."

"Yeah," Billy said. "He stayed until he killed somebody else."

16

When Martin reached the paper, he found that Patsy McCall had left three messages since noontime. Martin called immediately and Patsy said he didn't want to go near the newspaper but would pick Martin up by the post office dock on Dean Street in ten minutes. His tone admitted of no other possibility for Martin.

Patsy showed up alone, driving his Packard, and when Martin got in, Patsy gunned the car northward on Quay Street and into Erie Boulevard, a little-traveled dirt road that paralleled the old Erie Canal bed, long since filled in. Patsy said nothing. The road bumped along toward the old filtration plant and led Martin to the vision of Francis running, and to echoes of long-dead voices of old North End canalers and lumber handlers. Immigrants looked out forlornly from the canal boats as they headed west, refused entrance to Albany in the cholera days.

Patsy pulled the car to the side of the road in a desolate spot near the Albany Paper Works. Along the flats in the distance Martin could see the tar-paper shacks hoboes had built. Did Francis have a reservation in one?

"They picked Berman as go-between," Patsy said.

During the morning, Morrie had sent word to Bindy through Lemon Lewis that a letter had been left for him at

Nick Levine's haberdashery. "We got Charlie Boy and we want you to negotiate," it said. "If you agree to do this, go to State and Broadway at one o'clock today and buy a bag of peanuts at Coulson's. Cross the street and sit on a bench in the Plaza facing Broadway and feed the pigeons for fifteen minutes." The letter was signed "Nero" and also bore Charlie McCall's signature.

Almost simultaneously Patsy received a letter in his mailbox at the main post office on Broadway, the third letter since the kidnapping. "We want the cash pronto and we are treating your boy nice but we can end that if you don't get the cash pronto. We know all about you people and we don't care about your kind so don't be funny about this." It was also signed "Nero" and countersigned by Charlie.

"You're not surprised they picked Berman?" Martin said.

"Not a bit," said Patsy. "I always thought the son of a bitch was in it."

"But why suspect him out of everybody else?"

"It's an Albany bunch did this, I'll bet my tailbone on that and so will Bindy. They know too much about the whole scene. Berman's always been tied in with the worst of the local hoodlums—Maloy, the Curry brothers, Mickey Fink, Joe the Polack. We know them all, and they'd need Morrie because he's smarter than any of them."

"Me, Patsy. What am I doing here?"

"Morrie's playing cute. He says he really doesn't want to do this thing but he will as a favor. He wants somebody there when they deliver Charlie, a witness who'll take some of the weight off his story. He asked me to pick somebody and when I gave him four or five names, he picked yours. He thinks you're straight."

"What do I do?"

"Go with him. Do what he says and what they tell you to

do. If he's their man, you're ours. And take care of Charlie when you get to him."

"When does this happen?"

"Now. Morrie's waiting for me up in the Washington Park lake house. Can you do it?"

"You'll have to tell Mary something to put her mind at ease. And clue Emory in somehow."

"Here's a couple of hundred for lunch money. And put this in your pocket, too." And Patsy handed Martin a snub-nosed thirty-eight with a fold of money.

"I wouldn't want to use a gun."

"It won't hurt to take it."

Patsy then drove north on Erie Boulevard to Erie Street and turned on it toward Broadway, past the car barns Edward Daugherty had written about. Scabs clung to the frame of a trolley as it rocketed through the gauntlet of stone throwers. Across Erie Street from the barns the old wooden Sacred Heart Church once stood, long gone now, Father Maguire on horseback with his whip, his church plagued by pigs and chickens. God be good to Charlie Boy, and all the sick and simple, and all the unhappy dead in Purgatory, and Mama and Papa.

Patsy drove up Broadway through North Albany and up Lawn Avenue to Wolfert's Roost, where the tony Irish played golf. Martin took Peter there one day and the boy fired a hole in one on a par three and thought he'd learned the secret of the game. The car sped along Northern Boulevard, through a rush of memories now for Martin, who considered that on this day, or another very soon, he might be dead. All the history in his head would disappear, the way his father's history was fading into whiteness.

Patsy drove over Northern Boulevard and into Washington Park, past the statues of Robert Burns and Moses, and up to the gingerbread yellow-brick lake house. Patsy parked and Martin got out of the car and stared at a stunning sight: a maple tree shedding its yellow leaves in a steady, floating rain. The leaves fell softly and brilliantly into a perfect yellow circle, hundreds of them constantly in the air, an act of miraculous shedding of the past while it was still golden. The tree was ancient, maybe as old as the park, or older. Martin had walked through the park with his father an age ago. Young people with sleds rolled in the snow and embraced and kissed behind bushes glittering with icy lace. Young people rode together in the summer in open carriages. They held hands and walked around the spectacular Moses fountain. Martin's father stood at the edge of these visions, watching. This is no country for old men, his father said. I prefer, said Edward Daugherty, to be with the poet, a golden bird on a golden bough, singing of what is past.

The land was a cemetery before it was a park. To prepare the park, men dug up the old bones and carted them to new cemeteries north of the city.

"Come on, let's move," Patsy said to Martin.

Martin touched the pistol in his pocket and took a final look at the yellow rain of leaves, a sunburst of golden symmetry. On a day such as this, God rescued Isaac from his father's faith.

Morrie Berman, looking sharp in a gray fedora and blue pinstripe suit, sat alone on a bench inside the desolate lake house, legs spread, elbows on knees, blowing smoke rings at the tile floor. He stood up and stepped on his cigarette when Patsy came through the door. Patsy shook his hand and said, "I brought our friend." Then Martin too shook Morrie's hand, enriching with a quantum leap his comprehension of duplicity.

"They just said a heavy no to the twenty," Morrie told Patsy. "I got the message just before I came up here."

"What else did they say?"

"They think you're trying to chisel them. They called you a muzzler and said they want at least seventy-five."

"I got everything here the family can scrape together," Patsy said, tapping the black leatherette suitcase he carried in his left hand. "Matt just came back from New York with the last five and now there's forty here. And that's all there is, Morrie, that's all there is. I don't even have enough left for a shave. Morrie, you know we wouldn't chisel on Charlie's life. You got to make them know that."

"I'll do my level best, Patsy."

"I know you will, Morrie. You're one in a thousand to do this for us."

Patsy handed Morrie the suitcase. "Count it, make sure."

Morrie opened the suitcase and riffled swiftly, without counting, through the wrapped tens and twenties, then closed it.

"What about their letters?"

Patsy took a white envelope from his inside pocket and handed it to Morrie.

"One more thing. How do I account for all this cash if I get stopped?"

Pat took the envelope back from Morrie and wrote on it: "To whom it may concern. Morris Berman is carrying this money on a business errand for me. To confirm this, call me collect at one of these telephones." And he wrote the numbers of his home and his camp in the Helderberg Mountains, and then signed it. Patrick Joseph McCall.

"Is there anything special I need to know?" Martin asked.

"Morrie will tell you everything," Patsy said. "Just do what needs doing."

"They didn't like it you were a newspaperman," Morrie said, "but I convinced them you were okay."

"Do we need my car?" Martin asked.

"We drive mine," said Morrie.

"You tell them we want that boy back safe," Patsy said.

Morrie smiled and Patsy embraced him.

"They'll know if I'm followed," Morrie said.

"You won't be followed."

And then the three men went out of the lake house, one behind the other. Indian file. The truculent Mohawks once walked this same patch of earth. The Mohawks were so feared that one brave could strike terror into a dozen from another tribe. When the six tribes met to talk of land on Long Island ceded to the white man in exchange for guns and wampum, the lone Mohawk delegate asked whose decision it had been to cede the land. The Long Island chief said it was his. The Mohawk then stood up from his place in the tribal circle, scalped the chief, and left the meeting, a gesture which called the validity of the land transaction into some question.

In 1921, when Martin walked through the park with his father, they talked of Martin's novel in progress. Martin had just returned from Europe, where he had written about the war. His articles had been published chiefly in the Albany press by Martin H. Glynn, and several of his longer pieces were printed in The Atlantic and Scribner's and the North American Review, which had once printed the writing of his father. Certain editors regarded Martin as a writer of notable talent and encouraged him to challenge it. Accordingly, he wrote two-thirds of a novel about reincarnation.

He traced the story of the soul of the Roman soldier who diced for Christ's cloak, and who was subsequently to live as an Alexandrian fishwife, a cooper in Constantinople, a roving gypsy queen, a French dentist, the inventor of a spring popularized by Swiss watchmakers in the late seventeenth century, a disgraced monk in Brittany, a bailiff in Chiswick, an Irish sailor in the American Fenian movement, and finally a twentieth-century Mexican trollop who marries into the high society of Watervliet.

"You have excellent language at your disposal, and a talent for the bizarre," said the elder Daugherty, "but the book is foolish and will be judged the work of a silly dilettante. My advice is to throw it away and refrain from writing until you have something to say. A novel, Martin, is not a book of jokes."

As a retort, Martin told his father of a former schoolmate, Howie McMahon, who was obsessed with the fate of the oiler in Crane's open boat. Howie taught it to his students at Albany State Teachers College, wrote of it, spoke frequently of it to Martin. My struggle, Howie said, has no more meaning than the life of the oiler with his lifeless head bobbing in the surf after such a monumental struggle to survive. The oiler lived and died to reveal to me the meaning of his life: that life has no meaning. And Howie McMahon, Martin told his father, on a Sunday morning while the family was at high mass, hanged himself from a ceiling hook in the coal bin of his cellar.

"My response to the ravings of a lunatic like your friend," said Edward Daugherty, "is that whether he knows it or not, his life has a meaning that is instructive, if only to illuminate the impenetrability of God's will. Nothing is without purpose in this world."

Martin plucked a crimson leaf from a maple tree and tore it into small pieces.

"That leaf," said the elder writer, "was created to make my point."

17

By late afternoon on Saturday, the Albany newspaper and wire service editors decided they could no longer withhold news of the kidnapping from the world, and they told this to Patsy McCall. He said he understood but had no further comment. At seven o'clock Saturday night, sixty-three hours after Charlie had been taken, his story was told in print for the first time. Headlines seemed not to have been so fat and febrile since the Roosevelt landslide.

The nation's press sent its luminaries of the word to Albany to pursue the story: Jack Lait, Meyer Berger, James Kilgallen, and Damon Runyon among many, forcing comparisons with the 1931 killing of Legs Diamond in an Albany rooming house, the last time America had cast such a fascinated eye on the underside of Albany life.

Shortly after nine-thirty Saturday night, Billy bought one of the last of the *Times-Union* extras, an early edition of the Sunday paper, at the Union Station newsstand. The story of the kidnapping carried Martin's byline. Billy read his own name in the story. No mention was made of any intermediary having been chosen, and no member of the McCall family would speak for publication.

The confirming source for all information was the district attorney, Dick Maloney, who complained that neither he nor the police could convince the McCalls to cooperate with their investigation. Governor Herbert Lehman suggested a reward for the capture of the kidnappers but Patsy told the governor, no, this is between us and them.

Billy folded the newspaper, shoved it into his coat pocket and crossed Broadway to Becker's. The bar was busy, but he found a spot and caught Red Tom's eye. Red Tom nodded but made no move to come near him. "A beer, Tom," Billy finally said, and Red Tom nodded again, drew a beer, and placed it in front of Billy.

"Only one, Billy."

"What do you mean, only one?"

Red Tom put up his hands, palms out, and said nothing. A stranger at the bar looked Billy over, and Red Tom walked away. Billy sipped his beer and waited for enlightenment. When the stranger left the bar, Red Tom came down to Billy and whispered: "Gus don't want your business."

"Why not?"

"I don't know. What'd you do to him?"

"Nothing. I haven't saw Gus in weeks to talk to. And I don't owe him a nickel."

"Tell Billy Phelan we don't want his business is his exact words," said Red Tom. "Why not? I says to him. Because he's no good, he says. Wait a minute, I says to him, Billy is all right, he's a good friend of mine. Okay, you open up your own place and serve him. Here he don't get served, do you get my meaning? I get his meaning. I can't serve you, Billy, and I don't know why. Do you know?"

"Maybe I know," Billy said.

"We're friends, Billy, but I got to work."

"I know that. I don't blame you for anything."

"If I did own the joint, nobody'd keep you out."

Billy managed a small smile and finished his beer. "Have you seen Martin tonight?"

"Not yet. He must be on the story."

"I'll catch you later, Tommy."

And Billy went out of Becker's, feeling a door close on his life when the outside door clicked behind him. He stood looking around Broadway, which was at its Saturday night brightest, bustling with the traffic of cars and people, the usual bunch thickened by the showgoers and nightclubbers.

Not wanted in Becker's? That's like a ball game with no home plate.

Billy walked down Broadway and up the stairs into the Monte Carlo. The horse room was dark but the bird cage, the crap table, and two roulette wheels were all busy, and in the back Billy saw lights on in the card room. He stepped to the crap table, where Marty Mitchell was on the stick and Bill Shea, who ran the Monte Carlo for Bindy, was watching the play. Billy didn't know the shooter, who was trying to make a six. He made it, and then threw an eleven. He doubled his bet to forty dollars and threw a seven. "That's five passes," somebody whispered, and Billy pulled out the exchequer, sixty-two dollars, and put twenty on the come line.

"That twenty is dead," Bill Shea said, and the game stopped.

"What's the problem?" Billy said as the stickman nudged the twenty off the line and back toward Billy.

"No problem," Shea said. "Your money's no good here, Phelan."

"Since when?"

"Since now. And you're not wanted on the premises."

"Is this Bindy's orders?"

"I wouldn't know that. Now, be a good fellow and take your money and get out."

Billy put the twenty around the rest of his cash and backed away from the table under the silent eyes of the players. As he went out the door, the game resumed and the stickman called: "Seven again." Billy walked slowly down to the street.

He found the same response in three more Broadway bars, in Louie's pool room and at Nick Levine's card game. Nick, like Red Tom, apologized. No one gave Billy a reason for turning him away. In Martha's, he sat at the bar and she poured him a double scotch and then told him he'd been marked lousy.

"It was Bindy, I know that much," Billy said. "When did you hear about it?"

"This afternoon," Martha said.

"How?"

"Mulligan, the ward leader, called me. Said you might be mixed up in the kidnapping and to give you the treatment. I said, I got no argument with Billy, and he said, You don't do what I ask, your taxes go through the roof. So bottoms up, honey, and find someplace else to drink."

"That's a lie about the kidnapping. They wanted me to inform on somebody and I wouldn't. That's what it's about."

"Don't make no difference to me what it's about. Them taxes are what this place is about all of a sudden. They go through the roof, Martha goes back on the street, and Martha's too old for that."

"I'm not your problem, Martha. Don't worry."

"You hear about Louie?"

"Louie?"

"Louie Dugan. He died about two this afternoon. Cop who took him to the hospital last night came by and took a statement. I liked that crazy old man. He was mean as a goose but I liked him."

"What'd he die of?"

"Stuff he swallowed in his lungs, the cop says. Drink up, Billy. Don't make me no trouble."

"I'll catch you later, Martha."

"Not till things is straight. Then you catch me all you like."

Billy called Angie at the Kenmore, and while he waited for her room to ring he decided to ask her: How'd you like some fingerprints on your buns? But what he really wanted was to talk to her. Her phone never rang. The operator said she'd checked out and left no message. He went up to the Kenmore anyway and found the bar was out of bounds for him. Wally Stanton, a bartender, said the word came from Poop Powell, not Mulligan. Bindy had a whole team on the street fencing Billy out. Broadway gone, now Pearl Street.

He walked up Pearl toward Clinton Avenue and stopped in front of Moe Cohen's old jewelry store. Now the store was a meat market and Moe was meat, too; hired three punks to get himself killed, gave them five grand in diamonds and two hundred in promised cash. They shot him in the head and all it give him was a headache, and he says, Do something else, I'm dying of cancer and heart trouble, hurry, and they let him have it in the wrist and then in the shoulder and hit him with seven shots before they got one through the eye to do the trick. When they checked his pants for the two hundred, all they found was twenty-eight cents. The bum robbed us. They all went to jail, but nobody could figure out why Moe wanted to die. He didn't have cancer or heart trouble, he had something else.

My father has something else, is what Billy thought.

He thought of Moe among the sausages and turned around and headed toward South Pearl Street. Clinton Avenue would be fenced off by Bindy, too, but he probably wouldn't bother with State Street or South Pearl. That wasn't Billy's territory. Billy might even get a game on Green Street. Dealers didn't know him very well there. But the Cronins ran Green

Street for Bindy and they knew Billy and they'd get the word around sooner or later. It'd be a game of recognition. Anybody know Billy Phelan? Throw the bum out. What it came down to was Billy could go anyplace they didn't recognize him, anyplace he'd never been before. Or he could leave town. Or hire some of those fellows like Moe. Or go off the Hawk Street viaduct like Georgie the Syph.

No.

All his life Billy had put himself into trouble just to get himself out of it. Independent Billy. Now, you dumb bastard, you're so independent you can't even get inside to get warm, and it's getting chilly. Night air, like watching the last games of the Albany baseball season. Up high in Hawkins Stadium and the wind starts to whizz a little and you came in early when it was warm and now you're freezing your ass only the game ain't over.

Tommy Dyke's Club Petite? No. Bob Parr's Klub Eagle? No. Packy Delaney's Parody Club? No. Big Charlie's? No. Ames O'Brien's place? No.

Billy didn't want to think about his problem in solitude. He wanted to watch something while he was thinking.

The University Club? Dopey B-girls. Club Frolics? The emcee stinks.

Hey. The Tally Ho on Hudson Avenue. Billy knew the Hawaiian dancer. She was Jewish. And the comic was Moonlight Brady. Billy went to St. Joseph's school with him. He turned off Pearl toward the Tally Ho.

Billy ordered a triple scotch and kept his hat on. The place was jammed, no elbowroom at the bar. The lights were dim while the adagio dancers did their stuff. When the lights went up Billy looked at the half-naked-lady mural among the champagne glasses and bubbles on the wall. Some singer did a medley of Irish songs, for what? It ain't Saint Patrick's Day.

The shamrocks are growing on Broadway. Oh yeah. And the Hudson looks like the Shannon. Right. Betty Rubin, the Hawaiian dancer, had fattened up since Billy last saw her and since Billy likes 'em thin, he'll keep his distance and check out the toe dancer.

Billy had been chain smoking for an hour and the tip of his tongue was complaining. He wanted to punish himself for his independence. He could punish himself by going to Bindy and apologizing. Yes, you may kiss my foot. He'd already punished himself by throwing the pool match to the Doc.

Moonlight Brady came on and told a joke about Kelly, who got drunk and fell into an open grave and when he woke up he thought it was Judgment Day and that an Irishman was the first man up. He sang a song: Don't throw a brick at your father, you may live to regret it one day.

Billy's brain was speeding from the scotch, speeding and going sideways. Moonlight came out to the bar when the show ended, a chunky man with a face like a meat pie. All ears and no nose so's you'd notice and built like a fire plug. Billy bought him a drink to have someone to talk to. He would not apologize to Bindy, he decided, but what else he would do was not clear.

"I saw your story in the paper," Moonlight told him.

"What story?"

And Moonlight told him about Martin's column on the two-ninety-nine game and the hex. Billy took the paper out of his pocket and found the column and tried to read it but the light was bad.

"I bowled two-ninety-nine and two-ninety-seven back to back about six years ago," Moonlight said.

"Is that so?"

"Damndest thing. I was in Baltimore and just got red hot."

Billy smiled and bought Moonlight another drink. He was the greatest liar Billy ever knew. You wouldn't trust him if he just came out of Purgatory. He dove into Lake George one day and found two corpses. He put a rope around his chest and swam across Crooked Lake pulling three girls in a rowboat. He was sitting at a table with Texas Guinan and Billy Rose the night Rose wrote the words to "Happy Days and Lonely Nights." He gave Bix Beiderbecke's old trumpet to Clara Bow, and she was such a Bix fan she went to the men's room with Moonlight and he screwed her on the sink. He pimped once for John Barrymore in Miami and got him two broads and a dog. He took care of a stable of polo ponies for Big Bill Dwyer, the rum-runner. Billy's line on Moonlight was that some guys can't even lay in bed straight.

Morrie Berman was probably one of those guys. What if he was in on the kidnap? They took Charlie Boy's world away from him and maybe they'll even kill him. When Billy's father was gone for a year, his Uncle Chick told him he might never come back and that Billy would pretty soon forget his father and develop all sorts of substitutes, because that was how it went in life. Chick was trying to be kind to Billy with that advice. Chick wasn't as bad as the rest of them. And did Billy develop substitutes for his father? Well, he learned how to gamble. He got to know Broadway.

He wanted to see his father and ask him again to come home.

If there was a burlesque show in town he'd go to it.

He watched Betty Rubin, who was beginning to look good.

Billy hated the sons of bitches who closed the town to him, including Red Tom, you prick. Why don't you yell at them that it ain't right to do such a thing?

He would not test out any more places. He would do something else.

Tough as Clancy's nuts.

And to think, Billy, that you were afraid they'd mark you lousy if you finked.

"Oh yeah, I forgot," Moonlight Brady said. "I saw your father's name in the paper. That vote business. Funny as a ham sandwich on raisin bread."

"That's in the paper, too?"

"Same paper. They mentioned how he played ball so I knew it was him."

"Where's your father now, Moonlight?"

"He died ten years ago. Left me a quarter of a million he made on the stock market, every nickel he had, and I went through it in eighteen months. But it was a hell of an eighteen months. What a guy he was."

Billy laughed at that. It was one of Moonlight's wilder, more unbelievable lies, but it had what it takes, and Billy's laughter grew and grew. It took on storm proportions. He coughed and tears came to his eyes. He hit the bar with his hand to emphasize the power of the mirth that was on him, and he took out his handkerchief to wipe his eyes.

"What got him?" the barman asked.

"I did," Moonlight said, "but I don't know how." Moonlight was doing his best to keep smiling. "If the line is that funny, I oughta use it in the act," he said to Billy.

"Oh absolutely, Moonlight, absolutely," Billy said. "Use that one in the act. You gotta use that one in the act."

Billy walked down Green Street and looked at the whorehouses with their awnings, the sign. They were houses that used to be homes for Irish families like his own. Chinks on the street now, and second-hand clothing stores and the grocery where George used to write numbers upstairs. Bucket-of-blood joints and guinea pool rooms where the garlic smell makes you miscue. Bill Shea lives on Green Street, the son of a bitch. Billy brought him home one night in a cab, sick drunk from Becker's, and he forgets that and says my twenty is dead.

Billy walked into a telephone pole.

Really in the guinea section now. Billy went with a guinea for two years. Teresa. Terrific Teresa. A torch singer. "Along Came Bill," she'd sing when he showed up. She wanted to get married, too.

Angie, you bitch, where are you when I need you?

Would Billy marry Angie? "Frivolous Sal." Peculiar gal.

Angie got Billy thinking about marriage, all right, and now he thinks of Peg and George and the house they've got, and Danny. They can't fence you out of your own house. They can't fence you away from your kid.

His father fenced himself out of the house because he thought they were ready to fence *him* out.

Billy can hear a mandolin being played in a second-floor apartment and he can taste the dago red. He got drunk once on dago red with Red the Barber, dago red and mandolins, and he went out like a light and woke up the next day and lit a cigarette and was drunk all over again. So he don't drink dago red no more.

After he crossed Madison Avenue, the bum traffic picked up. He turned on Bleecker Street toward Spanish George's. It was moving toward eleven o'clock. Hello, Bill.

The stench of Spanish George's hit Billy in the face when he walked through the door, the door's glass panel covered with grating on both sides. A dozen bums and a woman were huddled around five round wooden tables, three of the bums asleep, or dead. The stench of their breath, their filth, their shitty drawers, the old puke on their coats and shirtfronts, rose up into Billy's nose like sewer gas.

George was behind the bar in his sombrero, propped

against the wall on the back legs of a wooden chair. Billy ordered a scotch, and George delivered it in a shot glass. Billy tossed it off and asked for another.

"You know anybody named Francis Phelan?" he asked George.

George eyed him and touched the handle of his six gun.

"You ain't a copper. I know coppers. Who are you?"

"I'm a relative. The guy's my father."

"Whoosa guy you want?"

"Francis Phelan."

"I don't know nobody that name."

Billy ordered another scotch and took it to the only empty table in the room. The floor beneath his feet had been chewed up long ago by old horses' hooves and wagon wheels. It looked like the faces in the room, old men with splintered skin. The wagons of the old days had rolled over them, too, many times. Most of them seemed beyond middle age, though one with a trimmed mustache looked in his thirties. Yet he was a bum, no matter what he did to his mustache. His eyes were bummy and so were his clothes. He was at the table next to Billy and he stank of old sweat, like Billy's locker at the K. of C. gym. Billy was in the Waldorf one night, and an old drunk was raving on about his life. Not a bum, just an old man on a drunk, and he looked clean. He got Billy's eye and told him, Son, have B.O. and they'll never forget you.

Unforgettable stench of right now. They oughta bottle the air in this joint and sell it for stink bombs.

The man with the mustache saw Billy looking at him.

"You fuck around with me," the man said, "I'll cut your head off." The man could barely lift his glass. Billy laughed out loud and other men took notice of him. He could lick any four of them at once. But if they got him down, they'd all kick him to death. Billy saw that the men had no interest in him beyond the noise he made when he laughed.

The woman at the far table was drinking beer and sitting upright and seemed the soberest one in the room, soberer than Billy. Old bat. Fat gut and spindle legs, but her face wasn't so bad. She wore a beret off to the left and smoked a cigarette and stared out the front window, which was also covered with grating. Bums like to put their hands through windows. And their heads.

The man next to the woman lay with his face on the table. He moved an arm, and Billy noticed the coat and remembered the twill. Billy went across the room and stood beside the woman and stared down at his father. The old man's mouth was open and his lips were pushed to one side so that Billy could see part way into the black cavity that had once been the smile of smiles.

"I don't want any," the woman said.

"What?"

"Whatever it is you're gonna ask."

"Conalee Street."

"I don't want any."

"Neither do I."

"Go way and leave me alone. I don't want any."

"Is he all right?"

"Go way."

"Is he all right? I asked a polite question."

"He's all right if he ain't dead."

Billy grabbed a handful of her blouse and coat just below the neck and lifted her halfway to her feet.

"Holy Mother of God, you're as crazy as two bastards."

"Is he hurt?"

"No, he's passed out, and he'll probably be out for hours."

"How do you know that?"

"Because he drank whiskey. He had money and he drank whiskey till he fell over. He never drinks whiskey. Who the hell are you?"

"I'm a relative. Who are you?"

"I'm his wife."

"His wife?"

"You got very good hearing."

"His wife?"

"For nine years."

Billy let go of her coat and slumped into an empty chair beside her.

When he told his mother he'd met him he made sure Peg was in the room. They sat in the breakfast nook, just the three of them, George still working. Billy was looking out at the dog in the back yard, and he told them all that had happened and how he wouldn't come home. The response of the women bewildered Billy. His mother smiled and nodded her head. Peg's mouth was tight, the way it gets when she fights. They listened to it all. He didn't say anything about Gerald just then. Just the bail and the turkey and the money he had and the way he looked and the change Billy saw from the photograph. I'm goddamn glad you didn't bring him home, Peg said. I don't ever want to see him again. Let him stay where he is and rot for all of me. And Ma said, No, the poor man, the poor, poor man, what an awful life he's had. Think of what a life he could've had here with us and how awful it must've been for him as a tramp. But neither of them said they were sorry he didn't come home. They think of him like he was some bum down the block.

So Billy told them then about Gerald, and Peg couldn't believe it, couldn't believe Ma hadn't told us, and Ma cried because of that and because your father didn't mean it, and how he apologized to her and she accepted his apology, but she was numb then, and he took her numbness for hatred, and he went away. But she wouldn't hold an accident against a man as good as Francis was and who loved the children so

248

and was only weak, for you can hate the weakness but not the man. Oh, we're all so weak in our own ways, and none of us want to be hated for that or killed for that. He suffered more than poor little Gerald, who never suffered at all, any more than the innocents who were slaughtered suffered the way Our Lord suffered. Your father was only a man who didn't know how to help himself and didn't know better. I kept it from you both because I didn't want you to hate him more than you did. You couldn't know how it was, because he loved Gerald the way he loved both of you, and he picked him up the way he'd picked you up a thousand times. Only this time the diaper wasn't pinned right, and that was my fault, and Gerald slipped out of it, and your father stood there with the diaper in his hand, and Gerald was already dead with a broken neck, I'm sure of that, the way his little head was. I'm sure he never suffered more than a pinprick of pain and then he went to heaven because he was baptized, and I thanked God for that in the same minute I knew he was gone. Your father knelt over him and tried to pick him up, but I said, Don't, it might be his back and we shouldn't move him, and we both knelt there looking at him and trying to see if he was breathing, and finally we both knew he wasn't, and your father fell over on the floor and cried, oh, how he cried, how that man cried. And I cried for him as well as for Gerald, because I knew he'd never get over this as long as he lived. Gerald was gone but your father would have to live with it, and so we held one another and in a minute or so I covered him with a blanket and went up the street for Doctor Lynch and told him I put him on the table to change his diaper and then he rolled off and I never knew he could move so much. He believed me and put accidental death on the record, and it surely was that, even though your father was drinking when it happened, which I know is the reason he went away. But he wasn't drunk the way he got to be in the days after that, when he never saw a sober minute. He had just come home after the car barns and a few jars at the saloon, and he wasn't no different from the way he was a thousand other nights, except what he did was different, and that made him a dead man his whole life. He's the one now that's got to forgive himself, not me, not us. I knew you'd never forgive him because you didn't understand such things and how much he loved you and Gerald and loved me in his way, and it was a funny way, I admit that, since he kept going off to play baseball. But he always came back. When he went this time I said to myself, He'll never come into this house again, and he never did, and when we moved here to North Pearl, I used to think, If he does come back he'll go to Colonie Street and never find us, but then I knew he would if he wanted to. He'd find us if he had to.

Sweet Jesus, I never thought he'd come back and haunt you both with it, and that's why I'm telling you this. Because when a good man dies, it's reason to weep, and he died that day and we wept and he went away and buried himself and he's dead now, dead and can't be resurrected. So don't hate him and don't worry him, and try to understand that not everything that happens on this earth has a reason behind it that we can find in the prayer book. Not even the priests have answers for things like this. It's a mystery we can't solve any more than we can solve the meaning of the stars. Let the man be, for the love of the sweet infant Jesus, let the man be.

Billy stared at the woman next to him and smiled.

"What's your name?"

"Helen."

"Do you have any money, Helen?"

"There's a few dollars left of what he had. We'll get a room with that when he wakes up."

Billy took out his money, fifty-seven dollars, and pressed it into Helen's hand.

"Now you can get a room, or get as drunk as he is if you like. Tell him Billy was here to say hello."

Billy tossed the newspaper on the table.

"And tell him he can read all about me and him both in the paper. This paper."

"Who are you?"

"I told you. I'm Billy."

"Billy. You're the boy."

"Boy, my ass. I'm a goddamn man-eating tiger."

He stood up and patted Helen on the beret.

"Good night, Helen," he said. "Have a good time."

"God bless your generosity."

"Generosity can go piss up a rainpipe," Billy said, and he started to laugh. The laugh storm again. The coughing, the tears of mirth. He moved toward Spanish George's door, laughing and telling the old bums who watched him: "Generosity can go piss up two rainpipes for all I give a good goddamn."

He halted in the doorway.

"Anybody here like to disagree with me?"

"You fuck with me," said the bum with the trimmed mustache, "I'll cut your head off."

"Now you're talkin'," Billy said. "Now you're talkin'."

18

Billy could go anywhere now, anywhere in town. He was broke. All the way broke.

He began to run, loping across a vacant lot, where a man was warming himself by a bonfire. It had grown chillier. No place for that fellow to go.

Billy could always get a buck. But where now?

He padded down Madison Avenue to Broadway, where the ramp to the Dunn bridge began. Tommy Kane's garage, where George got his car fixed. He turned up Broadway, still running, putting distance between him and the drunken dead. He wasn't even winded when he reached the Plaza and the D&H building. But he stopped running at Coulson's and went inside for a later edition of the *Times-Union*. The front page was different, but the kidnapping news was the same. He turned to Martin's column and read about himself. A gamester who accepts the rules and plays by them, but who also plays above them. Billy doesn't care about money. A healthy man without need for artifice or mysticism.

What the hell was Martin talking about? Whose rules? And what the hell was that about money? How can anybody not care about money? Who gets along without it? Martin is half crazy, a spooky bird. What is that stuff about mysticism? I still believe in God. I still go to the front.

He folded the paper and went out and crossed State Street and walked north on Broadway past Van Heusen Charles, which always reminded him of the goddamn house on Colonie Street, where they bought their junk. And Cottrell and Leonard and the mannequins in the window. Two bums broke that window one night, drunked up on zodiac juice, everybody's bar dregs, beer, whiskey, wine, that old Lumberg kept in a can and then bottled and sold to the John bums for six bucks a gallon. When the cops caught up with the bums, one of them was dead and the other was screwing the mannequin through a hole cut in its crotch.

Jimmy-Joe's shoeshine stand. Jimmy-Joe told his customers he shined Al Smith's shoes once, and Jack Dempsey's. Everybody's a sucker for big names. Bindy McCall. I kissed Bindy McCall's foot. Suckers.

Broadway was slowing down at one o'clock, all the trains in except the Montreal Limited. Traffic down to nothing, shows all let out. Bill's Magic Shop in darkness. Billy was sweating slightly and breathing heavily. Get the blood pounding and sober up. But he was still drunk as a stewbum, and reeling. Scuse me.

"Where the hell you walkin'?" said Mike the Wop coming out of Brockley's.

"Hey, Mike."

"That you, Billy?"

"Me."

"Whataya know. You got yourself in trouble, I hear."

"What do you hear?"

"That you got yourself in trouble and nobody'll take your action."

"They'll get over it."

"Didn't sound that way."

"Hey, Mike, you got a double sawbuck? I need coffee money and cab fare."

"Double sawbuck?"

"Don'tcha think I'm good for it?"

"You're a bad risk all of a sudden, Billy. You ain't got a connection. You can't even get a drink on this street."

Mike pulled out his roll and crumpled a twenty and tossed it up in the air at Billy. Billy bobbled it and the bill fell to the sidewalk. He picked it up and said nothing. Mike grunted and walked up Broadway and into Becker's. Billy walked toward Clinton Avenue, considering a western at the Grand Lunch. Martha's across the street. Martha's door opened, and Slopie Dodds came out wearing his leg. He saw Billy and crossed the street.

"Hey, man, how you makin' it?"

"I'm coastin', Slope."

"You got a little grief, I hear."

"Little bit."

"How you fixed? You need anything?"

"I need a drink."

"She don't want you over there."

"I know all about that. That ain't the only place in town."

"You ain't mixed up in that snatch, Billy. That ain't true."

"It's bullshit, Slope."

"I knew it was."

"Hey, man. You got a double sawbuck?"

"Sure, I got it. I got fifty if you need it."

"All right, twenty-five. That'll cover me." And Slopie counted it out for Billy.

"Where's your bootlegger?" Billy asked.

"Spencer Street. You want a whole bottle?"

"Yeah. Let me make a visit first and we'll go up."

"Fine with me. I'm done playin'."

They walked back toward the station and Billy went into Becker's. The bar was crowded and Red Tom looked at Billy and shook his head sadly. Oh, Billy. But Billy asked for nothing. He saw Mike the Wop at the bar and went to him. He threw the twenty, still crumpled up, onto the bar in front of Mike and said, "We're even."

"You pay your debts fast," Mike said.

"I pay guys like you fast," Billy said, and he went out. Then with Slopie he walked up to Spencer Street.

The last time Billy needed action from a bootlegger was in Prohibition. And he'd never used a nigger bootlegger before. George had been a bootlegger for about three weeks. Made rye in the kitchen in a wash tub, and Billy peddled it for eight bucks a quart and kept four. Then George got the job writing nigger numbers and gave up the hooch, and a good thing, too, because his rye was moose piss.

The bootlegger was in one of the last houses, a dim light in a first-floor flat. Quarts and pints for five and three, a good price at this hour. The bootlegger was a woolly-headed grandpa, half asleep. Probably made a fortune before it went legal, and now the bottles catch dust. He went to the kitchen to get Billy some Johnnie Walker. Billy opened the bottle and drank and passed it to Slopie.

"Take it outside," the old man said. "This ain't no saloon."

Billy and Slopie went down the stoop and stood on the sidewalk.

"Where you wanna go, Billy?"

"Go someplace and build a fire."

"A fire? You crazy?"

"Gettin' chilly. Need a little heat."

"Go over to my place if you like to warm up. I got some chairs. What the hell you want a fire for?"

"I wanna stay outside. You up for that?"

"Well, I give you a little while. Till my bones freeze over."

"It ain't that cold. Have a drink," and Billy upended the bottle.

"You in a big hurry to fall down tonight, Billy."

255

"I got a hollow leg, Slope."

"You gonna need it."

Slopie took a swallow and they walked toward the river, crossed the D&H tracks, and headed toward the station on a dirt path under the brightest moon Billy ever looked at. Billy picked up wood as they walked, but a bit of kindling was all he found. They walked past the sidings where Ringling Brothers unloaded every year. Billy had brought Danny down here at four in the morning two years ago and they'd seen an elephant get off the train and walk up to Broadway.

"I'm a little cold, Billy. I ain't sure I'm ready for this."

"Down by the river. There'll be some wood there."

They walked toward the bridge, toward Quay Street, and looked at the Hudson. Just like the Shannon. Billy never swam down this far but he skated on it sometimes when it wasn't all buckled, or snowed over.

"Ever skate on the river, Slope?"

"Never owned no skates."

On the riverbank, Billy found a crate somebody had dumped. He broke it up and made a pile on the flat edge of the bank. He wadded up the *Times-Union*, page by page, and stuck it between the boards. In the moonlight he saw the page with Martin's column and crumpled it. But then he uncrumpled it, folded it and put it in his inside coat pocket. He lit the papers, and then he and Slopie sat down on the flat sides of the crate and watched the fire compensate for the shortcomings of the moon.

"I hear Daddy Big kicked it," Billy said.

"What I hear."

"What a way to go."

"You did what you could, Billy. He'da been dead in the gutter on Broadway, wasn't for you."

"I didn't even like the son of a bitch."

"He was a sorry man. Never knew how to do nothin' he

256

wanted to do. He spit in your eye and think he's doin' you a favor."

"He knew how to shoot pool."

"Shootin' pool ain't how you get where you're goin'."

"Goin'? Where you goin', Slope?"

"Goin' home outa here pretty quick and get some winks, wake up and cook a little, see my woman, play a little piano."

"That where you started out for?"

"I never started out for nowhere. Just grifted and drifted all my life till I hit this town. Good old town."

"How is it, bein' a nigger, Slope?"

"I kinda like it."

"Goddamn good thing."

"What, bein' a nigger?"

"No, that you like it."

Billy passed the bottle and they drank and kept the fire going until a prowl car came by and put its searchlight on them.

"Everything all right here, girls?" one cop asked.

"Who you talkin' to, peckerhead?" Billy said. Slopie grabbed his arm and kept him from standing up. The cops studied the scene and then moved on. The fire and the moon lighted up the night, and Billy took another drink.

He woke up sick. Slopie was gone and Billy remembered him trying to talk Billy into going back to Broadway. But Billy just burned the rest of the crate to keep the fire going. He remembered watching the fire grow and then fade, remembered watching the night settle in again without heat, with even the light gone cold. The darkness enveloped him under the frigid moon, and he lay back on the grass and watched the sky and all them goddamn stars. The knowledge of what was valuable in his life eluded him, except that he valued Slopie now as much as he valued his mother, or Toddy.

But Slopie was gone and Billy felt wholly alone for the first time in his life, aware that nothing and no one would save him from the coldness of the moon and the October river.

He heard whisperings on the water and thought they might be the spirits of all the poor bastards who had jumped off the bridge, calling to him to make the leap. He became afraid and listened for the voices to say something he could understand, but they remained only whisperings of words no man could understand at such a distance. They could be understood out on the water. He edged himself upward on the bank, away from the voices, and took a drink of whiskey. He was still drunk and he had a headache. He was out of focus in the world and yet he was more coherent than he had been since this whole business began. He knew precisely how it was before the kidnapping and how it was different now, and he didn't give a shit. You think Billy Phelan gives a shit about asskissers and phonies? Maybe they wanted Billy to run. Maybe they thought if he got shut out of a joint like Becker's, he'd pack his bag and hop a freight. But his old man did that, and all he got was drunk.

The fire was out, and so Billy must have slept a while. He felt an ember. Cold. Maybe he'd slept an hour.

What I learned about pool no longer applies.

What Daddy Big learned no longer applies.

He took a swig of the whiskey, looked at the bottle, still half full, and then flung it into the river.

He saw a train coming in over the Maiden Lane trestle and watched the moving lights. He stood up and saw mail trucks moving in the lights of the post office dock on Dean Street. Up on the hill, he could see lights in the Al Smith building, and street lights blazed across the river in Rensselaer. People all over town were alone in bed. So what the hell's the big deal about being alone in the dark? What's the big deal about being alone?

258

Billy saw the elephant going up toward Broadway, a man walking beside it, holding its ear with a long metal hook on a stick.

Billy brushed off the seat of his pants, which was damp from the earth. He went to touch the brim of his hat but he had no hat. He looked around but his hat was gone. The goddamn river spirits got it. What do they want with my hat? Well, keep it. That's all you're gonna get out of me, you dead bastards.

Billy knew he was going to puke. He kept walking and after a while he puked. Good. He wiped his mouth and his eyes with his handkerchief and straightened his tie. He brushed grass off the sleeves of his coat, then took the coat off and brushed its back and put it on again. He bent over and pulled up his silk socks.

He walked toward Broadway.

No money.

No hat.

No connection.

The street was bright and all but empty, a few lights, a few cars, two trainmen waiting for a bus in front of the station, carrying lunch pails.

The street was closed, not only to Billy.

Billy knew he'd lost something he didn't quite understand, but the onset of mystery thrilled him, just as it had when he threw the match to the Doc. It was the wonderment at how it would all turn out.

Something new going on here.

A different Broadway.

He walked into the station and went to the men's room. He washed his face and hands and combed his hair. The tie was fine. He inspected his suit, his tan glen plaid, for grass and dirt, and he shined the toes of his shoes with toilet paper. He pissed, shat, and spit and went out and bought the New

York *News* and *Mirror* with his last half a buck. Forty cents left in the world. He looked at the papers and saw Charlie Boy's picture on page one of each. The news of the day is Charlie McCall. A nice kid, raised like a hothouse flower. He folded the papers and put them in his coat pocket. In the morning, he'd read Winchell and Sullivan and Dan Parker and Nick Kenny and Moon Mullins.

He would have an orange for breakfast to make his mouth feel good.

He went out of the station and climbed into a parked Yellow cab. He rode it to North Albany, to Jack Foy's Blackout on Erie Street and Broadway, and told the cabbie to wait. Jack hadn't heard the news about Billy yet and so Billy hit him for a deuce and paid the cabbie and then hoisted two cold beers to cool his throat. He knew Jack Foy all his life and liked him. When the word came down from Pop O'Rourke, Jack would not let him inside the joint.

Erie Street'd be as dead as Broadway downtown.

The word would spread and every joint in town would be dead.

Billy drank up and walked across Broadway and up through Sacred Heart Park to North Pearl Street, which was deserted, silent at four in the morning. He walked up Pearl, Joe Keefe sleeping, Pop O'Rourke sleeping, Henny Hart sleeping, Babe McClay sleeping.

He was in front of his house when he heard what he heard. First came the quiet snap, then almost simultaneously the streetlight exploded behind him like a cherry bomb, and he ran like a goddamn antelope for the porch.

He crouched behind the solid railing of the porch and listened for new shooting, but the street was already re-enveloped by silence. Still crouching, he leaped for the door to the vestibule and, with key at the ready, he opened the inside door and crawled into the living room. He locked the door and peered over the radio, out a front window, then out a dining room and a kitchen window, without moving any curtains, but he saw nothing. He heard movement upstairs and went toward it.

The door to the attic stairway was ajar.

Peg was in bed, but no George. Danny was in bed.

Billy went back to the attic door and climbed the stairs. The upper door to the attic was also ajar. He opened it all the way.

"Hello," he said. Who the hell to?

He smelled dust and old cloth and mothballs. He waited for noise but heard nothing. He went in and pulled the string of the ceiling light and stood in the midst of family clutter that belonged mostly to a child. Boxing gloves and bag, fire engine and steam locomotive, a stack of games, toy animals, skis, two sleds, a collection of matchcovers, a large pile of funny books, a smaller pile of pulps—*Doc Savage*, *The Shadow*, *The Spider*. On a rack in transparent bags hung George's World War uniform, his satin-lapeled tux, a dozen old suits, and, unbagged, a blue woolen bathrobe full of moth holes. Peg's old windup Victrola sat alongside a dusty stack of records, half of which Billy had bought her, or boosted. There was the fake Christmas tree wrapped in a sheet, and the ornament boxes, and a dozen of Peg's hatboxes.

The front window was open. Two inches.

Under it Billy found a flashlight and a copy of *The Spider Strikes*, a pulp Billy remembered buying five years ago, anyway. Richard Wentworth, the polo-playing playboy, is secretly The Spider, avenger of wrong. More than just the law, more dangerous than the underworld. Hated, wanted, feared by both. Alone and desperate, he wages deadly one-man war against the supercriminal whose long-planned crime coup will snuff a thousand lives! Can The Spider prevent this slaughter of innocents?

When he put the magazine back on the floor, Billy found an empty BB package.

He put the light out and went downstairs and met Peg coming out of her bedroom, pushing her arm into her bathrobe.

"What's going on? I heard walking upstairs."

"Is that all you heard?"

"What is it?"

"Somebody shot out the street light out in front."

"Shot it out?"

Billy showed her the BB package.

"The Spider carries the most powerful air pistol there is."

"Oh," she said.

They went into the room of Daniel Quinn, and Billy snapped on the wall switch, lighting two yellow bulbs in the ceiling fixture. The boy pulled the covers off his face and looked at them. Billy held up the BB package.

"Did you shoot out the streetlight?" Peg asked.

The boy nodded.

"Why?"

"I wanted it dark so when Billy came home the police wouldn't see him. I didn't know it was you, Billy. I thought you'd have your hat on."

"The police were here tonight," Peg said. "He was very impressed."

"What'd they want?"

"I don't know. They didn't come in. They just stopped out front and shone their searchlight in the front window. We had all the lights out, because George got a call they were coming to see him."

"Him? What the hell they want with him?"

"Nobody knows."

"Were they looking for me, too?"

"Only George, from what we heard. But they never came in."

"Where is George?"

"He went out for a while." She turned her head away from her son and winked at Billy.

Billy went to Danny's bedside and poked a finger in his ear.

"Thanks for the protection, kid, but you scared the bejesus out of me. I thought I was bushwhacked."

Daniel Quinn reciprocated the remark with a smile.

"You got a hell of an aim with that pistol. That's gotta be twenty-five yards, anyway."

"I had to hit it thirty-two times before it busted."

"An eye like that, you'll make a hell of a dart shooter."

Daniel Quinn reciprocated that remark with another smile.

Billy went to bed after he poured himself a glass of milk. Peg told him George had gone to Troy to stay at the Hendrick Hudson Hotel under the name of Martin Dwyer and would stay there until someone called him and said it was all right to come home. Billy pulled up the covers and thought of taking a trip to Miami or New York, if this was how it was going to be. But where would the money come from? Clean out the kid's bank account? He's been saving since he was in first grade. Probably got fifty by this time. Hock George's golf clubs for train fare?

Billy had a vision of wheat pouring into a grain elevator.

He saw Angie in bed with his twins.

When Billy was a kid he had no attic, no pile of toys, no books. He didn't want books. Billy played on the street. But now Billy has a trunk in this attic with his old spikes and glove in it, and old shirts, and pictures Teresa took of him in his bathing suit out at Crystal Lake. What the hell, it's his attic.

The kid was protecting himself and his mother. George was

gone and Billy wasn't home. The kid must've felt he was alone.

Billy thought of the carton of tuna fish Toddy won at a church raffle and how he took a taxi and left the tuna on Billy's stoop because Toddy never ate fish.

Billy thought of all the times he'd been suckered. In high school, it was a blonde who said she would and then didn't after it took him two days to find somebody who'd sell him cundrums. Plenty of bums stiffed him on horse bets, but then Pope McNally, a friend of Billy's all his life, welshed on a fifty-dollar phone bet and said he'd never made it. And that whole Colonie Street bunch. Presents at Christmas and your birthday, and in between you couldn't get a glass of water out of any of them. You think you know how it is with some people, but you don't know. Billy thought he knew Broadway.

He listened to the night and heard a gassy bird waking up. The light of Sunday morning was just entering the sky, turning his window from black to dark blue at the bottom. The house was silent and his brain was entering a moment of superficial peace. He began to dream of tall buildings and thousands of dice and Kayo and Moon Mullins and their Uncle Willie all up in a palm tree, a scene which had great significance for the exhausted man, a significance which, as he reached for it, faded into the region where answers never come easy.

And then Billy slept.

19

ree the children. The phrase commanded the attention of Martin's head the way a war slogan might. Stop the fascists.

Charlie McCall was the child uppermost in his thought, but he kept receiving images of Peter as a priest in a long, black cassock, blessing the world. He'd be good at that. Free Peter. Let him bless anybody he wants to bless.

It was three o'clock Monday morning and Martin was sitting alone in Morrie's DeSoto in an empty lot on Hudson Street in Greenwich Village, Patsy's loaded pistol in his right coat pocket. Hudson Street was deserted, and in the forty minutes he'd been sitting here, only two cars had passed.

This was the finale. Perhaps.

With Morrie, he'd left Albany and driven to Red Hook and then onto the Taconic Parkway. They stopped at the second gas station on the parkway and waited half an hour by the pay phone for a call. The caller told them to go to the Harding Hotel on 54th and Broadway in Manhattan, check in, and wait for another call. They did. They listened to "The Shadow" on the radio, and dance music by Richard Himber and the orchestra, and ordered coffee and sandwiches sent up. They played blackjack for a nickel and Martin won four dollars. Jimmie Fiddler was bringing them news of Hollywood when the phone rang and Morrie was given a circuitous route to deliver the money. Change cabs here and then there, take a bus, take two more cabs, get out at this place and wait to be picked up. Morrie was gone two hours and came back with the money.

"They threw it at me," he said. "They looked at it once and saw right away it was marked."

Martin called Patsy, who took two hours to call back. Go to a Wall Street bank on Sunday morning and the manager will give you new, unmarked money. Martin and Morrie slept and in the morning went together to the bank. They were watched, they later learned, by New York detectives, and also by the kidnappers, whose car Morrie recognized. With the new money, Morrie set off again on a new route given in another call. He was back at noon and said they took the money and would call with directions on where to get Charlie.

Martin and Morrie ate in the room and slept some more and exhausted all card games and the radio. Martin ordered a bottle of sherry, which Morrie would not drink. Martin sipped it and grew inquisitive.

"Why did they pick you, Morrie?"

"They know my rep."

"You know them?"

"Never saw any of them before."

"What's your rep?"

"I hung around with guys like them a few years back, tough guys who died with their shoes on. And I did a little time for impersonating a Federal officer during Prohibition. I even fooled Jack Diamond with that one. Our boys had the truck half loaded with his booze when he caught on."

"What'd he do?"

"He congratulated me, with a pistol in his hand. I knew him later and he bought me a drink."

"Were you a street kid?"

"Yeah. My old man wanted me to study politics, but I always knew politics was for chumps."

"The McCalls do all right with it."

"What they do ain't politics."

"What would you call it?"

"They got a goddamn Roman empire. They own all the people, they own the churches, they even own most of the Jews in town."

"They don't own your father."

"No. What'd he tell you when you talked to him?"

"I already gave you that rundown. He said you two didn't get along, but he gets along with your sisters."

"When my mother died, they worked like slaves around the house for him. But he was never there when I was a kid. He worked two jobs and went to college nights. I had to find a way to amuse myself."

"You believe in luck, Morrie?"

"You ever know a gambler who didn't?"

"How's your luck?"

"It's runnin'."

"How's Charlie's luck?"

"He's all right."

"You saw him?"

"They told me."

"And you believe them?"

"Those fellas wouldn't lie."

To free the children it is necessary to rupture the conspiracy against them. We are all in conspiracy against the children. Fathers, mothers, teachers, priests, bankers, politicians, gods, and prophets. For Abraham of the upraised knife, prototypical fascist father, Isaac was only a means to an enhanced status as a believer. Go fuck yourself with your knife, Abe.

When Martin was eight, he watched his mother watching

Brother William chastising fourth graders with a ruler. She watched it for two days from the back parlor and then opened her window and yelled into the open window of the Brothers School: If you strike any more of those children, I'm coming in after you. Brother William closed the window of his classroom and resumed his whipping.

She went out the front door and Martin followed her. She went down the stoop empty-handed and up the stoop of the school and down the corridor into the classroom opposite the Daugherty back parlor. She went directly to the Brother, yanked the ruler out of his hand, and hit him on his bald head with it. She slapped him on the ear with her left hand and slapped his right shoulder and arm with the ruler. He backed away from her, but she pursued him, and he ran. She ran after him and caught him at a door and hit him again on his bald head and drew blood. Brother William opened the chapel door and ran across the altar and escaped. Katrina Daugherty went back to the classroom and told the boys: Go home and tell your parents what happened here. The student who was being whipped when she came in stopped to thank her. Thank you, mum, he said, and half genuflected.

The last time Martin went to Hibernian Hall for Saint Patrick's Day a woman danced for an hour with her mongoloid son, who was wearing a green derby on his enormous head. When the music stopped, the boy bayed like a hound.

The call about Charlie came at midnight. Go to Hudson Street near the meat market with your friend and park in the empty lot. Your friend stays in the car. You walk to Fourteenth Street and Sixth Avenue and get a cab and go such and such a route. You should be back in maybe an hour with the property.

Martin felt the need to walk. He got out of Morrie's car and crossed the empty lot. He looked across the street at a car and saw its back window being lowered. Resting on the window as it rolled downward were the double barrels of a shotgun. Martin felt the useless weight of Patsy's pistol in his pocket, and he walked back to the DeSoto.

At four-fifteen a taxi pulled up to the lot and stopped. When two men got out, the shotgun car screeched off in the direction of the Battery. Martin opened the back door of the DeSoto and helped Charlie Boy to climb in and sit down. Martin snapped on the interior light and saw Charlie's face was covered with insect bites. The perimeter of his mouth was dotted with a rash where adhesive tape had been. He reeked of whiskey, which Morrie said the kidnappers used to revive him from the stupor into which he had sunk.

"Are you hurt anyplace?" Martin asked him. "This is Martin Daugherty, Charlie. Are you hurt?"

"Martin. No. They treated me all right."

"He's hungry," Morrie said. "He wants a corned beef sandwich. He said he's been thinking about a corned beef sandwich for three days."

"Is my father with you, Martin?"

"He's in Albany waiting for you. Your mother, too. And Patsy. Your whole family."

"It's good to see you fellows."

"Charlie," said Martin, "the whole world's waiting for you to go home."

"They hit me on the head and then kept me tied to a bed."

"Is your head all right?"

"One of them put ice cubes on the bump. I want to call up home."

"Were they tough on you?" Morrie asked.

"They fed me and one of them even went out and got me a couple of bottles of ale. But after I'd eat, they'd tie me down again. My legs don't work right."

Martin's vision of his own life was at times hateful. Then a new fact would enter and he would see that it was not his life itself that was hateful but only his temporary vision of it. The problem rests in being freed from the omnipotence of thought, he decided. The avenue of my liberation may well lie in the overthrow of my logic. Not until Charlie Boy was kidnapped did Patsy and Bindy think of electrifying the windows of their homes. Given the benign nature of most evenings on Colonie Street, there is a logic to living with nonelectrified windows. But, of course, it is a dangerously bizarre logic.

"It's time to move," Martin said, and he put out the car light and sat alongside Charlie Boy in the back seat. Morrie took the wheel and moved the DeSoto out of darkness onto the West Side Highway. It now seemed they were all safe and that no one would die. History would continue.

"Stop at the first place that looks like it's got a telephone," said Martin, to whom the expedition now belonged.

We move north on the Henry Hudson Parkway.

When we free the children we also drown Narcissus in his pool.

On the day after Charlie Boy returned home, Honey Curry was shot dead in Newark during a gun battle with police, Hubert Maloy was wounded, and ten thousand dollars of ransom money, identifiable by the serial numbers of the bills as recorded by the Wall Street bank, was found in their pockets.

When Charlie Boy was returned to Patsy McCall's cabin in the Helderberg Mountains, Morrie Berman and Martin Daugherty became instant celebrities. The press tracked them everywhere, and even Damon Runyon sought out Martin to interview him on the climactic moments on Hudson Street.

"Martin Daugherty," wrote Runyon, "climbs out of the DeSoto with the aim of stretching his legs. But he does not get very far with his stretching before he is greeted by a double-breasted hello from a sawed-off shotgun peeking out

270

of the window of a parked car. Being respectful of double-breasted hellos of such size and shape, Martin Daugherty goes back where he comes from and ponders the curious ways kidnappers have of taking out insurance on their investments."

Eight hours after Charlie Boy's return, the Albany police arrested Morrie Berman at the ticket office in Union Station, just after he had purchased a ticket to Providence. He was taken to the McCall camp for interrogation, and, Martin later learned, dunked in Patsy's new swimming pool, which was partly filled for the occasion, until he revealed the kidnappers' names. Curry and Maloy were among the names he disclosed, along with the nicknames of four hoodlums from New Jersey and Rhode Island.

The Newark shootout proved not to be the result of Morrie's disclosures, for no amount of dunking could have forced him to reveal a fact he did not know. He thought Maloy and Curry had gone to Providence. Maloy, under interrogation on what he erroneously thought was his death bed, said his flight with Curry from Greenwich Village to Newark was his own decision. He was tired and did not want to drive all the way to Rhode Island at such an hour.

None of the kidnappers had been in Newark before, during, or after the kidnapping. None of them had any way of knowing that the hangouts of criminals in that city had been under the most intensive surveillance for several days.

When Martin heard of Billy's status as a pariah on Broadway, he wrote a column about it, telling the full story, including how Berman saved Billy's life in a brawl, and wondering: "Is betrayal what Billy should have done for Berman by way of saying thank you?" He argued that Billy's information on Newark, and only Billy's information, brought Maloy and Curry to justice and saved the McCalls ten thousand dollars.

Yet even this was not a betrayal of Berman, for Berman had told Billy the truth about Newark: Maloy was not there, and had no plans to go there.

"Though I doubt he believes it," Martin wrote, "Billy knew Maloy would go to Newark at some point. He knew this intuitively, his insight as much touched with magic, or spiritual penetration of the future, as was any utterance of the biblical prophets which time has proved true. Billy Phelan is not only the true hero of this whole sordid business, he is an ontological hero as well.

"Is it the policy of the McCall brothers to reward their benefactors with punishment and ostracism? Is this how the fabled McCalls gained and kept power in this city of churches for seventeen years? Does their exalted omnipotence in this city now have a life of its own, independent of the values for which so many men have struggled so long in this country? If the McCalls are the forthright men I've always known them to be, they will recognize that what is being done to Billy Phelan is not only the grossest kind of tyranny over the individual, but also a very smelly bag of very small potatoes."

Emory Jones refused to print the column.

"If you think I'm going to get my ass into a buzz saw by taking on the McCalls over a two-bit pool hustler," he explained, "you're a certifiable lunatic."

Martin considered his alternatives.

He could resign indignantly, the way Heywood Broun had quit *The World* over the Sacco-Vanzetti business. But this was not in character for Martin, and he did like his job.

He could send the column in the mail to Patsy or Bindy, or handcarry it to them and argue the case in person. Possible.

He could put it in the drawer and forget about it and recognize that children must free themselves. True, but no.

The condition of being a powerless Albany Irishman ate holes in his forbearance. Piss-ant martyr to the rapine culture, to the hypocritical handshakers, the priest suckups, the nigger-hating cops, the lace-curtain Grundys and the cut-glass banker-thieves who marked his city lousy. Are you from Albany? Yes. How can you stand it? I was there once and it's the asshole of the northeast. One of the ten bottom places of the earth.

Was it possible to escape the stereotypes and be proud of being an Albany Irishman?

Martin awoke late one morning, hung over and late for a doctor's appointment. He dressed and rushed and when he stripped for the examination by the doctor, a stranger, he could smell the stink of his own undershirt. He yearned to apologize, to explain that he was not one of the unwashed. Sorry I stink, Doc, but I had no time to change. I got up late because I was drunk last night. Oh yes.

The quest to love yourself is also an absurd quest.

Martin called Patsy and told him he was wrong in what he was doing to Billy.

"I am like hell," said Patsy, and he hung up in Martin's ear.

Mary Daugherty agreed with Patsy McCall.

She sat in the Daugherty living room, reading in the evening paper the latest story on the kidnap gang. When Martin raised the issue of Billy Phelan by way of making polite conversation, she dropped the paper in her lap and looked at him through the top of her bifocals, her gaze defining him as a booster for the anti-Christ.

"The boy is evil," she said. "Only an evil person would refuse to help bring back young Charles from the clutches of demons."

"But Billy gave them the information that caught the demons," Martin said.

"He didn't know what he was doing."

"Of course he knew. He knew he was informing, which was why he refused to inform any further."

"Let him go to hell with his evil friends."

"Your tone lacks charity."

"Charity begins at home," said Mary, "and I feel first for young Charles, my own flesh and blood, and for his father and his uncles. Better men never drew breath."

Martin silently charted the difference between his wife and Melissa. Michelangelo and Hieronymus Bosch, Saint Theresa and Sally Rand. In the sweetness of her latter-day bovinity, Mary Daugherty swathed herself in immaculate conceptions and divine pleasure. And with recourse to such wonders, who has need of soiled visions? Life is clean if you keep it clean. Hire the priests to sweep up and there will be no disease. Joan of Arc and Joan Crawford. Hell hath no fury like a zealous virgin.

"What are we having for dinner?" Martin inquired.

Martin decided to send the column to Damon Runyon, for the recent edict from Hearst on Runyon was still fresh in his mind. Runyon was now the oriflamme of the Hearst newspapers, and yet editors across the country were cutting and shaving his column regularly. "Run Runyon uncut," came the word from The Chief when he heard what was happening.

"If you find a way to get this piece into print," Martin wrote Runyon, "I will try to find it in my heart to forgive you for those four bum tips you gave me at Saratoga in August."

And so, on a morning a week after he wrote it, Martin's defense of Billy Phelan appeared in Runyon's column in full, with a preface reminding his readers who Martin was, and suggesting that if he only gambled as well as he wrote, he would very soon make Nick the Greek look like a second-class sausage salesman.

The day it appeared in the *Times-Union*, the word went out to Broadway: Billy Phelan is all right. Don't give him any more grief.

Red Tom called Billy with the news and Billy called George Quinn at the Hendrick Hudson Hotel in Troy and told him to come home.

And Martin Daugherty bought himself six new sets of underwear.

Martin visited his father in the nursing home the afternoon the Runyon column appeared. His purpose was to read the old man a letter from Peter. Martin found his father sitting in a wheelchair with a retractable side table, having lunch. His hair had been combed but he needed a shave, his white whiskers sticking out of his chin like bleached grass waiting for the pure white lawnmower.

"Papa," he said, "how are you feeling?"

"Glmbvvvvv," said the old man, his mouth full of potatoes.

By his eyes, by the movement of his hands over the bread, by the controlled hoisting of the fork to his mouth, Martin perceived that the old man was clear-headed, as clear-headed as he would ever again be.

"Did I tell you I had lunch with Henry James?" the old man said, when he had swallowed the potatoes.

"No, Papa, when was that?"

"Nineteen-oh-three, I think. He and I had just published some of our work in the *North American Review*, and the editor dropped me a note saying James was coming to America and wanted to talk to me. He was interested in Elk Street. His aunt had lived there when she married Martin Van Buren's son, and he wanted news of the Coopers and the Pruyns and others. I had written about life on Elk Street and he remembered the street fondly, even though he loathed

Albany. We had lunch at Delmonico's and he had turtle soup. He talked about nothing but his varicose veins. An eccentric man."

"Mary and I had a letter from Peter," Martin said.

"Peter?"

"Your grandson."

"Oh yes."

"He's gone off to become a priest."

"Has he?"

"He likes the idea of being good."

"Quite a novel pursuit."

"It is. He thinks of Saint Francis as his hero."

"Saint Francis. A noble fellow but rather seedy."

"The boy is out of my hands, at any rate. Somebody else will shape him from now on."

"I hope it's not the Christian Brothers. Your mother was very distrustful of the Christian Brothers."

"It's the Franciscans."

"Well they're grotesque but they have the advantage of not being bellicose."

"How is the food these days, Papa?"

"It's fine but I long for some duck. Your mother was always very fond of duck à l'orange. She could never cook it. She could never cook anything very well."

"Melissa was in town this week."

"Melissa was in town?"

"She appeared in your play."

"Which play?"

"The Flaming Corsage."

"Melissa appeared in The Flaming Corsage?"

"At Harmanus Bleecker Hall. It was quite a success. Well attended, good reviews, and quite a handsome production. I saw it, of course."

"What was Melissa's last name?"

276

"Spencer."

"Ah yes. Melissa Spencer. Quite a nice girl. Well rounded. She could command the attention of an entire dinner table."

"She asked for you."

"Did she?"

"She's writing her memoirs. I presume you'll figure in them somewhere."

"Will I? How so?"

"I couldn't say. I'll get a copy as soon as they're published."

"I remember her profile. She had a nose like Madame Albani. Exactly like Madame Albani. I remarked on that frequently. I was there the night Albani came to Albany and sang at the Music Hall on South Pearl Street. In 'eighty-three it was. She drew the largest crowd they ever had there. Did you know she lived in Arbor Hill for a time? She played the organ at St. Joseph's Church. She always denied she was named for Albany, but she wouldn't have used the name if she hadn't had a fondness for the city."

"Papa, you're full of stories today."

"Am I? I didn't realize."

"Would you like to hear Peter's letter?"

"Peter who?"

"Your grandson."

"Oh, by all means."

"I won't read it all, it's full of trivial detail about his trip, but at the end he says this: 'Please tell Grandpa that I already miss him and that I am going to pray every day for his good health. I look forward to the day when I will be able to lay my anointed hands on his head in priestly blessing so that he may have the benefit, in the next, of my vocation. I know that you, Papa, and Grandpa, too, have been worldly men. But for me, I am committed to the way of the Cross. "Live in the world but be no part of it," is what I have been instructed and I will try with all my heart and soul to follow that guidance. I love you and Mother and bless you all and long for the time when next we meet. Your loving son, Peter.' "

"Who wrote that?" the old man asked.

"Peter."

"Peter who?"

"Peter Daugherty."

"He's full of medieval bullshit."

"Yes, I'm afraid he is."

"It's a nice letter, however."

"The sentiment is real."

"What was his name?"

"Peter Daugherty."

"Daugherty. That's the same name as mine."

"Yes, it is. Quite a coincidence."

"The Irish always wrote good letters. If they could write."

Martin's view of his meeting with his father was this: that all sons are Isaac, all fathers are Abraham, and that all Isaacs become Abrahams if they work at it long enough.

He decided: We are only as possible as what happened to us yesterday. We all change as we move.

20

Billy Phelan came into Becker's at early evening wearing a new hat and a double-breasted gray topcoat. The fall winds howled outside as the door swung closed behind him. He walked to the middle of the bar and stood between Footers O'Brien and Martin Daugherty.

"The magician is among us," Footers said.

"I could've done without that line, Martin," Billy said.

"Magic is magic," said Martin. "Let's call things by their rightful names."

"What're you drinking, Billy?" Red Tom asked.

"You still sellin' scotch?"

"Most days."

"A small one, with water."

"On the house," Red Tom said, setting the drink down in front of Billy.

"Times certainly do change," Billy said.

"Hey, Billy," Footers said, "there's a hustler upstairs looking for fish. Why don't you go give him a game?"

"I'm resting," Billy said. "Too much action all at once gives you the hives. Who's running the pool room now?"

"Nobody yet," Footers said. "Just the helpers Daddy had. Did you hear? They had to take up a collection to pay the undertaker. Bindy bought the coffin, but that still left a hundred and ten due. All they got was seventy-five."

"Who passed the hat?" Billy asked.

"Gus. Lemon. I scraped up a few bucks for the old bastard. Let this be a lesson to us all. He who lives by the tit shall die by the tit."

Gus Becker came out of the kitchen and saw Billy.

"So the renegade hero returns."

"The door was open."

"Give the man a drink on me, Tom," Gus said.

"I already did."

"Then give him another one."

"I don't need free booze, Gus. I got money."

"Don't hold it against us, Bill," Gus said. "When the word comes down, the word comes down. You understand."

"Sure, Gus. You got your business to think of. Your wife and kids. Your insurance policies."

"Don't be difficult, Bill. There was no other way."

"I understand that, Gus. I really understand that now."

"That a new hat, Billy?" Red Tom asked. "It looks like a new hat."

"It's a new hat. The river spirits got my old one."

"The river spirits?" Martin said.

"He's over the edge," said Footers. "You started this, Martin."

"You wouldn't want to explain that, Billy?" said Martin.

"No," Billy said.

"In that case," Martin said, "did you hear that Jake Berman raised two thousand dollars to have Marcus Gorman defend Morrie? It'll be in the paper tonight, without mentioning the fee, of course."

"I thought old Jake didn't like Morrie."

"He doesn't."

"Yeah. What star is that up there?" Billy said. "The one in the back row. That's new."

"That's Curry," Red Tom said.

"Curry? I didn't know he was in that picture. I must've looked at it five thousand times, I never saw him."

"It's him. He hung in here a lot in those days."

Curry was a gen-u-ine crazy," Footers said. "I saw him and another guy steal a billy club away from a sleeping cop one night over in the station. But the billy club wasn't enough so they took the cop's pants and left the poor sucker in the middle of the station in his long underwear."

"And Daddy's got his star, too," Billy said. "That's three in a couple of weeks."

"They go," Red Tom said.

Billy looked at the picture and thought about the three dead. They all died doing what they had to do. Billy could have died, could have jumped into the river to earn his star. But he didn't have to do that. There were other things Billy had to do. Going through the shit was one of them. If Billy had died that night, he'd have died a sucker. But the sucker got wised up and he ain't anywheres near heaven yet. They are buying you drinks now, Billy, because the word is new, but they'll remember you're not to be trusted. You're a renegade, Billy. Gus said so. You got the mark on you now.

Lemon Lewis came in the front door with red cheeks. Never looked healthier.

"Cold as a witch's tit out there," Lemon said.

"Don't talk about witches," Footers said. "The magician is here."

"What magician?"

"Don't you ever read the papers, Lemon?"

"Oh, you mean Phelan. Aaaaah. So they let you back in, eh, hotshot?"

"They just did it to make you feel good, Lemon," Billy said.

"Hey, Phelan," said Lemon, "that card game at Nick's that night of the holdup. Did you really have that ace in the hole?"

All Billy could do was chuckle.

"You'll never know, will you, Lemon?"

"You ready for another?" Red Tom asked Billy. "You got a free one coming from Gus."

"Tell him to give it to the starving Armenians. Footers, what about that guy looking for fish. You ready to back me till I figure him out? Fifty, say?"

"How does twenty-five grab you?" Footers said.

"In a pinch I'll take twenty-five," Billy said.

Billy drank his scotch and said, "Come on, Martin, maybe we'll get even yet."

And with Footers beside him, and Martin trailing with an amused smile, Billy went out into the early freeze that was just settling on Broadway and made a right turn into the warmth of the stairs to Louie's pool room, a place where even serious men sometimes go to seek the meaning of magical webs, mystical coin, golden birds, and other artifacts of the only cosmos in town.